The Conspiracy

PAUL NIZAN was born in Tours, France in 1905, the son of a railway engineer. A close friend of Sartre at the Lycée Henri IV and at the Ecole normale supérieure, he joined the Communist Party in the late 1920s and became one of its best-known journalists and intellectuals. His works include *Aden, Arabie*; *Les Chiens de Garde*; *Antoine Bloyé*; and *Le Cheval de Troie*. In 1939, following the Molotov–Ribbentrop Pact, Nizan left the party and was killed the following year in the Battle of Dunkirk fighting against the German army.

The Conspiracy

Paul Nizan

TRANSLATED BY QUINTIN HOARE
FOREWORD BY JEAN-PAUL SARTRE

Including a previously unpublished letter by Walter Benjamin

VERSO
London • New York

English-language edition first published by Verso 1988
This updated paperback edition published by Verso 2011
© Verso 2011
Translation © Quintin Hoare

First published as *La Conspiration* © Editions Gallimard, Paris 2005
Foreword by Jean-Paul Sartre from his *Situations* (vol. 1) © Editions
Gallimard 1948

Letter to Max Horkheimer (dated 24 January 1939), aus: Walter Benjamin,
Gesammelte Briefe. 6 Bände Band VI: Briefe 1938 1940 © Suhrkamp Verlag
Frankfurt am Main 2000
Translation © Esther Leslie

1 3 5 7 9 10 8 6 4 2

Verso
UK: 6 Meard Street, London W1F 0EG
US: 20 Jay Street, Suite 1010, Brooklyn, NY 11201
www.versobooks.com

Verso is the imprint of New Left Books

ISBN-13: 978-1-84467-768-9

British Library Cataloguing in Publication Data
A catalogue record for this book is available from the British Library

Library of Congress Cataloging-in-Publication Data
A catalog record for this book is available from the Library of Congress

Typeset in MT Janson by Hewer UK Ltd, Edinburgh
Printed in the US by Maple Vail

Contents

Translator's Note

In *The Conspiracy,* Nizan draws on cultural, political and historical sources that will often be unfamiliar to English-speaking
readers, half a century after its original publication. A few
explanatory notes have, therefore, been provided at the end of
the book, to which readers may if they wish refer – but without
burdening the text of the novel itself with any inappropriate
apparatus of reference numbers.

Perhaps the most important thing to explain is something
about the French system of higher education, in which a particular role is played by a group of elite *Grandes Écoles* in Paris, most
of which go back in their present (approximate) form to the
Revolutionary or Napoleonic period, and which flank the
University of Paris (Sorbonne). Rosenthal and his friends attend
what is still the best known of these, the Ecole normale
supérieure in Rue d'Ulm. This is entered by annual competition, open to pupils from lycées (roughly equivalent to grammar
or high schools) all over France. However, certain well-known
Parisian lycées like the Louis-le-Grand of this book (which the
author himself attended with Jean-Paul Sartre in the early twenties, and which stands next door to the Sorbonne) specialize in
preparing for the Ecole Normale Supérieure entrance: pupils
from less prominent lycées throughout the country transfer
there at the age of eighteen for this purpose. At the Ecole
Normale Supérieure, students are prepared not simply for a first
degree (*licence*), but also for the more difficult *agrégation,* a
competitive examination which qualifies successful candidates

to apply for a strictly limited number of teaching posts (in history, mathematics, philosophy, etc.) in lycées – posts which carry higher salaries than those open to teachers who only have ordinary degrees.

Other *Grandes Écoles* figuring here include the Ecole Nationale des Chartes, for archivists and librarians; the Ecole Libre des Sciences Politiques (now the Institut d'Etudes Politiques) in Rue Saint-Guillaume; the Ecole Polytechnique (familiarly known as X), which has a military status and qualifies pupils either for technical branches of the armed services or for engineering branches of the public services, through an education specializing in mathematics and the physical sciences; and, in the domain of technical and vocational education, the Ecole Centrale des Arts et Manufactures and the Conservatoire National des Arts et Métiers.

The Conspiracy is set in the political context of France between 1924 and 1929. In 1924, the Right-dominated Horizon-Blue Chamber (so called after the colour of the French Army's field uniform between 1915 and 1927) was replaced in general elections which led to a coalition government of the Left Cartel. Poincaré, the conservative politician most identified with France's hard line towards defeated Germany and in particular with French occupation of the Ruhr (1923), was replaced as Premier by the Radical-Socialist Herriot, while Millerand was similarly replaced as President by Doumergue. By 1925, however, the Right held governmental power once more, with a series of ministries headed for the most part either by Briand (1925–26 and again in 1929) or Poincaré (1926–29).

I should like to express my gratitude to Christine Donougher, Marie-Thérèse Weal, and especially Madame Rirette Nizan, for their kind help when I was finalizing this translation.

Foreword: On The Conspiracy

Nizan speaks about youth. But a Marxist has too much historical sense to describe an age of life – such as Youth or Maturity – in general, just as it marches past in Strasburg Cathedral when the clock strikes midday. His young men are dated and attached to their class: like Nizan himself, they were twenty in 1929 – the heyday of 'prosperity' in the middle of the post-war period that has just ended. They are bourgeois, sons for the most part of that grande bourgeoisie which entertains 'anxious doubts about its future', of those 'rich tradespeople who brought up their children admirably, but who had ended up respecting only the Spirit, without thinking that this ludicrous veneration for the most disinterested activities of life ruined everything, and that it was merely the mark of their commercial decadence and of a bourgeois bad conscience of which as yet they had no suspicion.' Wayward sons, led by a deviation 'out of the paths of commerce' towards the careers of the 'creators of alibis'. But in Marx there is a phenomenology of economic essences: I am thinking, above all, of his admirable analyses of commodity fetishism. In this sense, a phenomenology can be found in Nizan: in other words, a fixing and description, on the basis of social and historical data, of that essence in motion which is 'youth', a sham age, a fetish. This complex mixture of history and analysis constitutes the great value of his book.

Nizan lived his own youth to the dregs. When he was immersed in it and it barred his horizon on every side, he wrote in *Aden, Arabie:* 'I was twenty, I won't let anyone say those are the best years of your life.' He felt then that youth was a *natural* age, like childhood, although far more unhappy, and that responsibility for its miseries should be laid at the door of capitalist society. Today he looks back on it and judges it without indulgence. It is an artificial age, which has been made and which makes itself, and whose very structure and existence depend upon society: the age of inauthenticity, par excellence. Workers at twenty, however, are protected from it by misfortunes, by worries, by the contact they must make in order to survive: they 'already have mistresses or wives, children, a profession . . . in short a life'; once they leave adolescence, they become young men, without ever having been 'young people'. But Laforgue and Rosenthal, sons of bourgeois families, students, live that great abstract ennui to the full. Their fatal lightmindedness and their aggressive futility are due to the fact that they have no duties and are by nature irresponsible. They 'improvise' and nothing can engage them, not even their membership of extremist parties: '. . . these diversions . . . had no great consequences for the sons of bankers and industrialists, who could always return to the embrace of their class. . . .' Very wise perhaps, if these improvisations sprang from a brief contact with reality. But they remain in the air and their authors forget them at once. Their actions are puffs of smoke, they know this and it is what gives them the courage to undertake things – though they pretend not to be aware of it. What are we to call them, these undertakings so serious yet so frivolous, if not 'conspiracies'? But Laforgue and Rosenthal are not Camelots du Roi: young bourgeois can come and make their plots at the other end of the political spectrum, even in the parties of grown men. We can see what that fine word 'conspiring' hints at in the way of whisperings, little mysteries, hollow consequence and invented dangers. Tenuous intrigues: a game. A game – that great 'Dostoievskyan' plot hatched by Rosenthal, the only traces of which will be two incomplete and in any case totally uninteresting files at the back of a drawer. A feverish, angry game, an abortive conspiracy, that manufactured love which Rosenthal entertains for his sister-in-law. From calling it a game, moreover, it is but one short step to calling it play-acting: they lie to themselves because they know they are running no risk; they strive in vain to frighten themselves, in vain – or almost – to deceive themselves. I can just imagine the great, dumb sincerity of labour and physical suffering and hunger that Nizan would counterpose to their endless talk. Bernard Rosenthal – who from anger and sloth has performed the irreparable actions of suicide – will in fact know no other reality than the agony of death. The agony of death alone will show him – but too late – that 'he had missed love . . . that . . . he no longer even loved Catherine and he was going to die cheated'. Yet those young people have the semblance of good intentions: they want to live, to love, to rebuild a world that is tottering. But it is at the very heart of these good intentions that the abstract, self-assured frivolity lies which cuts them off from the world and from themselves: 'their politics is still based only upon metaphors and shouts'. For youth is the age of resentment. Not of the great anger of men who suffer: these young people define themselves in relation to their families; they 'tended to confuse capitalism with important people'; they expect to find 'a world destined for great metamorphoses', but what they want above all is to give their parents a bit of trouble. The young man is a product of the bourgeois family, his economic situation and his world-view are shaped exclusively by the family.

These young people are not all bad men. But Nizan shows very clearly how only through revolution can one leave this age, which Comte called 'metaphysical'. Youth does not bear its solution within it: it must collapse and be rent apart. Either it is the young man who dies, like Rosenthal, or he is fated by his family inferiority complex like Pluvinage to drag out a perpetual, wretched adolescence. There is a breakdown of youth for Nizan as there is a breakdown of childhood for Freud: the pages in which he shows us Laforgue's painful initiation to man's estate are among the finest in the book.

I do not think Nizan wanted to write a novel. His young people are not novelish: they do not do much, they are not very sharply distinguished from one another; at times they seem only an expression, among many others, of their families and their class; at other times, they are the tenuous thread connecting a number of events. But this is intentional: for Nizan, they do not deserve more; later, he will make them into men. Can a communist write a novel? I am not convinced of it: he does not have the right to make himself the accomplice of his characters. But in order to find this book strong and fine, it is enough that on each page you find the obsessive evocation of that unhappy, guilty time of life; it is enough that the book constitutes a hard, true testimony at a time when 'the Young' are forming groups and congratulating themselves, when the young man thinks he has *rights* because he is young, like the taxpayer because he pays his taxes or the father because he has children. It is a pleasure to find, behind these derisory heroes, the bitter and sombre personality of Nizan – the man who does not forgive his youth – and his fine style, taut and casual: his long Cartesian sentences, which sink in the middle as though no longer able to sustain themselves, but all at once spring up again to finish high in the air; and those rhetorical transports which suddenly come to a halt, giving way to a terse and icy verdict. Not a novelist's style, sly and hidden: a style for combat, a weapon.

Jean-Paul Sartre
November 1938

Part One

The Conspiracy

I

— Well, said Rosenthal, we might name the journal *Civil War*...

— Why not? said Laforgue. It's not a bad title, and it says what we mean all right. Are you sure it hasn't already been taken?

— Civil war's an idea that must be in the public domain, said Rosenthal. It's not something you could copyright.

It was a July evening, at that hour after dusk when the sweat dries on your skin and all the dust of the day has finally settled like the ash from a spent conflagration. A broad expanse of sky stretched above the gardens, which were merely a small enclosure of parched trees and sickly grass, but which nonetheless, there amid the stone hills of Paris, gave as much pleasure as a meadow.

In the apartments of Rue Claude-Bernard, which Laforgue and his friends sometimes spied on for hours as though they harboured important secrets, people were beginning to get ready for the night. A bare arm or shoulder could vaguely be discerned passing in front of a lamp: women were undressing, but they were too far away for one to be able to make out whether they were beautiful. They were not. Actually they were middle-aged ladies, removing corsets, girdles and suspender-belts like pieces of armour. The younger female inmates of these dwellings – those whose songs would sometimes well forth from the recesses of a kitchen – slept in garrets where they could not be seen.

Loudspeakers spewed forth from their maws in a confused babble strains of music, speeches, lessons, advertisements; every now and then you could hear the screech of a bus at the stop in Rue des Feuillantines; yet there were moments when a kind of vast, marine silence swirled lazily over the reefs of the city.

Rosenthal was speaking. He always spoke a lot, since he had the voice of a prophet and thought its timbre gave him powers of persuasion. His companions, as they listened to him, contemplated the raspberry shimmer of Paris above their heads; but they were thinking confusedly about the women readying themselves for bed and addressing mechanical words to their husbands and lovers – or, perhaps, phrases overflowing with hatred, passion or obscenity.

They were five young men, all at that awkward age between twenty and twenty-four. The future awaiting them was blurred, like a desert filled with mirages, pitfalls and vast lonely spaces. On that particular evening, they gave it little thought: they were merely longing for the advent of the summer vacation and for the examinations to be over.

— All right then, said Laforgue, we'll manage to publish this journal next term, since philanthropists can be found naive enough to entrust us with funds they'll not see again. We'll publish it, and after a certain time it will fold . . .

— Of course, said Rosenthal. Is any one of you so depraved as to imagine we're working for eternity?

— Journals always fold, said Bloyé. That's a simple empirical fact.

— If I knew, Rosenthal continued, that any undertaking of mine would involve me for life and pursue me like some kind of ball-and-chain or faithful dog, I'd sooner go and jump in the river. To know what you're going to be is to live like the dead. Just imagine us forty years from now, with ugly ageing mugs, editing an aged *Civil War* like Xavier Léon and his *Revue de Métaphysique*! A splendid life would be one in which architects built houses for the pleasure of knocking them down and writers wrote books only in order to burn them. You'd have to be pure enough, or brave enough, not to require things to last . . .

— You'd have to be freed entirely, said Laforgue, from the fear of death.

— Cut out the romanticism, said Bloyé, and the metaphysical anguish. We're making plans for a journal, and we're having high-faluting discussions because we haven't got either women or money – there's nothing to get excited about. Anyway, one has to do things, and we're doing them. It won't always be journals.

— How about going for a drink, said Pluvinage.

— Let's go, said Jurien.

They left the gardens to go drinking and had all the cafés that lie between Place du Panthéon and the Jardin des Plantes to choose from. They went down Rue Claude-Bernard then up Avenue des Gobelins till they arrived at the Canon des Gobelins, which still stands at the corner of the Avenue and Boulevard Saint-Marcel. The café's pavement seats were full of people shattered by work and the heat, who mumbled absurd, truncated conversations or told each other insulting truths, as they waited until it was time to go off and sleep two by two in damp beds hidden away in wretched rooms; there were also a few showy pieces with watchful eleven-o'clock eyes, one of them a rather buxom young woman whose tight curls were faintly repulsive, reminiscent of an armpit or a pubis, but she had handsome knees that gleamed like black stones.

They sat down and looked at the drinkers around them, but it was too hot to get very excited about other people's existence or even convince oneself very easily that they were anything but images, projections, reflected forms. Laforgue was more interested in the woman with curly hair and eventually she rose from her chair and went inside the café; Laforgue followed her to the cloakroom in the basement. The cloakroom lady said:

— We've still got fine weather ahead: the glass is set fair.

— But it's thundery, said the young woman. I don't know if you're like me, Madame Lucienne, but it makes a person all tense. If you ran a hand through my hair, it would crackle like the fur on a cat's back.

Laforgue asked for a telephone number that did not exist.

— There's no reply, said the cloakroom lady.

— That doesn't surprise me, said Laforgue.

The woman had applied powder, rouge and – after spitting on a little brush – mascara. She smiled at Laforgue and started off ahead of him; on the steps of the narrow, winding staircase she asked him:

— Is tonight the night, then?

Laforgue was standing three steps below her and, at the level of his eyes, could see a belly which bulged slightly beneath the black crêpe-de-Chine of her dress.

— That's just what I was wondering, he replied. But we'd better make it some other day, the weather's not right, the glass is set too fair.

— It's a shame, she said, we'd have been good together. You'll regret it, and as for me, I'll have been downstairs for nothing.

— You'll have a drink all the same, won't you? said Laforgue.

They sat down at a table in the café's deserted interior: the percolator hissed over the till-lady's head, the waiter was nodding – they woke him up. Through the open window they could see a row of necks that told a lot about their owners' faces. The woman drank green peppermint cordial and began talking, and since he had followed her for the sake of one action alone, Laforgue began to caress her knees; then he rose and rejoined his companions.

— You were hitting it off? asked Bloyé.

— As you say, replied Laforgue. She was a woman with a thirst, especially for affection; she was tender; she was just getting round to making plans for the future. One Sunday, she was saying, we might go and see my little daughter, she's with a wet-nurse near Feucherolles, perhaps you know it, you get out at Saint-Nom-la-Bretèche, beyond Marly-le-Roi, you must like children. A fine Sunday was in the making – for someone fond of children, canaries and cats.

When it was almost midnight Rosenthal left, since his home was far away from that neighbourhood, at La Muette, where people live in over-large stone shells, on streets as clean as the avenues in cemeteries where plots are leased in perpetuity.

Rosenthal, as he stood on the platform of the AX carrying him from the Jardin des Plantes towards the Gare de Passy, was thinking furiously about the potent domain of families. Since he had been breathing that La Muette air (no match for the breeze wafting at midnight over the paulownias of Parc Mont-souris, but still . . .) for twenty-three years now, he had the wherewithal to fill the time of his homeward journeys with childhood memories: the gatherings of nannies and nurses on the lawns of La Muette, round perambulators drawn up in a circle like the wagons of nomads none too sure about the darkness; the games with the children in the Bois who play in white gloves, who play without disarranging their silken hair; and later, after a day at Janson, the walks in Allée des Acacias or Allée de Longchamp thinking about Odette de Crécy, and the Sunday-morning girls beneath the flowering chestnuts on the avenue in the Bois when everything is redolent of spring, petrol, horses and women.

There is more than one Jewish quarter in Paris. The 16th arrondissement was not the one where Bernard Rosenthal would most readily have chosen to live, but each time he thought of Rue Cloche-Perce and Rue du Roi-de-Sicile, that was not possible either: the corkscrew ringlets of the latest immigrants from Galicia did not strike him as much less revolting than the Charitable Works of the Rothschild family; and he did not think a leap from the twentieth century and La Muette into the sixteenth century and Vilna or Warsaw was such a brilliant solution.

When a young French bourgeois like Laforgue is seized by a desire to rebel against the condition his class imposes upon him, he experiences less complex problems in making the break: the race and its mythologies, the complicities of church, clan and charity, do not long mask from him society's true contours. A deviation from the path traced for him, like the reaction of a foal that takes fright and shies; the rift with paternal allegiances: these are enough to cast him back into the midst of a human space bereft of history, or which history scarcely trammels. Everything sorts itself out quite speedily: if, in an attempt to find his bearings, he seeks a bit of posthumous advice from his peasant forebears, they are never far away. Disloyal to his father who has done so much for him and, by God, makes no bones about telling him so, he can console himself by exclaiming that he is at least loyal to his grandfather: nothing threatens bourgeois stability more fundamentally than this constant interchange of compensatory betrayals, which are simply the normal consequences of the celebrated stages of democracy.

Rosenthal really did not know which way to jump, whom to be loyal to. His rabbi forebears were no joke, and in Paris what use was their advice full of Zohar and Talmud? He had too much self-esteem not to admit to himself – in spite of that human respect which does so much for the defence of lost causes – that the humblest of his relatives disgusted him no less than the richest and most triumphant; than those who had ended up acquiring an astonishing security like that of Catholics – as if Heaven and Hell belonged to them too. The pathetic synagogues on the first floor of some fissured building in the Saint-Paul neighbourhood, from which on Saturdays such unkempt old men would descend; the kosher inscriptions on the butchers' windows; that incense-laden aroma of the East you can inhale only two hundred metres away from the Hôtel de Ville emporium and the church of Saint-Gervais; the tall girls, somewhat too pale-skinned and disdainful, beside a bowler-hatted father on the threshold of a tailor's shop; the little gangs of pickpockets in the Polish bars; the white silk scarfs woven with threads in the hues of twilight and the moon – Bernard could no more put up with all this than with his cousins' grand weddings in the temple on Rue de la Victoire or Rue Copernic, with the top-hats in a ring round the *hupa* and the ladies' fur coats in the left bay; with tales of contango and backwardation, of outside market and official market; with the young girls who, when he met them at his beautiful sister-in-law Catherine's, would speak to him in careless tones with the hint of an English accent of their holiday cruises to Spitzbergen or in the Cyclades, for which the fashion was then beginning. Bernard had no desire to exchange prisons.

Nor were the impassioned fur-trade workers' meetings, in the little hall on Rue Albouy, any great help to him: the speakers held forth almost exclusively in Yiddish, he did not know a word of it. In his family, no one uttered a word of the forgotten language any more without laughing, ever since they had forsworn poverty, exile and anger. He did not in any case believe Jews had the right to a special liberation, a new act of alliance with God: he saw their liberation as submerged in a general emancipation, wherein their names, their misfortune and their vocation would disappear all at once. Besides, Bernard still wished only to be freed – he gave little thought to freeing anybody else.

It was quite hard actually for Rosenthal to forget that he was Jewish: his name sometimes inspired him with a kind of shame, which he considered ignoble and blushed for; it inspired him also with pride, and among his friends he would sometimes begin a sentence with the words 'As a Jew, I . . .', as though he had inherited secrets of which they would always remain ignorant – recipes for knowledge of God, intelligence or revolt; as though, for his salvation, he had had an exhilarating and bloody history to exploit, a history of battles, pogroms, migrations, legal proceedings, exegesis, knowledge, real power, shame, hope and prophecy. But he had only to find himself among his kinsfolk to detest them, to tell himself that the Jewish bourgeoisie was more dreadful than all others, Jewish banks more ruthless than Protestant banks or Catholic banks: he had scant acquaintance with the economy of other faiths.

How hard it was to be burdened by the problems of two millennia, the tragedies of a minority! How hard, not to be alone!

The Rosenthals lived in Avenue Mozart, at a time when almost all their relatives and friends still remained loyal to the Plaine Monceau, sending their sons to the Lycée Carnot or Lycée Condorcet and their daughters to the Dieterlen School; when the great movement towards Passy and Auteuil had not yet assumed the remarkable dimensions it was to assume in the years that followed.

First you went down a spacious corridor in white marble set off with long mirrors and blood-red wall-settees in garnet velours, then you arrived at the Rosenthals' ground-floor apartment. This was large, its french windows opening onto a damp garden enclosed by railings and shaded by tall white buildings. The large and small drawing-rooms were crammed with statues, bound volumes, gloomy paintings and console tables with gilt feet: there was a grand piano, a great glossy saurian protected by a Seville shawl; a harp; and canvases by Fantin-Latour and Dagnan-Bouveret, dating from the period when painters had everything to gain by adopting double-barrelled names that endowed them with a plebeian nobility.

M. Rosenthal was a broker, but you would have thought

yourself in the home of some great surgeon. On days when Mme Rosenthal received, her guests would all have the air of people waiting for an appointment and a verdict on the condition of their appendix or their ovaries. The moment had not yet come to yield up those apartments, furnished twenty years earlier with distraught passion, to the decorators of nineteen hundred and twenty-five. It was only young married couples who were beginning to set up house in white rooms furnished in glass and metal – and the atmosphere still remained medical.

Bernard entered his domain. In that stately apartment, his room's sole ambition was to be austere. It was furnished with a large table, a brass bed that Bernard had deemed less frivolous than a divan, and an English wardrobe: on the walls there were shelves of books (not many of them bound like the ones in the large drawing-room), a poor lithograph of Lenin, a fairly good reproduction of Hals's *Descartes*, and a little metaphysical landscape by de Chirico rather reminiscent of a provincial museum's reserve collection beneath a stage moon – and which dates the period when this tale of young people unfolds. Bernard took a bath and went to bed, thinking that he had definitely smoked too much and that he was rather hungry. He then thought vaguely about the Revolution, and with exactitude about his family, the furniture in the large drawing-room, and the kitchen where there must be things left in the refrigerator. He told himself things had to be settled one way or another, without really knowing whether it was a matter of covering Paris with barricades; catching a train next morning that would take him for a few weeks far away from his father and mother, his brother, his sister-in-law and the servants; or simply going down to the kitchen – he was really too sleepy, eventually he fell asleep.

A quarter of an hour after Rosenthal, Pluvinage in turn had left the Canon des Gobelins. Pluvinage, who was preparing for his *agrégation* in philosophy at the Sorbonne, lived alone in a fairly dismal room in a hotel in Rue Cujas inhabited by Chinese students and by whores from the Pascal, the d'Harcourt and the Soufflot. As always, his companions felt faintly relieved by his departure; but since they regarded this as a pretty unworthy sentiment, they did not speak of it. Laforgue, Bloyé and Jurien did their best to postpone the moment of going home to bed. Luckily, they were passionately attached to Paris, their neighbourhood and night strolls.

Nine years ago the neighbourhood round the Panthéon still formed a fairly enclosed little world, its frontiers following Rue Gay-Lussac, Rue Claude-Bernard, Rue Monge, Rue des Ecoles, Rue de la Montagne-Sainte-Geneviève, Place du Panthéon, Rue Soufflot and Rue Saint-Jacques; the authorities had not yet begun bisecting the houses with streets of hospital severity, overlooked by sheets of glass and by brick and concrete towers dedicated to Knowledge. The passer-by would proceed through winding lanes frequented by flocks of Irish seminarists, through alleys that boasted food and destitution round Place Maubert, without any desire to go beyond the frontiers down towards the banks of the Seine, the gusts of Notre-Dame, the long funereal shelters of the Gare, and the barren, hopeless folly of the skeletons of fish and monsters, the gemstones, the culinary herbs, the animals and the palm-trees imprisoned in dreamlike dens and glasshouses at the Jardin des Plantes.

It was a neighbourhood that gave its inhabitants all they needed: their greatest demands were gratified by the rural memories still lingering round Rue Lhomond, Rue Rataud and Rue du Pot-de-Fer, in the depths of leafy yards and acacia-shaded lodges, towards the Panthéon riding-school with its gilded horses' heads. Nowhere could you hear more cocks crow at dawn; and even in the afternoon, on stormy days, their rain calls would suddenly ring out through the lulls of Paris. It had not been so long since the last stock-rearers had abandoned the courtyards of Rue Saint-Jacques, where they had been replaced by cabinetmakers, sculptors, teachers of painting and dance;

among the *polytechniciens* going up Rue Lhomond of a Wednesday, you would not have been surprised to encounter a cow or a sheep-dog.

Behind the worn façade of great Louis XV town-houses, abandoned gardens proliferated where weeds and brambles overran stone vases and statues the weather had beheaded like queens; where, as dusk fell, the children of concierges and button-sellers used to organize never-ending games and chase one another, twittering like swallows and squeaking like mice; and in Rue Lhomond there still existed houses where the arm of the hay-winch jutted out above the rotting loft-door.

In Rue Mouffetard that evening, odours of dead meat, cat and urine hung about, along with the invisible flakes of poverty; as ever, in those sleeping wildernesses of Paris, Laforgue and his comrades saw flitting away only the last prowlers down on their luck: those old women, trundling from doorway to doorway with shopping bags full of papers, crusts, rags and the same shiny fragments of iron, bone, mother-of-pearl and pottery that lunatics in asylums sew onto their coarse petticoats; those Negroes and Algerian labourers, who can be heard singing so late in summertime under the green-paper trees of Place Maubert, as though on an African rooftop. As ever, all that remained for them to do was decide to go to bed, telling each other this was really no life at all – then they went home. It was no use their dreamily probing the day's little pile of rubbish, they did not find anything much there: nothing had happened.

In order to keep young people quiet, men of forty tell them that youth is the time of surprises, discoveries and great encounters; and tell all those stories of theirs about what they would do if they were twenty years old again and had their youthful hopes, teeth and hair, but also their splendid experience as fathers, citizens and defeated men. Youth knows better, that it is merely the time of boredom and confusion: nary an evening, at twenty, when you do not fall asleep with that ambiguous anger a giddy sense of missed opportunities engenders. Since the consciousness you have of your existence is still uncertain and you rely on adventures capable of furnishing proof that you are alive, late nights are none too cheerful. You are not even tired enough to experience the joy of sinking into slumber: that kind of joy comes later.

No one thinks more steadfastly about death than young people, though they are reticent enough to speak of it only rarely: each empty day they deem lost, life a failure. Better not risk telling them that such impatience is unfounded, that they are at the lucky age and preparing themselves for life. They retort that such an existence – as infant larvae waiting to be brilliant insects at the age of fifty – is a merry one indeed! Everything for our future wings – do you take us for hymenoptera? What is this insect morality? At the age of thirty, it is all over, you make your peace; since you have begun to grow accustomed to death and tot up the remaining years less frequently than at twenty, what with all the work you have, the appointments, the obligations, women, families and the money you earn, you end up believing in your existence entirely. Youth has had its day, you go and pay little visits to the corpse, find it touching, happy, crowned with the pathetic halo of lost illusions: all this is less hard than seeing it die in vain, as one does at twenty.

This is why Laforgue and his friends stayed awake so late, as if to multiply their chances. But at two o'clock in the morning in Paris, you can really count only on picking up a girl with legs so exhausted by her vigil and with such a longing for sleep that her bedroom is no place to expect much from life, as she undresses, all yawns and without any thought for those heart-rending gestures of coquetry, or humility, which women resort to when awake, to hide some defect of their breasts, a crease in the stomach, a scar, or age, or the flaccid symptoms of misfortune.

Every evening they went home cheated. Should they then have stuck it out to the end, not slept at all, seen the day born in the whitening of the stubbly small hours when, at least for a moment, one can believe that everything is beginning, that one will see everything, that one will be able to sing like the colossi of the dawn? But at their age, eyes close . . .

II

Two days later, Rosenthal came to meet with his friends again.

All these encounters take place at the Ecole Normale, in Rue
d'Ulm. This is a large square building dating from the time of
Louis-Philippe; a courtyard forms its centre, with a cement pool
where goldfish circle lazily; a festoon of great men runs between
the windows, to set an example; a cold stench of refectory soup
hangs about the glazed arcades; a naked man dying against a
wall, proffering a stone torch that nobody is willing to take from
his hands, symbolizes the War Dead; flanking Rue Rataud there
is a tennis court, and between Rue Rataud and Rue d'Ulm a
garden embellished with a carved stone bench and two naked
women of somewhat flabby outline, often decorated with
obscene inscriptions. At one extremity of the tennis court stands
a little physics laboratory, in the style of the historic sheds where
famous inventors discovered the internal combustion engine or
the wireless detector; at the other extremity ten years ago there
used to be a gymnasium and some plant biology laboratories,
falling into ruins round a little botanical plot dubbed 'Nature'.
  From the rooftops you can discern – with the feeling of exaltation and power that altitudes inspire – the entire southern half
of Paris and its misty horizon, bristling with domes, steeples,
clouds and chimneys. It is on these roofs that Laforgue,
Rosenthal, Bloyé, Jurien and Pluvinage spoke again about *Civil*

War, without exaggerating the importance it might have, but reckoning all the same that it would take its place as one of the thousand little undertakings thanks to which, when you come right down to it, the world is thought to change.

It was the end of June in the year nineteen hundred and twenty-eight. As these young people were living in a country quite as good as any other, but where the Prime Minister was just then explaining in a speech to the Chamber that he was not sorry to have been nicknamed by the communists Poincaré-la Guerre and Poincaré-la-Ruhr – because if he had not visited the wartime front lines with his puttees and his little chauffeur's cap, and if he had not gone across to the other bank of the Rhine, where would France be? – and as they were not driven by the depressing need to earn their daily bread immediately, they told each other it was necessary to change the world. They did not yet know how heavy and flaccid the world is, how little it resembles a wall that can be knocked to the ground in order to put up another much finer one, how it resembles instead a headless and tailless gelatinous heap, a kind of great jelly-fish with well-concealed organs.

It cannot be said that they are entirely taken in by their speeches about transforming the world: they view the actions that their phrases entail simply as the first effects of a duty whose fulfilment will later assume forms altogether more consequential; but they feel themselves to be revolutionaries, they think the only nobility lies in the will to subvert. This is a common denominator among them, though they are probably fated to become strangers or enemies. Spinoza, Hegel, Marxism, Lenin – these are still just great pretexts, great muddled references. And since they know nothing about the life men lead between their work and their wives, their bosses and their children, their little foibles and their great misfortunes, their politics is still based only upon metaphors and shouts . . .

Perhaps Rosenthal is simply destined for literature and is only provisionally constructing political philosophies. Laforgue and Bloyé are still too close to their peasant great-grandfathers to commit themselves, without many *arrière-pensées* and mental reservations and serious mystical revelations. Jurien lets himself be drawn along by comrades remarkably different from himself; he has the feeling he is sowing his wild oats, as his father – a radical schoolteacher in a Jura village – puts it, and that Revolution is less dangerous to health than women: admittedly, it gives less pleasure at first and does not prevent him from having bad dreams. Pluvinage is perhaps the only one among them who adheres fully to his action; but it is an adherence that cannot but end badly, because he is basically concerned only with vengeance and believes in his destiny without any ironic reflection upon himself.

All this is terribly provisional, and they are well aware of it. It is at twenty that one is wise: one knows then that nothing commits or binds, and that no maxim is more unworthy than the notorious saying about the thoughts of youth being realized in maturity; one consents to commit oneself only because one senses the commitment will not give one's life a definitive shape; everything is vague and free; one makes only sham marriages, like colonials looking forward to the great wedding organs of the mother country. The only freedom seen as desirable is the freedom not to choose at all: the choice of a career, a wife or a party is just a tragic lapse. One of Laforgue's comrades had just got married at twenty; they spoke of him as of a dead man, in the past tense.

For nothing in the world would they have confessed these convictions: his wisdom does not prevent the young man from lying. Two days earlier, it had taken an hour of indolence on the grass, the temptations and the inimitably confidential tone of the night, for Rosenthal to slip into speaking out loud about demolished buildings and burned books. They treated their improvisations as lifelong decisions, for they still accompanied their actions with illusions that did not deceive them. They were not even misled about the meaning of their friendship, which was merely a rather strong complicity among adolescents too threatened not to feel the worth of collective bonds, too lonely not to strive to replace the reality of their nocturnal playmates by the images of virile comradeship. Basing the future upon the connivances of youth seemed to each of them the height of cowardice.

On the cover of the journal – whose dummy they settled upon that day, stretched out on the burning metal of the roofs with their heads buzzing from the sun – they decided to have a machine-gun engraved; it was Pluvinage who made the suggestion.

The year was ending. Rosenthal wanted everything to be ready for November. He invested the same impatience in this project that could sometimes draw him into pursuing a woman. Everything that Bernard undertook had to be accomplished at such a rapid pace that he seemed to have little time for living; to be preparing himself for a death full of regrets, memories, plans. His friends dared not resist him: such impatient individuals do sometimes play the role of leaders. Besides, it was Rosenthal who had found the funds for the journal: those twenty-five thousand francs, that skill in worldly matters, gave him the right and the means to convince young people who had not yet emerged from their studies and the confinement of the lycée, and to whose eyes money seemed absolutely magical.

III

In Rue d'Ulm it was that uncertain time when examinations are over and you have to wait for the results in a state of extreme idleness that is full of charm for naturally lazy adolescents forced for years into absurd labours.

Laforgue used to spend whole afternoons on a divan covered in a golden material now grown very dark. He would take a book and begin to read, but he would soon fall asleep. When he was too hot, he would go down to the ground floor and take a shower, or a glass of something in a bar in Rue Claude-Bernard.

One afternoon at around four, someone knocked: it was Pauline D., a young woman (no longer all that young) who from time to time used to come and see Laforgue in Rue d'Ulm, when she felt like being kissed. Laforgue had met her on a little beach in Britanny, where the young men would kiss the young women after strolls back and forth along the sea-wall, when they had stretched out on the sand and were disarmed by the darkness, the stars or the green phosphorescence of the sea which came to sputter out at their feet. Philippe always had great trouble keeping the conversation going with Pauline: he told himself he had never detested a woman as much as her, but since he did not have all that many opportunities to caress a bosom and legs, he made the best of it. He used to tell her roughly:

— You know incredible people, like the parish priest of the Madeleine and the military governor of Paris. To think you're the niece of a police commissioner! What on earth do you come here for?

One day Pauline had taken him to a charity sale in the Hôtel des Invalides. It was spring on the streets. War invalids, sitting in their little carriages, read their newspapers in the sun. General Gouraud was parading his empty sleeve among the ladies of the Union of the Women of France; these former nurses, forewarned about the illusion amputees entertain (as much of a byword as Aristotle's marble, or the well-worn quips of opticians), would move aside to avoid knocking against the empty sleeve, the phantom arm: did they picture the general suddenly letting himself go and releasing the scream of pain he had suppressed to the last on the fields of battle? Objects were being sold that nobody wanted to buy – it is always like that at sales, but luckily gifts are always needed for housekeepers or poor relations – cushions, mats, brushes and utensils made by blind veterans and sad as their guide-dogs, or by the yellow and black wards of the French nuns of Annam and the Somali Coast. Pauline always reminded Laforgue of wartime in the provinces, when he used to go each Thursday to the Sainte-Madeleine convent hospital to see the wounded making macramé or knitting mufflers and the sisters running about – those holy young women who had never had such a good time – and when, on Sunday evenings after he had served at the Office, tinkling the altar bells in front of the soldiers who would be dozing and thinking they were as well off there as anywhere, the convalescents used to give him cigarettes which made him throw up; returning home in a taxi with Pauline kissing him, he told himself that she was acceptable only as a childhood memory, the image of the blue-veiled nurses with their breasts so lovely beneath their square tuckers, beneath the throb of their epidemic medallions.

Pauline began talking about the Conservatory auditions and the exhibition of artworks on loan from Rome; she never had a great deal to do, she did not miss a concert, an exhibition or a big sale;

she used to go one day a week to a surgery and advise young mothers about the feeding of newborn infants and the illnesses of early childhood; she did not have much money; she was not getting married.

Laforgue affected never to set foot in a picture gallery or an art dealer's, in the Opera House or the Salle Pleyel: this was typical of him. Like his friends, he used to proclaim proudly to all and sundry that he didn't give a fig for painting, music or the theatre, and that he preferred bars, fairs at the Belfort Lion, neighbourhood cinemas and the festivals in Avenue des Gobelins. This was a kind of challenge they threw out to people for whom the arts served as a merit, a justification or an alibi. Since he knew Spain and Italy quite well, Philippe could have spoken all the same about painting; but Pauline did not come to Rue d'Ulm to have a serious talk about pictures or music, and Laforgue considered there was no good reason to take the trouble to be polite. He sat down next to Pauline on the divan and she told him he wasn't very chatty.

— I'm sorry Pauline, he said. And Heaven knows there's a lot going on! Thirty degrees in the shade at Perpignan, an anticyclone from beyond the Sargasso Sea is moving towards the Azores. The financier Loewenstein has drowned in the Channel, and the Amsterdam Stock Exchange is significantly affected. *Maya* is playing at the Théâtre de l'Avenue, where we shall not be going. There were forty-eight dead at Roche-la-Molière, but since they're miners the accident is hardly of much consequence; and M. Tardieu has had an informal chat with the wounded, which was extremely helpful. In Paris . . .

— Just kiss me, said Pauline.

Philippe kissed her and found a slightly irritated pleasure in doing so, because summer perspiration made Pauline's lips rather salty, her lipstick had an odd taste, and she was one of those impossible women who parade all their feelings, tremble when you touch their breasts and late in life will stage perfectly faked nervous breakdowns.

'Such airs and graces!', thought Laforgue. 'How would I look if Bloyé came home, with this histrionic girl apparently in a trance? Perhaps I'd better go and lock the door.'

He detached himself from Pauline and went over to shoot the bolt.

— Do you by any chance have evil intentions? she asked with a little contrived laugh. I'd probably better take off my dress.

— I think so too, said Laforgue.

Pauline stood up and took off her dress, a dress the colour of dead leaves that actually made a dry little rustle like dead leaves; she was wearing a mauve slip with broad strips of ochred lace running across her bosom and her legs.

'This woman has no taste,' Philippe said to himself: he liked women to wear either virginal underwear or the extravagant artifices of the tarts at the Madeleine or the Opéra.

She had a rather skinny torso and shoulders, but fairly heavy legs and hips for which Philippe had a sufficient liking to forgive her her underwear. She stretched out on the divan and spread her dress over her knees; Laforgue, lying alongside that moist body, was thinking he ought to have drawn the curtain, what with all that sun they had full in their eyes and which was high-lighting the freckles on Pauline's white skin above the broad hem of her stockings; but he was beginning to purr and couldn't face getting up. Pauline was not a woman with whom there was any question of going all the way; she used to defend herself with a stubborn presence of mind that scarcely hampered her pursuit of pleasure. She closed her eyes; the make-up disap-peared from her cheeks; the movement of her belly was reminiscent of the spasmodic, dreamy throbbing of an insect's abdomen; she was alone, absolutely enclosed within herself and the strange concentration of pleasure; her heart beat strongly throughout this intense labour; Laforgue remembered that he had not shaved that morning, and that Pauline would get red spots round her mouth and pink patches in the hollow of her shoulder – but since he was thinking about this alien being with resentment, he congratulated himself on that. These caresses, these movements, these jerky exhalations involved a mute and shifting torpor, a blind urgency, a grimness that seemed never-ending. Suddenly, however, Pauline clenched her teeth, opened her eyes again, and Laforgue was furious to see that distraught look – that anguish of the runner who has given his all – and the girl's body grew taut, her thighs locked with incredible force upon Laforgue's wrist, while he himself achieved a dubious pleasure.

Pauline sank back, laying one hand on her breast:

— We're crazy, she sighed.

She stretched, closed her eyes again. Later, she raised herself on one elbow, took a mirror from her handbag and looked at herself:

— I do look a sight! she exclaimed.

— A sorry sight, said Philippe.

She was dishevelled, beads of sweat still bedewed her temples, her nostrils, the roots of her hair, after the hard begetting of pleasure. Laforgue looked at those pale lips:

'Love doesn't suit women,' he said to himself.

— Wipe your mouth, said Pauline. If your friends saw all that lipstick . . .

She covered her breasts, which were set rather low, then stood up to slip on her dress. Pauline accomplished with admirable promptitude the difficult transition from the disorders of pleasure to life in society: with her clean face, her smooth hair, her ankle-length dress, nobody would have dreamed of showing her insufficient respect. She wanted to talk: idle chatter was one of the last echoes of pleasure for her. She read the titles of the books lying about everywhere; Laforgue had just finished a Greek year, the books were austere, on his table there were the *Politics,* the *Nicomachean Ethics* and *Simplicius' Commentary.* Pauline sat down again on the divan. Her dress revealed the great silken beaches of her stockings; she looked at Philippe with a killing smile intended to speak volumes.

'That's quite enough for today,' thought Laforgue. 'We're not accomplices on the strength of so little.'

— How exciting it must be, all that Greek wisdom! she exclaimed.

— As if I didn't know! replied Laforgue.

— So much more exciting than a woman like me, isn't that so? sighed Pauline. A woman of no importance . . .

— No comparison, said Philippe, telling himself: 'She's simpering, this is the limit.' But you remind me, I was busy working when you arrived. It was one of my good days, would you believe . . .

— Which must mean, replied Pauline, that I might perhaps now relieve you of my presence.

Laforgue shrugged his shoulders slightly, but Pauline smiled: it was over, she was dressed again, she knew she could not demand of men any passionate gratitude for what she gave them.

Laforgue accompanied her to the Rue d'Ulm door, she went off in the direction of the gate and the porter's lodge.

'One's really too polite,' he thought. 'This time I should have had that girl.'

Bloyé arrived at the foot of the portico steps, he was returning from the gardens. Laforgue said to him, rather loudly:

— Bloyé, do you see that lady? Well, she doesn't go all the way!

Pauline turned round and cast an angry glance at them. Laforgue told himself ashamedly that the insult would not prevent her from returning, that she was not so proud – and he went back inside to wash his hands.

This is how some of their love affairs used to pass off: it will perhaps be understood why these young men generally spoke of women with a crudity full of resentment. This department of their lives was not in order.

At parties, at dances, during the holidays, they would meet girls whose lips before too long they could almost always taste, whose breasts and nerveless legs they could caress; but these brief strokes of luck never went very far, and left them irritating memories that engendered rage more than love. They thought with fury about how the girls were waiting for older men than they to marry them: how they were reserving their bodies. Philippe, when he danced with them, would sniff them with an animal mistrust; he preferred the insolent perfume of the tarts with whom he used to form easy liaisons on Boulevard Montparnasse or Boulevard Saint-Michel. Those gaudy women would permit silent relations, free from the theatricals of language and protocol; they were labourers in an absent-minded eroticism denuded of anything resembling an unlawful complicity.

Rosenthal did not breathe a word about any women he might know. Bloyé used to go once a month to a house in Boulevard de Grenelle, from which he would hear, in the furthest bedroom, the trains roaring past on the elevated track where it entered the La Motte-Picquet Métro station. Jurien was sleeping with the maid from a little bar in Rue Saint-Jacques, a red and tawny woman with a missing incisor. Pluvinage's lady friend was a tall, mannish girl who worked in an office.

'What a dreadful creature!' thought Laforgue in his bed that evening, mulling over Pauline's visit before falling asleep and thinking with some distress that he really should have had her. 'I don't like this little war of escapes, these solitary pleasures. Let's hurry up and be done with onanism for two.'

He is a bit quick to generalize his own experiences. The fact is, he knows only whores or young girls, no women: which amounts to saying he knows nothing about anything. As yet, he has access only to that desert of solitude and bitterness through which a young man shapes his course towards love; of pleasure itself, he knows only a kind of organic wrench. He has never met a woman who has said to him dreamily after lovemaking:

— How painful it must be for you too!

He hopes to discover that love is a suspension of hostilities when, for a split second, a man and a woman escape from hatred and from themselves; when they forget themselves like two wartime soldiers fraternizing between the lines around a well or the burial of the dead.

'When I know that,' he said to himself, 'will it be much more fun?'

IV

Half-way through November and with the interminable family holidays now over, *Civil War* made its appearance, with Pluvinage's machine-gun, which they had finally adopted, in black on the blue cover. They were all rather proud of themselves because of their names in capitals on the contents page and Serge's machine-gun.

People took out subscriptions. At the editorial offices they had established in a damp and gloomy little shop in Rue des Fossés-Saint-Jacques, where the electric lamps were on all day, they received enthusiastic letters written by students from Dijon and Caen or Aix-en-Provence – people are so bored in the provinces that the faintest cry uttered in Paris will always find echoes there – or by country schoolteachers, sentimental and critical; by women; by lunatics, who would send them plans for perpetual Peace, suppressed inventions, symbolic fates, the imaginary documents and the defence speeches of never-ending trials, or heartrending appeals to Justice: their unknown friends consisted above all of defeated people. There also arrived abusive letters, and letters along the lines of Aren't-you-ashamed-of-yourself-young-man, because *Civil War* expressed rather well a natural state of fury, and its editors used to attack, by name, living and genuinely respectable individuals. The reasons they used to give for these indictments, though based on a great display of philosophy, were not all rigorous or valid; but when you think that France at that time, by way of great men, had Prime Minister Poincaré, M. Tardieu and M. Maginot, it must be admitted that their instinct ran no risk of leading them far astray.

The team's first political memory went back to nineteen hundred and twenty-four. That was a year which had begun with deaths, with the disappearance of the most considerable symbols or actors of the first years of the Peace: Lenin had died in January, Wilson in February, Hugo Stinnes in April. In May, elections full of poetic enthusiasm had brought the Left Cartel to power: having just got rid of the Horizon-Blue Chamber, people thought war was over and done with for good and they were going quietly to recommence the little regular shift to the left in which serious historians see the Republic's secret, finding that this providential inevitability solves many things and allows everyone to sleep like a log. In November, to please a country which in five months had not stopped hoping, it was decided to transfer the body of Jean Jaurès to the Panthéon, where the man who died in July '14 was awaited by the grateful Fatherland and the mortal remains of the Great Men – La Tour-d'Auvergne, Sadi Carnot, Berthelot, Comte Timoléon de Cossé-Brissac and Comte Paigne-Dorsenne.

That year Laforgue, Rosenthal and Bloyé were at Louis-le-Grand, preparing for the Ecole Normale. The lycée was a kind of great barracks of pale brick with sundials bearing gilded inscriptions, where boys of nineteen could not learn much about the world on account of having to live among the Greeks, the Romans, the idealist philosophers and the *Doctrinaires* of the July Monarchy: they were, however, as people say 'on the Left'. With what was going on in the world, even on their free days, they would have had to be blind . . .

A *normalien* of Rosenthal's acquaintance procured them invitations on 24 November to the lying in state. It was to take place at the Palais-Bourbon, in the Salle Mirabeau, which had that very morning ceased to be called the Salle Casimir-Périer: at the last moment people had judged the latter to be impossible, because of the memories that hyphenated name evoked. Echoes of the Lyon risings crushed in eighteen hundred and thirty-one by the Interior Minister grandfather would, after all, have jarred; nor could any great connection be discerned between Jaurès and the President of the Republic grandson. Mirabeau could be accommodated, by stressing his speeches and his historic sallies in the Summoned-here-by-the-will-of-bayonets style, while casting a veil over his intrigues with the Court. Since there was in any case no question of Robespierre, Saint-Just, or Babeuf . . .

Violet gauze hangings draped the stone walls, which recalled the Expiatory Chapel in Boulevard Haussmann and also, already, the cellars and subterranean glory of the Panthéon; they shrouded the chandeliers and diffused a gloomy mauve light, just right for half-mourning, over a fragile scaffolding that awaited the coffin and a black cloth with silver stars that had done sterling duty. The women seated at the foot of the walls were saying to themselves that this mauve lighting must give them an odd complexion, but that they would not solve the problem by putting on more powder. The guests all consisted of figures from a house of bereavement: little groups of individuals were chatting quietly in corners; deputies were shaking hands, with a mien and bowed shoulders imbued with grief-stricken familiarity; every now and then, the husky tones would be heard of someone who could not manage to keep his voice down. The ushers, who carried their little cocked hats with the tricolour cockades under one arm, marched in double slow time like Swiss Guards, in well-broken shoes that did not squeak; they kept a passage open between the catafalque and the door, through the crowd that had grown denser as though Jaurès had really had quantities of brothers, relatives and inconsolable friends. Every-one kept glancing towards the door. People were thinking about that great man, dead ten years and five months, who was still not arriving. They were vaguely uneasy: the news spread that the

Albi train had had an accident at Les Aubrais. Someone said in the vicinity of Laforgue and Rosenthal:

— It's really rotten luck.

Bernard sniggered.

Then they recognized Lucien Herr, who was chatting to Lévy-Bruhl and whom they respected, since being told that Herr still talked to young men about the will not to succeed. Lucien Herr, who already bore – along with the invisible weight of the great books he had not written – the burden of his imminent death, came up to them. They greeted him. Herr said to their companion from Rue d'Ulm:

— Don't go too far away now. I want to introduce you to Blum.

Herr moved off and returned with Léon Blum, who proffered them a long hand, which they found soft and burning, and said nothing to them. He did not seem to take much interest in these young men; after turning his head this way and that, like a large bird on the lookout, he moved away with a strange stiff, jerky gait.

At a quarter to eleven, the two leaves of the door at last slowly opened as if upon a scene at the Opera; everyone thronged forward, the crowd made the same noise as a theatre audience does when the curtain goes up. Outside there was a milky darkness astonishingly luminous for the end of November, as though somewhere behind the sky there had been a moon of frost or spring; those sparkling mists on the black courtyard of the Palais-Bourbon caused the insipid violet twilight of the Salle Mirabeau to grow pale; people felt cold and anxious to leave that long cavern to walk beneath the trees; the women shivered.

The bearers deposited the coffin on the bottommost tread of the stairway; their steps resounded heavily in the murmurous silence. Miners lined the way. An outburst of shouts exploded brutally like a great nocturnal bubble above the crowd that was surging against the gates of the Cour de Bourgogne and that had just rushed through the sleeping streets behind the hearse, after its departure from the Gare d'Orsay. But the coffin entered, the double doors fell shut again and the shouts were stifled. The Carmaux miners, who were wearing their black pit overalls and their leather caps, lined up clumsily around the catafalque where the ushers and undertaker's men were piling the withered wreaths which had just made the journey in the icy gloom of the goods van.

No one was weeping – ten years of death dry all tears – but men were fabricating masks for themselves: Saumande, who gave rather a good impersonation of a lizard's grief, Lautier of a pig's, François-Albert of a ferret's.

It was still necessary to wait, nobody knew for what – the dawn perhaps. From time to time a band would play Siegfried's 'Funeral March' to relieve the waiting. It was an unbearable night. In that great stone cell, Laforgue and his friends had the impression they were the silent accomplices of adroit politicians who had deftly filched that heroic bier and those ashes of a murdered man, which were destined to be the important pieces in a game whose other pawns were doubtless monuments, men, conversations, votes, promises, medals and money matters: they felt themselves less than nothing among all those calculating, affable fellows. Luckily, through the walls and above the muffled sound of trampling and music, there would sometimes arrive what sounded like a stormburst of shouts; they would then tell one another that in the darkness there must exist a sort of vast sea which was breaking with rage and tenderness against the blind cliffs of the Chamber: they could not catch the words that composed these shouts, but they sometimes thought they could make out the name Jaurès at the peak of the clamour. The guests looked at one another with a particular expression, like people warm and snug in a house near the sea on a stormy evening, who do not care to think about the squalls the night is fashioning.

Rosenthal felt like a smoke, and said to Laforgue in an undertone:

— Did you spot that society type Léon Blum shaking the miners' hands, those horny hands of theirs? Talk about old family retainers, I must say . . .

Around one in the morning, Laforgue said:

— I can't take any more of this. Let's get the hell out of this cellar!

They made their escape, taking precautions, but no one noticed their departure. Outside, Laforgue continued:

— Well, we'll have had the honour of keeping watch beside the body of Jean Jaurès.

— Yes, said Bloyé. It's even an honour we'll have shared with M. Eugène Lautier.

— And with Herr, said Rosenthal.

— Which is much odder, Laforgue went on. Because after all, with him you really don't have to worry, he's not got any little trick up his sleeve. He must have been the only person who was actually thinking, as if the body blow of July '14 had happened only yesterday, about Jaurès – a fellow who had been in the same year as Baudrillart and Bergson, and who had strength, hairs on his chin, courage, a voice and who, in his youth, had written a thesis in Latin on the reality of the sensible world . . .

People were beginning to move away from the Chamber, taking the Pont de la Concorde or Boulevard Saint-Germain, in order to catch the last Métros. Some groups lingered, however, still listening to the muffled strains of the funeral marches issuing from the loudspeakers between the columns. An imponderable haze submerged the flutings and the great tricolour drape that flapped from top to bottom of the Palais-Bourbon's façade; the Seine was unusually lonely and black, and in the silence of Paris you could hear it rending and gently hissing round the piles of the bridges as though you had been walking through open countryside beside its waters. When they reached the Légion d'Honneur building, Laforgue said:

— All in all, there was a prize little band of swine there this evening. Instead of playing at being pallbearers and pious young university types, we'd have done just as well being out on the embankment with the others.

The next day, at the start of the afternoon, they had positioned themselves on the corner of Rue Soufflot and Boulevard Saint-Michel, and were circulating from group to group: they were beginning to love the echoes and contingencies of large gatherings. It was 25 November, the weather was grey, the women were feeling none too warm with that little wind round their legs, under their coats. A voice was raised behind them:

— Proper All Saints' Day weather.

Another voice replied:

— It's the month, isn't it . . . Funeral weather, you might say. It must have been finer the day Jaurès died, in July '14 . . .

By and large, people were fairly content with this apposite climate, since it was a death parade that was about to take place, starting from the Palais-Bourbon and finishing in the frozen crypts of the Panthéon in a clutter of standards and immortelles, and people do not like contradictions between the heavens and humanity – funerals in spring when the cemeteries are flowering, or weddings beneath the rain.

The crowd was dense on the pavements all the way from the Law Faculty to Rue de Bourgogne: with crowd-like decorum, coughing and stamping its feet, it waited patiently for the great men in the cortège and for the communists, who had assembled around noon all along the Champs-Elysées as far back as the Marbeuf Métro station, so people were saying.

The boulevard was as empty as a dried-up riverbed. From time to time a dark police vehicle would pass slowly by, its tyres crunching over the sand. At last a noise was heard coming from the West, then a swelling tide of shouts in which were intermingled relief, anger and joy.

— If it's another instalment of last night, said Rosenthal, it's going to be a really trashy affair.

34

— Can't tell, said Laforgue. Let's not forget the people who were calling for Jaurès last night outside the Chamber, as if they had the power to raise him from the dead – and who weren't looking any too happy . . .

The mobile catafalque arrived, a strange scarlet-and-gold platform recalling the civic displays of the French Revolution, its draped daises, its baroque floats celebrating the harvest, youth, war, patriotism and death. The cortège followed: it was a narrow ribbon of men in mourning, and magistrates, professors, military officers, in which there were peaked caps, top-hats, white starched shirtfronts, sashes worn across chests and around bellies, ermines, taffeta robes, pale-blue masonic ribbons, medals, sabres, famous faces casting furtive glances to right and left, all along that petrified stream, at the two moving ridges of chests, heads, legs and shouts that were perhaps about to surge onto the carriageway. People were thinking, of course, about the crossing of the Red Sea: and the Prime Minister was doubtless not much prouder than Moses – with that Pharaoh and his war chariots galloping at his heels, and the two liquid walls growing impatient at being miraculous for so long – and was in a hurry to reach the shore of the Panthéon.

An empty space opened up, then voices in the ranks of the crowd said:

— There they are!

The boulevard filled up: it was the workers from the outlying districts, the masses from the city's densely populated eastern and northern neighbourhoods; they held the carriageway from one bank to the other bank, the river had finally begun to flow. The people in the first cortège, who were respectable people, did not sing, but these ones were singing, and since they were singing the Internationale, the tenants in Rue Soufflot and Boulevard Saint-Michel, who had never seen anything like it and who were beginning to feel rather small behind their looped drapes and their half-curtains, started shouting out insults and shaking their fists – but since no one heard their shouts, these demonstrations by the residents were of no particular importance.

The spectators on the pavements opened their eyes wide and craned their necks to read the inscriptions on the banners, which were along the lines of: 'Jaurès, a victim of war, is being glorified by his murderers', and which protested against the Dawes Plan, the Left Cartel, fascism and war, and called for Revolution and the arraignment before a revolutionary Tribunal of those responsible for the War: perhaps these were slightly Utopian slogans, but no doubt could be entertained as to the fresh truth of these rallying cries when people told themselves how the socialist deputies had just voted through the Interior Ministry's secret budget.

One could not help thinking of vigorous forces, of sap, a river, the flow of blood. The boulevard suddenly merited the appellation 'artery'. The men and women on the pavements had perhaps from the outset wanted to remain calm, because they had come here with their families, out of curiosity, or out of gratitude, or to see famous people pass by, or out of loyalty to the sentimental images Paris retained of Jean Jaurès and his boater and his old tailcoat and his fists uplifted against war, there beneath the wide skies of the Pré Saint-Gervais: but there was no way of remaining calm. It is of no avail being a Parisian and accustomed to great funerals – what with all the ministers and cardinals and academicians and generals who die – and to parades and cortèges; there is no fever that spreads faster than the flames of great processions, and since it had never crossed the minds of the demonstrators coming from the Champs-Elysées to assume suitable expressions, those on the pavements told themselves that if Jaurès were all at once to return, he would probably be rather pleased to see people happy at being two hundred thousand in his honour, and that the crowd filling the carriageway was in the right: this is why the pavements allowed themselves, after hesitating for a moment, to be seduced. The motionless men no longer resisted the moving men, nor the spectators the spectacle, nor the silent ones the singers; they stepped down to experience the river's movement. Laforgue, Rosenthal and Bloyé lost what deference to convention they had left, they too plunged in and began to sing.

Later, the Prime Minister slowly climbed the steps of the Panthéon, between two lines of miners who were still playing a decorative and symbolic role, and began to speak: he could be seen extending his arms, puffing out his chest, laying his hand on his heart, but not a word of his speech could be heard amid all the bursts of cheering and booing that were erupting from all sides on the black-and-grey square. The demonstrators, moving forward as slowly as lava, threw their placards against the railings; and the Thinker, who had never looked greener or more hungry, gazed vaguely with his eyes of bronze at that pyre of wood, calico, cardboard and everlasting flowers that rose up before Jaurès's coffin, like the crutches, votive offerings and sticks before a miraculous site. The whole crowd was drifting away via Rue Valette, Rue de la Montagne-Sainte-Geneviève, Rue Clovis and Rue de l'Estrapade: darkness began to fall and yellow lamps were lit over its dispersal.

Between the Hôtel des Grands Hommes and the corner of Rue des Fossés-Saint-Jacques, Laforgue said with a sigh:

— No question about it. One knows which side one should be on.

— That second cortège was needed, replied Rosenthal who was feeling a bit drunk, to cleanse us of our night of dissimulation . . .

Nothing is more difficult than the systematic exploitation of an event of the heart, nothing more swiftly damped than the reverberations of love at first sight. Examinations, laziness, literature, curiosity about women, all the false manoeuvres in which the arduous life of adolescents is dissipated, long prevented Laforgue and his friends from drawing from those violent memories of 24 and 25 November all the practical consequences they should have implied: for years, it was merely something they held in reserve.

It might be thought odd that they were not shaken by certain events in the years '25, '26, '27 and '28: but that would be to take insufficient account of the diversions into which so many young men are enticed, when at a stroke they discover books and women. In July '25, Laforgue was going for Sunday excursions out of Paris, and taking out dancing at Saint-Cloud and Nogent-sur-Marne a little salesgirl from the Faubourg Saint-Honoré, who seemed to him the most important thing in the world. In May '26, Rosenthal forgot everything in favour of the revelations in the *Ethics*. The war in Morocco, the Canton rising, the English general strike were barely anything more to them than great opportunities for a few days of political enthusiasm: they signed manifestos that committed them far less than their parents thought. The interest they took in the world lacked specificity. The Sacco and Vanzetti affair, with all those heads broken in Paris, might have played a role in their lives that would have marked them more severely than the Jaurès ceremonies; but it was the holiday period, none of them was in Paris, the whole business was simply an item of news that they read in the papers, with a forty-eight hour delay, in Brittany or in the Midi.

Throughout all these years, they would have periods of passion when they would resolve to go to bed at three in the morning: this was more than was needed to pass their examinations, it fell a bit short of forgetting themselves. They would espy a trail and plunge in, less to gain knowledge than with the hope of stumbling upon a mirror or a source. They discovered one after another Mendelssohn, the 'Unknown Philosopher' and Rabbi ben Ezra. After a couple of weeks, humour would prevail, they would wake up and return to the cinema almost every evening. They were eager young men, but lazy.

This superficiality did not prevent them from believing in Revolution: they cared little about appearing truly inconsistent. They sometimes examined their consciences – but only to conclude that they did not incline towards Revolution out of love for humanity, nor out of any strict adherence to events. It is quite true that there was not the least scrap of philanthropy in their natural impulse to revolt: humanitarianism struck them as entirely counterfeit, nor did they view Revolution as a secular rebirth of Christianity.

— What I like about Revolution, said Laforgue, is that the civilization it promises will be a hard civilization.

— Agreed, said Rosenthal. The age of ease is coming to an end ...

They were stirred more by disorder, absurdity and outrages to logic than by cruelty or oppression, and really saw the bourgeoisie, whose sons they were, less as criminal and murderous than as idiotic. They never doubted for a moment that it was in decline and doomed. But they wished to fight not for the workers – who, fortunately, had by no means waited for them – but for themselves: they viewed the workers merely as their natural allies. There is a great deal of difference between wanting to sink a ship and refusing to sink with it ...

The intense family repugnance they felt for the bourgeoisie might have led them to a violent, but anarchist, critique. Anarchism, however, struck them as illiterate and frivolous: their academic studies saved them. They scorned the generation that had immediately preceded them, for having expressed its revolt only in poetic vocabularies and upon poetic sureties: the moment seemed right to endow anger with philosophical guarantors.

— Let's start being serious, said Bloyé.

Rosenthal commented:

— It will be seen later that a historic change occurred, once Hegel and Marx superseded the Schools of Rimbaud and Lautréamont as objects of the younger generation's admiration.

They liked only victors and reconstructors; they despised the sick, the dying, lost causes. No force could more powerfully seduce young men who refused to be caught up in the bourgeoisie's defeats than a philosophy which, like that of Marx, pointed out to them the future victors of history: the workers, destined for what they somewhat hastily judged to be an inevitable victory. Moreover, they went so far as to convince themselves, with excessive complacency, that the Revolution was accomplished now that they themselves positively no longer identified with the bourgeoisie: a kind of smug pride made them speak of post-revolutionary consciousness. No one would have dreamed of finding them dangerous; they worked less to destroy the present than to define a dreadfully contingent future.

Civil War took up a great deal of their time during the first months: they had no suspicion at the time that what was most important about the venture was the fact that it gave them opportunities for extensive reading, and their first chance of sustained relations with workers, and that they would later recall, with the surprise which the memory of happiness gives, the hours they used to spend with deft, sardonic compositors in the little book printshop in Rue de Seine where they went to correct their proofs and lay out the journal.

They were not modest, they compared themselves to famous groupings, to the Encyclopaedists or the Hegelians.

Rosenthal thought their principal undertaking should be an encyclopaedic critique of values, and a sort of general reduction of ideas to their true motives: no study seemed to him more important than the critique of mystification and the exposure of mendacity. Laforgue dreamed of a kind of generalization of Marx's analyses on the fetishism of commodities – some universal charactery of deception.

It was, after all, the morrow of the War and the first peacetime disorders. They were emerging from a prodigiously mendacious time, when the entire education of the young had been accompanied by solemn twaddle, fuelled in turn by the requirements of prosecuting the War, then by the success of the grand machinations of the Peace. They realized they had been deceived no less at school than their fathers or elder brothers had been at the front. Their mothers, lonely and glibly heroic like all wives of men who will die in wars, had themselves lied with a disconcerting civic ease. Ten years after Versailles, almost all the men who had returned from the front, saved at the last instant when the clarion of the Armistice sounded, still hesitated to unmask the meaning of the rhetorical inventions for which they had fought: rarely does a person have the courage to retract and cry from the rooftops that he once took the word of liars; it is necessary to be strong indeed for such public confessions – people would rather have been accomplices than dupes. It will easily be understood why Laforgue and his comrades despised no one more deeply than War Veterans. The voices that had been raised after the last day of the War still seemed few in number: they did not compel the young men's recognition. Everything depended upon the chance of an encounter that did not always occur. By about a year Laforgue and Rosenthal had missed the Clarté movement, which was already disintegrating.

Behind the closed shutters of the shop in Rue des Fossés-Saint-Jacques, or in their lecture-rooms in Rue d'Ulm, they spent hours mulling over these matters. Comrades who did not form part of the team would come to visit them; they would talk till very late, drinking coffee that Bloyé handed round, until they were tipsy with words and smoke. For example, Rosenthal would say:

— A modern encyclopaedia could only be based on the sincerity of insolence. Nobody expects anything of us other than insolence. We must announce, with sufficiently prophetic means of expression to unsettle the smug, the decline of the age of mendacity. Such an annunciation will not be achieved without a system: that's why our special mission in philosophy consists in giving a new tone, and the accents of our age, to all the denigratory systems – Spinoza, Hegel, Marx . . . Our undertaking will thus be more like the Hegelian Encyclopaedia than the

Encyclopaedia of d'Alembert, which has all the defects of the bourgeoisie's compromises ... If people are at death's door, that's because they're suffocating inside shells of mendacity. We shall tell those hermit-crabs why they're dying! They'll be furious with us, nobody likes truth for its own sake. Marx said that men must be given consciousness of themselves, even if they don't want it. They don't like consciousness, they like death ... For a certain time, my friends, our sole task will be to denigrate their ideas and disaccustom them to flattery ... There's no phrase I admire more than Lenin's about the profanation of gold, do you remember? 'When we are victorious on a world scale, I think we shall use gold for the purpose of building public lavatories in the streets of some of the largest cities of the world.'

Then Laforgue said:

— What I'm a bit worried about is the possible duration of this mission ... Do you know whom I compare us to?

— No, Rosenthal replied.

— I compare us to that brilliant group of Young Hegelians, such as Bruno Bauer and his ilk, who definitely preferred revolutions in consciousness to the rough and tumble of actual revolutions. Don't you know that little epigram on the Doktorklub?

> *Unsere Täten sind Worte bis jetzt und nock lange*
> *Unter die Abstraktion stellt sich die Praxis.*

There are days when I wonder if it wouldn't be more worthwhile sticking posters up on walls, with the chaps in some party cell ...

— That's just inverted romanticism, and pretty low quality too, Rosenthal replied. Victory in thought must precede victory in reality.

— If only it could, said Laforgue. That's exactly why you strike me as idealist. Doesn't it really come down to the fact that reality strikes us as rather hard to shift?

— I don't agree, Rosenthal interrupted. The function of philosophy consists exclusively in the *profanation* of ideas. No violence is equal in its effects to theoretical violence. Later comes action . . .

— It comes, said Laforgue, when theory has penetrated the masses. Do you think it's our theory which the masses are just waiting to be penetrated by?

— We shall see, replied Rosenthal.

Yet Bernard was more impatient than all the rest. But nothing then seemed to him more urgent than to utter a few cries which he usually called messages – and which lacked simplicity. In December and again in February, Rosenthal published pages in *Civil War* that had no serious chance of shaking capitalism.

V

His first cries uttered, his first cries written, Bernard wanted action.

Civil War had been going for three months, it had five hundred subscribers and eight hundred single-copy purchasers, three publishing houses were giving it advertising. This was a great deal, it was a success, but it could not be called a historic upheaval in French thought. Rosenthal would no doubt have been content with talking about anger or the depreciation of values, or the ruses of bourgeois Reason, if such arguments had provoked legal actions – but with this absurd freedom of the press, the Public Prosecutor was still making no move. It was impossible to view the exercise of philosophy as an act.

Spring was about to arrive. People had been through hard months, but the ice was melting, winter was dying in showers of rain, one felt like rising early, the days were lengthening like the plants you see tremulously growing and unfolding on the cinema screen. In Rue de la Paix, the shop-girls came out in droves and crossed Place Vendôme and Rue de Rivoli arm in arm. From time to time the weather would be fine, as though summer, autumn or late-spring days that had not made their appearance months earlier – stifled by rain or a storm – were now dispensing their warmth upon still-numbed hands and still-chapped lips. There were still hoarfrosts on the lawns of the Luxembourg, but between two spring showers the sky would come back into view.

Apart from this oncoming spring, it was a bad time for impatient young men. Things seemed generally to be calming down, in economics and politics alike. There was a moment when the history of Europe appeared as slack as a neap-time sea, when people forgot war and peace, the Ruhr, Morocco and China. The season at Deauville had never been as brilliant as that year – indeed people would still be speaking of it during the summer of '37, not such a bad summer itself in terms of race-meetings and casinos. At Rosenthal's parents' house, ladies who had had their *belle époque* during the period of Mobilization-is-not-war would say:

— Don't you think, my dear, this spring has a little whiff, as it were, of pre-war days?

There really was not much happening. People were on the whole amused by the *Gazette du Franc* affair, Prime Minister Poincaré had hundred-vote majorities, the Briand–Kellogg Pact was perhaps going to make people feel a bit safer. There were a few strikes, of course, but Halluin and the textile industry of the Nord were far away, and the taxi strike was really quite pleasant for the private cars, which could at last drive about in Paris. People might perhaps have been moved by the thirty deaths in the Rhine Army during the month of March: how dreadful those epidemics are, mowing down young soldiers in faraway countries during the showery season – not so far away as Indochina or Madagascar, but all the same a long way from their mothers! Thereupon Marshal Foch had died, in the same month as the Rhine Army soldiers, to whom people had given rather less thought. What an opportunity to go and queue up at the end of Rue de Grenelle – in the heart of the Faubourg Saint-Germain, with Englishmen, nannies from the Champ-de-Mars, old ladies and priests – to see what the funerals of illustrious families are like, and how old victorious marshals settle into death wearing their chinstraps! But in April, when soldiers fraternized in the

45

Gard with the striking miners they were actually supposed to evict from the pits, people were fed up with all these stories about servicemen whereas only marshals – at most – were really tolerable. Eventually, however, the ladies felt easier in their minds. They were the same ones who, a few years later, would talk about pre-crash days as in '28 they had talked of pre-war days, and who could be heard in drawing-rooms saying that in the last war their sons had been taken, which for France's sake they could accept, but that in the next war their money would be taken too. Their minds had to be set at rest. Luckily, that year Prefect Chiappe showed that with him public order was in no danger: after 1 May and 1 August, people told themselves it would be a long while before the communists had bandaged all their wounds.

It was indeed a difficult year to get through, for young men who placed all their hopes in the aggravation of disorder, and for whom the only desirable future consisted in not having one. Already their parents, forever paved with good intentions, were reviving career plans for them about which they had long been doubtful, bearing in mind what this strange, tottering world of the twenties held in store. Laforgue's father, who had quite some time ago consoled himself for his son's refusal to enter the Ecole Polytechnique, spoke to him about doing a doctoral thesis, after his *agrégation*.

— Who do you take me for? Philippe exclaimed.

Was it all going to start up again, then? Were they finally going to be compelled, after invoking all the shipwrecks befitting great ornamental centuries, to sail upon the level waters of bourgeois life, observing nautical regulations and all the red signals on bridges?

The prosperity of '29, those Markets that were so healthy despite their ups and downs and any check in the contango rate, appeared as oppressive to them as the celebrated failed Revolution of '19, ten years earlier, had seemed to their elders.

They had lived amid such thrilling uncertainty, since the time when, at school, their classes had been interrupted by air raids and shellbursts and every door that banged had made them think of an explosion, that it seemed impossible to them that the sad age of indolence miraculously suspended by the four years of the War could ever resume its course.

Laforgue and Rosenthal dated history from nineteen hundred and fourteen: they would have liked to be able to call '29 Year XV, numbering the dates of a new era in the same way that the Russians spoke of Year XIII of the October Revolution. Were they now going to have to remain in the continuation of the Christian era, and feel themselves bound in perpetuity to Jesus, Charlemagne, Henri IV, Louis XIV, Voltaire, Napoleon and M. Thiers? For several months they foresaw the advent of an age of regress and boredom, such as had not been seen since the Restoration or the first years of the Third Republic, when they would lament the warlike and peaceful exploits of their elders, just as the young men of eighteen hundred and twenty had lamented the Revolutionary Wars, the Italian Campaign and Napoleon's anabases from one end of Europe to the other, or the young men of eighteen hundred and eighty had lamented the Burning of Paris and the Commune with its sixty days of great innovations. Would they then be reduced to writing poems?

They were well aware that the public authorities and their families were conspiring, as in the past, to make them relapse into brilliant futures, careers, worries about advance-ment, money and successful marriages. These pretensions struck them as repugnant, but they trembled to see them confirmed by the becalming of history: in their entire adoles-cence, there was perhaps no year more disturbing than that year of '29, when everything contributed to a non-stop purr of contentment.

Thank God, in November, the Wall Street crash was to reas-sure them: they welcomed it like news of a victory. Since they tended to confuse capitalism with important people, when they saw their fathers' faces they convinced themselves that they had been quite right to stake their lives on the cards of confusion, and that they could indubitably count upon a world destined for great metamorphoses. There was no question of settling down into an order that was about to die, no question of making their beds.

— Didn't we say so! they exclaimed.

But they had had a narrow escape.

None of them was more sensitive than Rosenthal to these plunges and abrupt recoveries of potential. You must picture Bernard founding *Civil War* only in order to play for time, in order to occupy his mind, until he got a chance to show what he was capable of. He would gladly have been heroic: there were no opportunities.

One evening towards the end of March, in Rue d'Ulm, Rosenthal exclaimed that the Revolution required far more than articles:

— One writes, he said, and one believes that the Revolution is made. One falls – we fall – into post-revolutionary fantasies. Are you satisfied? Yes or no? You're not saying anything? One's confidence in revolution can be measured only by the sacrifices one makes to it and the risks one runs for it . . .

— That's more or less what I've always had the honour of telling you, replied Laforgue.

Next day, Bloyé said to Laforgue:

— It's four months that the journal has been going now, that's a long time . . . Rosenthal must have some ideas at the back of his mind. You can detect that hypocritical self-satisfaction of men who are making plans . . .

— Yes, said Laforgue. He's slyly singing a new song to himself.

Rosenthal dropped hints, he said:

— Do you recall Dostoievsky and what he says about the Idea one must have and in whose power one must believe?

48

There's no living person to whom I feel closer than I do to Arkady Makarovich Dolgoruky...

His friends waited, however. Knowing his taste for mystery and coups de théâtre, they did not question him.

VI

One Saturday, towards evening, they all received an express letter inviting them to assemble next day at two o'clock opposite Saint-Germain-des-Prés: all of them – Laforgue, Bloyé, Jurien and lastly Pluvinage.

No group of young people exists in which hierarchies and distances are not established, as though some of them were credited by all the others with a more far-reaching future. Rosenthal, who was looked on as the leader and enjoyed this position, vaguely mistrusted Pluvinage and had hesitated before inviting him along: he would not have entrusted him with his secrets. Perhaps it was because of his name: nobody calls themself Pluvinage. But the day was not expected to be packed with great mysteries, so Bernard had notified Pluvinage after all.

It was a rainy early-April day, an icy aftermath of those March showers when all hopes placed in the establishment of spring burst as rapidly as the heavens. Because of that black Sunday rain, Paris was empty: umbrellas drifted between wind and water like shining jellyfish; couples made their way to tedious visits and slapped their children; gusts of damp wind closed down the newspaper vendors under the Abbey porch, where three beggars lay in ambush for the faithful at Vespers. Rosenthal was waiting in an old open car, parked between the Clamart tramway and the shop supplying insignia on Place Saint-Germain-des-Prés.

— You're a proper swine, said Bloyé, you really could have brought your old hearse up to Rue d'Ulm.

— Climb aboard, said Rosenthal. We've quite a way to go.

— Might one know where we're off to? asked Laforgue.

— You'll soon see, replied Rosenthal as he engaged the gears.

None of them insisted: they had not yet lost their taste for mystery games.

The car left Paris by Avenue de Neuilly and Route de la Défense; at Argenteuil, which they approached via the river embankment, batteries of factory chimneys rose behind the curtain of rain over flat meadows ruffled by the wind; acid fumes hung everywhere in the harsh Sunday air; after leaving behind Argenteuil and then Bezons, they crossed the Seine a second time by the Maisons-Laffitte bridge, then turned in the direction of Saint-Germain. A little before Mesnil-le-Roi, the car stopped with a screech of brakes in front of an old house built in that rather soft facing-stone which one soon encounters along the roads of the Vexin region. The rain had just stopped. Its branches still black, barely budding after the interminable winter, the wisteria over the gate was dripping. Rosenthal rang at the iron door; a young woman emerged onto the perron and shouted to them to come in, and they pushed open the garden gate.

— Hullo, Rosenthal, how are you? asked the young woman. Weren't you scared off by all that rain?

— Of course not, replied Bernard. It was even rather pleasant. Simone, these are the friends I've told you about.

— I'm sure François will be delighted to meet them, she said.

She clasped their hands at length, staring them rather myopically in the eye. She was fair, made-up, quite thin, her hand had bones of disturbing smallness and dryness. They went in; puddles formed at once beneath their raincoats. In the dining-room, there were crocheted covers, lampshades, plates bearing legends on the walls, a faded green cloth embroidered with yellow flowers on a round table where piles of journals and newspapers lay about. The young woman caught their glances:

— It's pretty squalid, isn't it? she said. But François needed a quiet place to work; in Paris, he can't do anything with all his appointments and that dreadful telephone. I'm going to make you some tea, you must be frozen . . .

She went out, they heard the clatter of cups. They gathered round the wood fire that was burning at the back of the black marble fireplace.

— Who ever is that lady? asked Laforgue, and who was she talking about?

— You're in the home of a friend of mine, Rosenthal replied. He'll be down.

The young woman returned. They waited a while longer, drinking tea with slices of lemon from glasses.

— Do you at least like Russian tea? she asked.

The conversation flagged. They could hear somebody pacing up and down overhead.

— When François is working, the young woman said, he's like a lion in a cage . . . I told him you were here.

They grew a little bored, but after all, for a Sunday in April . . . Through the panes they could see the valley of the Seine, which changed direction beneath the terraces of Saint-Germain, and on the blurred horizon a province of red roofs dropped at random, from the plain with its roads right up to the slopes of Mont Valérien.

— You've got a really splendid view, said Bloyé.

— As if I cared about that! she cried, crossing her bare legs. Nothing gets on my nerves worse than the countryside. And at this time of year!

A door closed on the first floor, footsteps could be heard coming down the stairs, which creaked, and their host entered. He was a tall man with something of a stoop, blue eyes which darted about with such mobility that at times he appeared to have a squint, and a bald forehead which gave him a faintly distraught air.

'I've seen that face somewhere,' thought Laforgue. 'That weak mouth ...'

— Régnier, said Rosenthal, allow me to introduce my friends. Meet Laforgue, Bloyé, Jurien, Pluvinage ...

Régnier shook hands with them. They all knew his name, they had read his books, he was the first well-known writer they had met. They immediately wanted to make an impression, compel him to admire them. It was not easy, and ultimately they did not succeed. François Régnier talked almost the whole time, in a jerky manner, about the weather they were having; about the book on which he was working, and which as it so happened was concerned with youth, and he was so very glad to be having a chat with them; about travelling – he mentioned Spanish and Greek dishes, one would have thought travellers never emerged from restaurants.

— At La Barraca in Madrid, he said, one can eat a truly exceptional *cocido* ... When you go to Madrid, you absolutely must go and see my old friend El Segobiano, who will make you an astounding bread soup ...

Or else:

— In Athens, at Costi's, the thing to eat is roast woodpigeon. But perhaps the best meal I ever had in Greece was really those eggs fried in olive oil that I ate at Eleusis, in the home of a grocer who was explaining some things to me about the Battle of Salamis.

They did not really find him very exceptional, indeed this superior tone of the man of forty who has seen it all made them quite cross. Every now and then, Régnier would stand up and walk round them.

— François, stop that, said the young women finally. You're making us seasick ...

— Simone, he replied, give me my plaid. It's perishing in this house.

He threw a Scottish plaid over his shoulders and did not sit down. He asked the young men questions about themselves, about their ideas on love and politics. They replied evasively – what business was it of his? He quoted things famous people had said, he seemed to know all Paris:

— Herriot was saying to me only last week, he began, 'My dear Régnier . . .'

Or:

— Philippe Berthelot was telling me that the day the Briand–Kellogg Pact was signed . . .

The name of Plato launched him into a brilliant variation on the theme of painting, about which as a matter of fact Berthelot had never understood a thing: however, these specialists fresh from their *Sophist* and *Politicus* judged it fallacious. Bloyé explained this to him with a certain insolent severity. They were not sorry to catch out in error such odious fluency, and to show Régnier that, even if he knew Berthelot, Herriot and Léon Blum, he was at any rate ignorant of Plato.

— It's quite possible, he replied, laughing in a careless manner, baring his teeth. What a time it has been since I construed the *Republic* at the Sorbonne, before the war! That isn't the least bit important, in any case. When you're my age, you won't give a fig for textual fidelity.

He went on explaining painting to them, which in those years played the role that the theatre had filled twenty years earlier, and since he was mentioning the names of painters they did not know, they found him vulgar.

A little later, he asked them:

— How old are you all?

— Twenty-two.

— Twenty-three.

— Twenty-three.

— Rosenthal I know, said Régnier.

— And you? asked Laforgue.

— Thirty-eight, he said. How young they are!

Régnier began to laugh once again with his disagreeable laugh.

At around half past five, they left. It was quite dark; beneath a ceiling of clouds, a vast jumble of winking lights stretched to the ends of the earth, far beyond Paris. As soon as Rosenthal accelerated, under the rotting trees in the forest of Saint-Germain, the cold cut into their cheeks. The wind smelled of moss, fungus and mould.

— What do you think of him? asked Rosenthal. How did you find Régnier?

— Not bad, said Bloyé weakly.

— Extraordinarily boring, said Laforgue.

— He wasn't on form, said Rosenthal. One shouldn't catch him on a working day, I'm afraid we may have disturbed him a bit, then he says any old thing, just banalities. But I wanted you to make his acquaintance, for later. Now it's done, you'll have other opportunities to know him better . . .

— Don't apologize, said Laforgue. The weather might have been even filthier.

Rosenthal was upset and fell silent. But near Bougival he suddenly said, in a defiant tone of voice:

— Régnier's the most intelligent man I know, all the same.

— Why not? said Laforgue. Perhaps he's keeping his cards close to his chest . . .

VII

BERNARD ROSENTHAL TO PHILIPPE LAFORGUE

Paris, 26 March 1929

Dear Philippe,

*It is time I finally put you in the picture about the project you have
all no doubt suspected me of having – I am writing to Bloyé and
Jurien as well. Let's say nothing for the time being to Pluvinage.*

*We have opted for Revolution as our reason for living. A reason
for living is not just an element of spiritual comfort to use at night
in order to fall asleep in the obscene embrace of good conscience. We
must reflect deeply upon the consequences which this reason entails:
this is how the totality of life may be arrived at. Without totality,
we shall not endure ourselves. Spinoza says: acquiescentia in se
ipso. That is what we shall demand. The essential lies in accepting
oneself.*

*Nothing appeals to me more than the idea of irreversible commit-
ment. We must invent the constraints that will bar us from
inconstancy; opting for Revolution must not be a promise for a term,
which it might one day be legitimate to reconsider. Let us beware of
our future infidelities . . .*

*A man who believes in God is a victim of the most squalid
sentiment in the world, yet his whole life is condemned, he is seamless,
there is not the fragment of belief and the fragments of normal life: it*

56

is impossible for him to retrace his steps and reverse his decision, without feeling destroyed. The Revolution demands deeds of us that are as effective as the Christian's, as far removed from inner life, and which compromise us enough for us never to be able to go back. What strikes me in Christian life is that it basically concerns itself only with works and demonstrations – good intentions are Protestant claptrap. That is how we shall understand commitment: as a premeditated system of rigorous constraints.

Anarchism was particularly favourable to works of this kind. Throwing a bomb, killing somebody important: after that, it was really impossible to go on living as before the bomb or the murder; never again was there a status quo; the lines of retreat were severed; one was in history up to one's neck; one could only plunge in, from the moment one had placed oneself outside the normal bounds. But anarchism has been killed off by history, by the revolutions of the twentieth century, by the masses the latter have brought into play and by the revolutionary's certain conviction that he will not, through a terrorist act, succeed in seriously frightening the enemy. Politics stripped of terrorism and its pure commitments confronts the individual with problems of another order, the highest of which is that of effectiveness. We must take a stand against excessive profundity that evades questions; we must simply aim for truth and Being, which are simple.

It was against quite remarkable government and police techniques that the old passions of anarchism shattered. The Revolution will be technical. The difficult part is to devise acts that serve the Revolution and at the same time constitute for us irreversible events. We must no longer believe that once the truth about evil is known, evil is abolished. It is necessary to destroy evil. To philosophize with hammer blows. To devise irreparable things.

It is clear, and you must feel it like me, that the articles we have published and the speeches we shall not fail to deliver do not commit us dangerously – at least, not for long. Just as there exist female accomplishments, these are scarcely more than youthful accomplishments, characterized by skilful artistry and self-satisfaction.

It seems to me – and François Régnier, with whom I have
spoken at length since our abortive visit to Carrières, has said
some really important things to me about this – that espionage
might at this moment constitute the simultaneously effective and
irremediable activity which I have so passionately in mind. The
legendary baseness of espionage has entirely to do with the
temporal interests that motivate spies and with the ignoble aims
their imperialist paymasters harbour. Espionage has not yet been
considered as one of the forms of intellectual activity. An act of
espionage absolutely disinterested in its motives, or whose deeply
interested nature is of a concrete and metaphysical order and
entirely pure in its aims, does not strike me as unworthy of us: no
means is impure.

There are two revolutions: one has been made, the other remains
to be made. The period of reconstruction from which the October
Revolution has yet to emerge places technical information in the first
rank of its needs. The USSR's watchword is to catch up with and
surpass the most advanced capitalist countries. We have the good
fortune to live in one of these. You can see that I am thinking here of
a form of industrial espionage, which does not seem to me impossible
from a practical point of view, inasmuch as we live within the
bourgeoisie, where no one would dream of mistrusting us on that
particular terrain. They do not alter their habits of 'thought' so
quickly, they will never mistrust anyone except traditional foes,
traitors dressed for the part.

The French Revolution that is being prepared, despite all
appearances and all signs of stability, must place in the forefront
of its concerns the issues of the seizure of power and the resist-
ance that may be put up in the first weeks of armed conflict. So
there exists a necessity to work politically in the Army, and a
conspiratorial necessity to gain possession, before the decisive
days, of various items of military information: security arrange-
ments, protective plans, arms dump locations, mobilization
centres, etc. If I still cannot see in detail the real conditions for
the success of industrial espionage – it will obviously be necessary

to create a complex network of absolutely reliable technicians, only a few of them in the Centrale and Polytechnique milieux, perhaps a rather larger number in Arts et Métiers, in the technical schools for the poor – I find it easier to imagine the fairly swift and widespread success of military espionage. We are all destined to carry out our military service as infantry or artillery officers, or as soldiers occupying (thanks to the virtues of Culture) privileged jobs. (Actually, we have been following a stupid policy up to now in systematically opposing higher military training and, like the normaliens of Quimper, organizing at the Ecole a struggle against the draft.) What defines military secrets is not so much profundity as repetition: nothing is more Kierkegaardian than a military headquarters. So a quite small number of comrades would be enough at the beginning to transmit what is really important, and to start organizing a network of informers which will not need to be of limitless dimensions. We shall speak again soon at our leisure about the concrete details: please do give the matter some thought.

The transmission to its final destination of the information we collect poses a problem that is of an ethical more than a practical nature: I regard it as indispensable that it should be effected anonymously. In no case should it be possible to establish any link between the intended recipients of our consignments, who must not be implicated, and ourselves. Besides, the private value of our actions would be utterly compromised by the expectation of any recognition or importance whatsoever. Virtue is its own reward. Yours.

P.S. Do you remember Simon, who was with us at Louis-le-Grand and went on to the Ecole des Chartes? He is secretary to his colonel at Clignancourt. We might make a trial run. I shall see him: I have always had a certain influence over him, up to now he has done almost everything I have suggested to him.

Strasburg, 28 March 1929

Dear old Rosen,

So that was your Dostoievskyan idea. I find it unbelievably romantic. If it's a matter of commitment, I somehow have the impression that a metalworker's commitment in a party cell, a factory cell, goes much further than any mystical – and also sly – demonstration: sly, because it is explicitly understood that fellows like us are never caught, are not catchable. The metalworker risks – and straight away, not in six months or outside time – his freedom, his job and his livelihood. Same thing with the fellows who get themselves nabbed in barracks for Inciting-military-personnel-to-disobey-orders-in-pursuance-of-the-aims-of-anarchist-propaganda. Perhaps, if we were not afraid of political servitude, and if it were not the case that nothing seems more important to us than not choosing, the true solution for us too would consist in joining the party without further ado, although life in it cannot always be easy for intellectuals. We shall have to see . . .

All the same, until such time as we make up our minds to take the plunge, and the Revolution is more visibly imminent than in this bitch of a period, we are having such a damnably tedious time living our young elite existence that I cannot see why we should not have a go at conspiracy, something along the lines of The Possessed or the Narodniks. Your clandestine dreams, though, strike me as more effective for the purposes of your personal perfection than for concretely achieving the conquest of political power by the proletariat.

But you are as you are, you will reply that man has no need, like a horse, for perfection.

It is not impossible that I might come across something to do in the industrial field, thanks to my father with his Polytechnique background who, as is only proper, is in the vanguard of technology. It would astonish me, however, if I found the energy for this at once, because of the atmosphere one breathes here while awaiting Easter.

Strasburg – gloriously reconquered from the enemy, to the great joy of the patriots, who brought out again quantities of little black-and-green ribbons; and also of the German officers of the Rhine flotilla, already sequestered by their rebellious sailors brandishing revolvers in docks filled with red flags, while the admiral paced up and down without a stitch on, at several degrees below – Strasburg, I say, even though its frivolous, musical character has been much weakened during the six years since my father arrived there in the victors' baggage train, still possesses the enchanting look of a Rhine resort where there is no question of taking things seriously. The time of the great madness is over, when the lieutenants of the French Army were lording it over the Broglie and on Rue de la Mesange, and when the most amazing schemes were within a week making rich men out of petty adventurers only just demobbed, whose wives were soon driving about in Mercedes and Rolls; a romantic trade in contraband currency was carried on by boat between the two banks of the Rhine, which, when all is said and done, was actually contained in Anglo-French glasses; military planes would smuggle bicycles and sewing-machines fastened between the wheels of their landing-gear; the customs men on the Kehl Bridge used to empty women's bodices stuffed with silk stockings, men's pockets, the robes of priests, all of them made dizzy by the abysses of the German inflation; powerful families of brewers and bankers would pay unattached young men from the interior to sleep with the daughters-in-law from whom they wished to deliver their sons; the high officials of Millerand and Alapetite's Commissariat were carrying off whole wagonloads of state property to France for their country houses; the surrealists used to come to Strasburg in quest of the well-springs of German romanticism. That's over, but one can still spend one's leisure time wandering along embankments flanked by steeples, bell towers, palaces, latticed gardens, churches and Protestant chapels, where the tourists go to meditate upon death as they peer at glass coffins containing little girls in dresses with farthingales, or stuffed and extremely moth-eaten eighteenth-century generals. There are spots

61

beside the canals and the Ill with trees, grass and silence; and
Weinstüben, where waitress-mistresses in black silk dresses reveal
their thighs so far up that you want to stroke them, even though
their skin has an off-putting salad whiteness: when you know
them quite well, they take you into the kitchen to kiss you expertly
on the lips and call you Dearest Soul in German. Easter is not bad
in Alsace, but nothing equals the snowy season in this town. Then
all the brothels have Christmas trees, round which the young
bourgeois of the town grow emotional in the company of the girls of
the house, while their parents attend Midnight Mass in the
Minster. These young men usually have mistresses, as they call
them, who are waitresses from some brasserie, in black aprons and
with big breasts, who give them a bit of pocket money. On Sundays
they go and dance with their sisters' friends in the ballrooms of the
Hôtel Hannong or the Maison Rouge, for it is still rather cool in
the restaurants of La Wanzenau and Le Fuchs am Buckel. In a
few days' time, these maidens will begin playing tennis on the
courts of La Robertsau, where there will be roses. All the lures of
the Family . . . Yours.

BERNARD ROSENTHAL TO PHILIPPE LAFORGUE

Paris, 30 March 1929

Dear Philippe,

I can overlook your epithet 'romantic': we'll have to argue it out,
because it seems to me to indicate a serious misunderstanding between
us. This is not the first time I have suspected you of a kind of casual
lack of passion. Watch out for the gardens of Ile de France, for the
speech of Touraine, for moderation, for useless moderation, for
Common-sense-the-most-widely-shared-thing-in-the-world, for the
idiocy of Anatole France, for the chicanery of Voltaire. Sometimes you
are terribly French.

We shall also have to speak further about joining the party,
because that is serious. Our function consists in inventing or

deepening beliefs, but not in dissolving them into politics. It must be possible to play an important role as irregulars. As old Uncle Spinoza says, there can never be too much liberty.

Thanks, whatever happens, for your acceptance in principle of my project: I would not have done anything without you, or without the others. Bloyé agrees too, with some objections in the caution department, and Jurien, which surprises me more. I did not have such high hopes of that future university lecturer, who will lose his taste for Revolution at the same time as his virginity, which by now cannot be long delayed. I have met Simon, much affected by military service. I have told him nothing as yet. It is obvious that there is not much to be discovered from his colonel's office, apart from the list of men in the regiment classified as PR. But he has independently conceived the ambition of getting himself posted as secretary to one of the offices of the Paris garrison, and has told me that he has asked to be transferred from the 21st Colonial at Clignancourt to the 23rd at Lourcine, where a job is about to fall vacant in the office of Area 2 of the garrison. He sees in this transfer, to which I have vigorously encouraged him, merely the advantages of indolence and the attractions of the locality. He has few Parisian contacts. But when we meet in a few days, we shall have to find a way of getting him recommended by Mr So-and-so, who knows Mrs X, who just so happens to be on ever such intimate terms with the supreme commander of the colonial troops. Are you yourself not more or less stabled with a filly from the Gouraud circle? Cheerio.

PHILIPPE LAFORGUE TO PAULINE D.

Strasburg, 2 April 1929

Dear Pauline,

I have a tiny favour to ask of you, which you must be in a position to do for me thanks to the bad company you keep. One of my friends, who is a private in the 21st Colonial at the

Clignancourt barracks, wants to come across to the Left Bank, and specifically to the 23rd Colonial at the Lourcine barracks. He has entirely serious reasons which are none of your business, as they are none of mine. Since you are up to your neck in generals, you might perhaps ask one of those fellows decked out in oak leaves how the matter should be tackled. I should add that my friend is particularly desirous of being assigned to a post which is about to fall vacant and which he says is a cushy number, that of secretary to Area 2 of the Paris Garrison, which is housed precisely in the Lourcine or Port-Royal barracks. He is called André Simon, private in the 21st Colonial Infantry Regiment, Headquarters Wing, Clignancourt Barracks, 18th.

P.S. After the Easter break is over, dear Pauline, if the notion takes you to come back to Rue d'Ulm, I should like it to be after nine at night. Given the house customs, there is no doubt about the porter letting you past, he has seen even nigger-women come in.

PAULINE D. TO PHILIPPE LAFORGUE

Paris, 9 April 1929

Philippe dear,

I do a favour for you! It is too diverting for me to refuse. As you can imagine, your conduct does not deceive me and I am too fond of our reprehensible little sessions at Rue d'Ulm to hold your bad manners against you. I found the right general, of course, he was an old friend of my uncle's and a telephone call was all it took. Your friend will be appointed to the post he set his heart on. Apparently this was not one of those ambitions that cannot be satisfied. Do not thank me, I detest written expressions of gratitude. I shall come and see you. After nine at night, since that is what you want. Till then.

Paris, 9 April 1929

My dear old Rosen,

It is all settled. Simon will go to Port-Royal. I arrived in Paris yesterday evening and think we shall see each other soon. Nothing is simpler than the beginning of a Great Conspiracy. Yours.

VIII

André Simon was a rather weak young man. He was the son of rich tradespeople from Nantes, who brought up their children admirably, but who had ended up respecting only the Spirit, without thinking that this ludicrous veneration for the most disinterested activities of life ruined everything, and that it was merely the mark of their commercial decadence and of a bourgeois bad conscience of which as yet they had no suspicion. They had plenty of excuses: never had the values of commerce and status attached themselves more powerfully to writers, artists and diplomats – to all creators of alibis.

This gifted boy – who would no doubt have settled for managing the purchases and sales of his father's silk business in Rue Crébillon, while consoling himself for having above him only the shipowners of Boulevard Delorme and the great maritime brokers of the Fosse – had entered the Ecole des Chartes. What an adventure!

There are few social movements more remarkable than the fate of certain great Nantes houses in the years following the War: the deviation which led Simon out of the paths of commerce towards the little curiosities of Diplomatics was at the same time propelling young men from his background – whom he may have known at the Lycée Clemenceau, in the years when old men and young women were replacing teachers away at the front or dead on the field of honour – towards the Ecole des Sciences Politiques and the little secrets of diplomacy.

Sons of wholesale grocers, brought up beneath the bell-towers of Sainte-Croix, in about 1925 discovered golf at La Baule, horses in Paris, and plunged into proud but obscure careers in the French legations of this Europe of Versailles, Saint-Germain and Trianon in which treaties with the names of châteaux and parks cannot conceal the blood and violence to come. Others, echoing Parisian appeals or Alsatian voices, hurled themselves blindly into poetical activity. Yet others, at a loose end thanks to easy money and the dispersal of their schoolfellows, with frivolous enthusiasm collected the records of the American hot jazz greats, played poker, chased married women impelled by boredom into provincial adulteries; they learned to find cocaine and ether in the shady chemist shops of the town, and borrowed one-hundred-franc notes from the antiquated whores of Place Royale and Place Graslin, who demanded them back with insults on the pavement of Rue Crébillon or beneath the white arcades of the Passage Pommeraye, which still displays its braces, etchings, jokes and novelties, sheaths, trusses, and the outdated model of the battleship *Jauréguiberry*. Jewellers' sons end up burgling their fathers' shop-windows, sparing neither First Communion medals, nor betrothal salvers, nor wedding rings, nor christening baubles. Youths, huddled behind the Quai de la Fosse or the embankments of the Ile Gloriette, in mouldy cellars which must remind them of London warehouses and the literary quaysides of Hamburg, organize secret societies bound by childish rituals and the practices of an eroticism as antiquated as the kept women of their native town.

This unruliness of youth commenced after the peace of '19 in the large provincial towns, at Nantes as at Rheims, Nancy, Bordeaux, Rouen or Lille, when the time came for the provincial grandes bourgeoisies to entertain anxious doubts about their future. It seemed that their heirs could choose only between two temptations: the son of a Bordeaux wine merchant, who on leaving the Ecole Normale goes off to Athens to prepare for digs in the Chersonese or at Delos, is perhaps no less wayward than the Rouen notary's son hauled before the assizes for a motor theft, a swindle or trafficking in drugs.

Eight or nine years later, when the time of Leagues, arms deals and plots came, people thought everything would be settled by political adventures: the unruliness of the sons then seemed to protect their fathers' Ledger.

What André Simon feared most of all was to be despised by Rosenthal, with whom he had graduated from Louis-le-Grand and whom he admired, as Bernard from time to time thought he admired François Régnier, but in a different way. What a concatenation of influences, what an interplay of mirror reflections, in the lives of young men who feel themselves still somewhat too spineless to walk without companions, confidants and witnesses. One day Simon wrote in a letter to his father:

> My friend Rosenthal is perhaps the only *living* philosopher there exists at present in France. People do not know this, and he probably does not know it either. But when he has published, or delivered, his first lectures, people will realize the truth, realize that they have a philosopher as important as Bergson.

These rhapsodies, however, were based only on a few sentences from Bernard.

The first effect of this admiration was that André Simon was doing his military service as a private. He could have been a second lieutenant, he even should have been if he had obeyed the laws on the military training of students; but Rosenthal had forbidden him to submit to those rules, against which many young men put up a violent resistance in '27 and '28.

— If you agree to become a reserve officer, said Rosenthal, I shall never speak to you again. We must remain in the ranks. They would like us to become their accomplices, utterly their accomplices; they believe almost sincerely, in any case, that this is our due, as it is theirs to command. But we shall give ourselves all the opportunities we can to be against them and with their enemies. Military service is the first chance we have to find ourselves mingling with peasants, workers and bank clerks. To separate ourselves from our class. Are we going to miss our first chance!

Now a private, Simon could never accustom himself to so inhuman a condition. Everything depressed him. The barbarous world which, at Clignancourt, extended between the walls of the outer boulevard and the muddy villages of the periphery was subjected to rules and customs of an astonishing violence, which would be given vent in its ways of eating, sleeping, washing, speaking about women, or passively receiving orders which had been passed down so many times that they seemed absurd by the time they reached the men.

Obscure passwords and an omnipresent wish to humiliate governs military life: on his arrival at the barracks, Simon had little idea of the refinements an NCO in a colonial regiment can achieve in the debasement of man.

The young Paris workers of the 21st Colonial – who used to defend themselves against army life with inimitably dexterous puns, jokes and ripostes; who in town had mistresses or wives, children, a profession which they sometimes continued to pursue between supper and lights out . . . in short, a life; who managed to ward off Breton sergeants and Corsican sergeant-majors by dint of levity, irony and a disdainful knowledge of men – to Simon appeared like heroes. This young archivist, barely emerged from the warmth of provincial life and from a kind of old bourgeois distinction, was possessed by the same hopeless love of freedom as young miners from the Pas-de-Calais whom war and the ravages of invasion had kept from learning to read; or as farm boys from the Vendée, dazed by their first weeks in the Army, who grew thin and at once fell ill.

Lieutenant-Colonel de Lesmaes – who sometimes used to summon Simon to his office to question him about the philosophies of China and India, in which he took an interest and whose great names and systems Simon, in order to avoid disappointing his superior, had to invent on the spot – Lieutenant-Colonel de Lesmaes said to him:

— You see, Simon, your comrades do not understand the need for external marks of respect: the halt at a distance of six feet, or the salute before addressing a superior, strike them as idiotic. But external marks of respect shouldn't be seen as pointless annoyances. It's quite obvious that a man's first reaction would be to kill his officer: a regiment is burdened with a vast quantity of explosive substances, so such impulses must be disciplined by the external marks of respect. Have you never seen an animal caught in a trap? No? It no longer moves, it knows there's nothing to be done. Standing to attention is a trap, military discipline a civility motivated by caution. There's no question of prostituting yourself to the men. Discipline means being the boss, and giving that lot the idea that they're buggered without you . . .

— You should reread Alain, Sir, said Simon, who was distressed by this philosophy of command.

He was quite aware that the system eventually won over many of his companions: it was on 1 May that he heard Corporal Palhardy, who was completing his service before returning to his Poitou smithy, declare:

— What do you expect the workers to do? They're not armed against us. And with old Papa Chiappe . . . They get taught some respect . . .

*   *   *

Simon saw his anger and concern as a systematic revolt against
the system that gives birth to modern armies. In reality they
were keen but unprincipled: the barracks was simply a place
where he could not breathe, as though it had been four thousand metres above sea-level, or below the ground. He often
used to go and lean on the parapet of the rampart-walk facing
the smoky district of Saint-Ouen, thinking in despair how in
the evening he would have to return to the office where he
slept beside the regimental flag and boxes full of war trophies,
helmets, German colours and braid torn from the sleeves of
dead men; opposite a window rent by the violet flashes of Paris;
hearing, when he could not sleep, the North trains whistle. He
thought only of escape, to which he devoted the same skill as
those old re-enlisted soldiers who used to be billeted for a few
weeks at the Clignancourt barracks between two terms in the
colonies: long enough to tell lurid tales from Cochinchina and
the Lebanon and find, among the black ruts of the periphery or
in the streets that climb towards the town hall of the 18th
arrondissement, women whom they still had the heart to argue
over with the pimps of Rue du Poteau. Simon had quickly
learnt to imitate fairly accurately all the signatures needed to
get him past the guardhouse or the little gate in the bastion
where the sergeants' families lived. That was nothing: life does
not consist in a few midnight passes, which do not prevent you
from relapsing into the nightmares that barracks and prisons
manufacture all night long. Simon was really proud of himself
on the day when he simulated a hepatic attack so well that the
regimental doctor sent him to spend three weeks in the
confined atmosphere of the fever wards and classic grey monas-
tery gardens of the Val-de-Grâce. Among his chance
companions, he really liked only the absent without leave, the
deserters, those whose Army file bore the fine black-and-red
arabesques of punishments for habitual misconduct, the insolent soldiers whose unauthorized absences expired an hour
before becoming desertion. Anything seemed to him better

than this blind servitude, this feverish barrack-room brooding: hospital, prison, suicide. Nothing discomfits the military authorities more than suicide, whereby a man craftily escapes all the Army's supernatural threats. But nothing seemed more natural to Simon, who as long as he lived would see as the most heartrending symbol of order, and the noblest image of courage, the plain wooden coffin of a peasant from the Vendée who had hanged himself one night with his tie, after sixty hours' confinement to barracks, from the banister on the top landing of the stairs in C Block: the officers were dreadfully put out, the men prowled about in front of the open door to the showers which were serving as a mortuary, the colonel's staff captain recalled the time when a forceful colonel would make all his men march past a swine of a suicide's corpse, exposed on the stable dungheap.

As he had hoped, at the Port-Royal barracks Simon found a few freedoms. In this barracks, an astonishing, easygoing disorder reigned, maintained by the to-ings and fro-ings of colonial arrivals and departures, which allowed many prisoners to escape. Those on secondment like Simon, since the sentries scarcely knew them, used to enter and leave their quarters without anyone dreaming of asking them to account for themselves.

The offices of Area 2 of the Paris Garrison were installed on the first floor of a main building facing onto Rue de Lourcine: it was an isolated refuge, where two secretaries lived – Simon and a private named Dietrich, whom he saw only rarely. Each morning, a company sergeant-major would come and smoke a cigarette in the office. Two or three times a week, a major would pay a brief visit to the men under his command, whose names he had forgotten, although he knew vaguely that one of them had been a student and had been recommended by the high command of the colonial regiments.

Sergeant-Major Giudici, while awaiting his retirement,

which would come soon what with his years of campaigning and his semi-campaigns at sea between Indochina and Marseilles, carried on an existence rich in complicated intrigues, centred upon a number of whores from Rue Pascal and the Carrefour des Gobelins.

He liked Simon, because he thought he could rely more upon men who had a mysterious education, and whose unknown concerns and civilian world were no doubt too far distant from his own for them to take a notion to intervene dangerously in his affairs: he did not imagine that a young bourgeois could ever become a rival, or a spy.

The discretionary power of military command, the baseness that habitually attaches itself to the sovereign exercise of absolute power, and the certainty of always being believed before an inferior, generally induce NCOs to look upon their men as servants and to force them into waiting upon their persons: the relationship of subordination which discipline establishes with a view to war turns in peacetime into a relationship of servility. A barracks is scarcely anything but a great assemblage of employers and servants – no feature of military life is more feudal than this. A strange game of social compensation and revenge takes place: a sergeant, who in civilian life has been unable to achieve anything, avenges himself for many former humiliations by ordering a young lawyer or engineer to sweep his room or empty his pail.

Sergeant-Major Giudici, who had always had underlings, promptly found it natural to entrust Simon with errands to the sombre bars on the streets that cross Boulevard de Port-Royal beneath iron bridges, linking the Mouffetard to the Broca and Santé neighbourhoods.

Simon at first endured with extreme impatience the obligation to act as the sentimental messenger and intermediary of a non-commissioned officer who was basically nothing but a pimp. He then told himself, recalling certain sergeants he had known at Clignancourt, that a procurer is at least better than an invert or a brute, and that this complicity would give him the right to demand of the Sergeant-Major, with the proper degree of insolence, certain favours and the right to lie low when he felt like it. Besides, Giudici had a kind of lazy affability which his smile, his Bastia accent and his colonial lies endowed with considerable charm. Simon ended by taking pleasure in his brief passages through a frivolous, turbulent and lax universe, of which he had hitherto had no suspicion and which never yielded up to him its true secrets. He would have been no intellectual if he had not been sensitive to all changes of scene and capable of romanticizing them: he was naively astonished to find himself in Rue Pascal, just as he would have marvelled to see himself in China or Peru.

So Simon would go into some bar, which would usually be painted in melancholy colours, and would ask at the counter whether Madame Jeanne or Madame Lucie was there: when she was absent, he would say that he would call again; when she was there, he would deliver a message from Giudici. The Sergeant-Major's lady friends would welcome him with the mechanical familiarity common to whores and soldiers.

— You're Sergeant-Major Giudici's orderly? he would be asked.

— Not exactly, Simon would reply. Just one of his men.

— You won't leave without a little drop of something . . .

He would sip drinks that filled him with the greatest mistrust while Madame Jeanne, or Madame Lucie, read the letter. Sometimes the recipient would exclaim:

— Oh, the swine! the swine! You can go and tell your sarge from me that he can just bugger off, and he'd better not set foot in here again! Not ever!

Some days, everything would go off peacefully and Simon would sit down and listen patiently, overcome by the paralysis that affects you when you are having a shoeshine or a haircut, to the rambling confidences of the Luxemburger girl from Rue Saint-Jacques or the mulatto girl from Rue des Feuillantines, as if these stories had been a kind of sweet, purring message. The women had tangled lives and an extraordinarily pernickety concern for their dignity, their *amour propre*, for absurd points of honour, like points of honour in the days of the Hundred Years War.

One evening, a young woman brought Simon back in a taxi to the barrack gates, all the way from the café in the 12th opposite the 46th Infantry barracks where he had gone to meet her. It was April, night was beginning to fall, the air was sharp and blue, it was pretty cold for the time of year. Simon, who was growing numb in that spring coolness, said nothing because those exuberant women intimidated him sufficiently for him to be convinced he was not attracted by them. Suddenly he felt a burning hand alight on his thigh and fumble at the buttons of his uniform breeches; he made to push it away, but a rather husky voice said:

— Just relax, my darling . . . It'll warm you up. The driver can't see a thing – as you see, he's got no rear-view mirror . . .

Simon released the wrist he was grasping and surrendered himself, till he was shaken by a pleasure whose violence shattered him and gave him ideas about the skill of whores that he had always regarded as mythical. In the darkness, he then kissed an invisible mouth filled with flowing, silvery saliva; he touched the tip of a flattened breast, a shaven sex of horrifying but fiery nakedness. The taxi steered a lengthy course over the icy waters of the evening to the winking lights of Lourcine. When he climbed out, the young woman, whose name it seemed was Gladys, told him to wipe the lipstick from his mouth.

Simon saw her again. When he left her, on the threshold of her room full of calendars, with its velvet clown cushions on the bed, Gladys would put packets of cigarettes into his greatcoat pockets and tell him that she loved him, using expressions of disgusting obscenity from which he derived a kind of pride.

These dealings no doubt degraded him, but everything seemed to him justified by the freedom he had to roam aimlessly through the streets of the Left Bank; to go and have a lie down in town, in a lonely hotel room inhabited in the morning by a whore who left in it her aroma of heliotrope and soap, sunk in a private sleep that no bugle tone, no second call, was likely to disturb. He was living in a half-dream that bore no relation to his former or his future life; and when he thought about his Chartes dissertation on Charles V, he mostly felt like laughing.

IX

A few days after 1 May, Rosenthal, who was trembling with anger at the thought of the four thousand five hundred preventive arrests which the commissioner of police had organized that year, sent Simon an express letter asking him to come and see him, as though he were in a hurry to retaliate against the forcible measures of the police. André went to put on some civilian clothes he had entrusted to Gladys, then made his way to Avenue Mozart. He would have been ashamed to show himself in the uniform of a colonial regiment anywhere except between the Observatory and the Jardin des Plantes.

Bernard asked Simon how things were going with him and – since it almost always happens that young men lie rather less to their friends than to their parents and are prone to boast to them about things they would hide from their fathers – Simon told him. It had been understood between them for years that they told each other everything. Or almost everything.

It made a lengthy recital – the two barracks, the sergeant-majors, the whores, and the story of Gladys and the taxi from the 12th. These confidences, imparted in Rosenthal's bedroom in front of the Lenin, the Chirico and the Descartes, suddenly appeared remarkable. Bernard grew annoyed: he had a moralistic side to him and found it hard to endure any of his friends enjoying a relaxed existence. Valuing nothing more highly than fullness and tension, he held the opinion that a man must be uneasy. Finally he upbraided Simon for seeming not to realize the baseness of his life, and told him that this indifference was worse than the enjoyment itself. Simon replied that he realized it perfectly well, but could not care less:

— My only pleasure consists in casting off all restraint, he said. This military life turns my very bones to jelly. I feel myself dissolving altogether. Luckily, I've discovered how to turn an idiotic bondage, from which I could get relief only by dint of constant guile and an extremely wearisome presence of mind, into a slightly dreary long vacation . . . My lack of restraint will be only temporary.

— No, said Rosenthal, whose one pleasure was giving advice and warnings to distraught or heedless people, writing MENE TEKEL PERES on every wall. No, this situation can't continue. It's high time to steel yourself. Do you want some tea?

Simon replied that he was thirsty and Rosenthal rang. A chambermaid knocked at the door and came in. Bernard gave her instructions with an embarrassed politeness: few practical problems struck him as harder to resolve than his relations with his parents' servants, whom he did not know what to call. Simon, who no longer doubted himself since the adventure with Gladys, looked at the chambermaid. During this brief scene, Rosenthal had time to tell himself that the moral neglect to which Simon had surrendered might perhaps favour his plans, and that an abandoned man must in fact wish to take a hold on himself. The chambermaid went out.

— Have you ever wondered, said Rosenthal, why I insisted on your going to Port-Royal?

— Not at all, answered Simon. I regarded your insistence as a favour, for which I'm grateful to you. I'd put in a request, but you know me, I'd have done nothing more about it.

— I never do favours, said Bernard.

— Sometimes, said Simon gently. In spite of yourself.

*   *   *

78

Rosenthal explained to Simon the metaphysical causes, the significance and the mechanics of the Conspiracy. Simon listened, and found all this audacity exceedingly futile. So when Bernard declared that he was reserving him a role in the very heart of the affair – and was, in effect, charging him with inaugurating the Conspiracy – André felt that he had no desire to act alone for a revolution which, as described by Rosenthal, appeared quite mythical and did not excite him. He answered that he did not want to get mixed up in the venture. Rosenthal then resorted to feminine arguments, which appealed to friendship, loyalty and memories and defied Simon to refuse. Simon continued to jib, adding that the whole business struck him as childish and utterly absurd; but after an hour he gave in, when Rosenthal had shifted the debate onto the plane of insult:

— If you don't want to follow us for the sake of either principle or friendship, that means you're afraid. Are you a coward then?

Telling himself that he could not bear the idea of being discredited in Bernard's eyes, Simon took the plunge. Rosenthal, who was delighted less by seeing his Idea start to be achieved and propel someone into real actions than by having once again imposed one of his wishes, reassured his friend:

— In any case, he said, what can happen to you? The risks are infinitesimal.

— Well, all right, Simon answered, we shall see.

They agreed upon a number of practical ways of transmitting the information that Simon would obtain: Simon was to go and mail his letters in a neighbourhood far away from Port-Royal, and to type the addresses . . . He stood up to leave.

— Now you've got an aim in life, said Rosenthal.

— Oh! an aim . . . replied Simon. Let's not exaggerate. Scarcely a pretext, at best . . .

* * *

The defence plan for Paris, Area 2, was locked up in a little deal cupboard, rather like the lockers in school dormitories in which pupils keep their shirts and brushes and the letters sent by their mothers and sisters, which they pretend have been sent by some woman. The familiar character of this grey-painted box fixed to the chocolate-coloured wall robbed of all seriousness the confidential documents which it was supposed to protect. A brass padlock with a four-letter combination was the door's sole defence: this childish fastening was fairly indicative of the nature of the military world's secrets.

After his visit to Avenue Mozart Simon waited another three days, telling himself that the exploits which Rosenthal's friendship required of him were decidedly a bit theatrical for his taste. Since he was after all his father's son, he thought modestly about his chances of success and about his future, destroyed perhaps if he were caught; about prison and about his court-martial: he saw himself arrested, interrogated, caught up in the inexplicable machinery of military justice and trials from which he would never emerge. Yet he had no doubt that this illegal undertaking was legitimate and even noble, even though it struck him as uncertain in its results and unworthy of exciting a man in the way that it did Rosenthal. 'After all, it's only an intellectual pastime,' he told himself, to reassure himself and convince himself that nothing would happen. He was true to his years: he was unable to believe that the actions of youth might have any consequences.

On the third day in the evening, when he found himself alone at Port-Royal with his iron bed and the secrets cupboard, Simon decided it was finally time to study the padlock: it took him two minutes to find the keyword, which was Siam. In barracks like this, almost everything is ruled by words from colonial expeditions and famous Great War battles: flags, messes, squadrooms, soldiers' clubs with stencilled decorations, State secrets – all can be discovered by the same methods as the solutions to crosswords and riddles.

Next day the other secretary, who had relatives in the Pas-de-Calais, went off on leave: with Dietrich out of the way, Simon was sure of being left alone in the evening for three days. At one of those dead hours between the end of supper and the desolate notes of lights out – when the squadrooms are empty, and the men are loafing along the boulevards, outside the cafés or in the amusement halls on Avenue des Gobelins – Simon opened the cupboard. There was no chance of seeing Sergeant-Major Giudici or Major Sartre arrive on the scene.

The cupboard was half-full of files whose folders bore the title 'Confidential' or 'Secret' written in roundhand. Simon had no difficulty in discovering the only important item, which was the defence plan for Area 2. It was a notebook which, with extreme baldness, evoked war, revolution, civil strife. This administrative anticipation of such cataclysms was sufficiently poetic for Simon to be affected by its calligraphic presentation of the future: he dreamed for five minutes over the blazing pictures of Paris that rose from every line, and began to copy the instructions in the note-book. At the Choisy-le-Roi waterworks, so many men, he read. At Villeneuve-Saint-Georges, so many machine-guns. At the Gare de Lyon, so many troops from the 21st Colonial regiment. He saw the Army occupy the strategic points of Paris, he heard commands echo back and forth in the silence of great historical tempests, the muffled breathing of the Parisians as they peered through the slats of their shutters at the menacing streets, without cars, without lamps, at night. Lights-out checked him.

Next day Simon resumed his work, and on the third day he sent Rosenthal what he had already copied – going to the Champs-Elysées to mail the letter. On the evening of the third day, the office door opened. Simon, who had forgotten to lock himself in, pushed back his chair and stood to attention. Major Sartre, who had left his gloves behind in the office that morning, came in. Simon really did look guiltier than he ought to have: the Major, though not good at reading faces, could make no mistake. Sensing that something was going on, he looked around him and noticed the open door of the secrets cupboard.

What most troubled Simon's officers was not perceiving the reasons which could have impelled him to copy secret documents. The Major had lodged Simon in prison the same evening, and this decision gave his commanding officers time for reflection. A worker would at once have been suspected of espionage and romantic links with Germany or with Moscow. But Simon? Lieutenant-Colonel de Lesmaes, who had learned of his former secretary's escapade, asked the Major:

— Well, can you please explain to me then, Major, what a young man from Simon's background, a former student at the Ecole des Chartes who, as we know, has never bothered himself with politics, could find interesting about the Paris defence plan!

The battalion commander raised his arms and said:

— This business is quite beyond me, Sir. I don't have the faintest idea.

Simon in his regimental prison was waiting to be interrogated: he felt as though he had reverted to school age, saw himself being questioned by a colonel/headmaster, a major/deputy-head, flabbergasted that so good a pupil should have provoked a scandal. He was thinking how people have very primitive ideas about a man, and how his action must seem obscure to them because it did not fit in with any notion a career officer could form of a well-bred soldier. At last he was interrogated: the Colonel appeared much more embarrassed than he. When he was asked:

— Come now, Simon, tell us whether there was anybody behind you. Bad influences? A woman?

Simon understood that he could say no and would be

believed. Military equality is a façade, in the name of which a person initially forgives the excesses of discipline in the belief that he is at least in the same boat as all the others – but such illusions do not withstand three months in barracks. Simon sensed from the tone of his officers that social complicities were capable of keeping all the Army's written laws at bay. He divined that they would reason like confessors, or like readers of detective stories, and that he could doubtless trick them.

Silence struck him as a manifest duty: there was no question of betraying Rosenthal. He did not feel noble: he was still at school, where you never tell on anybody. He was rather afraid his former friendship with Rosenthal would be discovered, and in this way a connection made with some revolutionary group: he was wrong to be worried, the inquiry carried out by military means had come up with nothing; it had been learned only that he did not meddle in politics, had no suspicious relationships or financial needs. Sergeant-Major Giudici had said nothing about the dubious associations in which he had himself involved Simon. The information reaching the barracks spoke only of his virtues.

Simon finally took a risk, telling himself that his version was going to seem a bit crude. He explained to the Colonel that his curiosity about military matters was keen, and that he had not been able to resist the temptation to cast a glance at the plans it was his mission to protect; the proximity of these documents had suggested to him the idea of composing a futuristic novel, for which he was taking notes at the moment when the major had surprised him; he was desperately sorry about this childishness, upon whose consequences he had not reckoned.

— But in that case, exclaimed the Colonel, why didn't you speak earlier? Your silence allowed every kind of conjecture!

Simon, who had just caught the look which Major Sartre had exchanged with the Colonel, told himself the battle was won.

This explanation, which would have seemed absurd from a soldier of any other background, actually struck them as acceptable.

— I was afraid of seeming ridiculous, Sir, said Simon, and I thought you wouldn't believe me. It seemed to me I could defend myself only by keeping quiet.

This yarn corresponded pretty closely to the idea the officers had of the man. The invention of a novel seemed to them to fit in well with the daydreams they associated with all intellectuals, in their conviction that they were themselves men of action. They breathed again, now that they were presented with a version of the incident that contradicted none of their values. It made them smile, and the Colonel told Simon that he had behaved like a child and that one cannot hide one's head in the sand. He was asked to give his word of honour that nothing had left the barracks: he gave this forthwith, and added that he had only just begun taking notes when the Major came in. He considered that his friendship with Bernard was worth any lie. Honour played so natural a role in the moral habits of Simon's officers that it never crossed their minds that a lad like him could perjure himself. They would perhaps not have taken the word of a worker's son, but Simon deceived them with the greatest of ease.

Since it was not possible for his indiscretion to go unpunished, he was sentenced to a fortnight's imprisonment with a week in solitary, which on passing upwards to the higher echelons of the military hierarchy became a month's imprisonment with a fortnight in solitary. He concluded that he was getting off lightly and that Gladys would not have long to weep over him.

Rosenthal, who had had no news of Simon since the dispatch of the first information, quickly grew worried. He thought of rushing to the Lourcine barracks, but reflected that if André had got himself caught, all visits would be suspect. He went and prowled about outside the barrack gates, on Boulevard de Port-Royal, at the hour when the unemployed wait in front of the guardroom for the soldiers to finish their evening meal, but he did not see Simon come out. He was convinced that all was lost. If ill, Simon would have made some arrangement to warn him. These anxieties gave him an exhilarating idea of the Conspiracy. When he saw Laforgue, he explained to him that everything must have been discovered.

— That poor fellow's going to be doing time, said Laforgue. Unless I'm much mistaken, it must be a court-martial affair.

— I know Simon, said Bernard, he won't open his mouth. They won't suspect a thing.

— It wasn't you I was thinking about, said Laforgue.

— How sentimental you are, answered Rosenthal.

The idea of danger excited him: for a few days, he felt alive, he thought about plots in Italian cities, about a world of conspiracies, police and music. He believed that police-detectives were following him and hid Simon's notes. But nothing happened: the policemen were always only passers-by.

His term of imprisonment completed, Simon renewed his acquaintance with the Clignancourt barracks, to which he had been sent back by the Paris Garrison. It was the beginning of June, the weather was quite perfect. On his first day of freedom, he wandered about in the barrack yard between the stables and the showers, from one end to the other of that crazy military planet, listening to the bugle calls whose meaning he had already forgotten. For one day more, high iron gates and grindstone-grit walls separated him from the world: long did he watch through the slats of the little guardroom gate as life's strange parade – workers, bare-headed girls, tramps, lorries, open trucks and women pushing baby-carriages alongside the flowering acacias of the Circle railway – passed by. On the other side of the yard lay the poor suburbs, with their meagre whisps of smoke, their flowering shrubs sprouting from the signs of secondhand dealers, restaurant advertisements, African huts of corrugated iron, planks and cardboard; dishevelled girls trudged through the white spring dust, their stockings round their ankles, and half-naked children played with old bicycle wheels on ground covered with loose stones, rubble, charred rags, empty cans and bed springs; the sad native land of the Parisians was studded with the black steeples of chimney stacks. For the first time for months, Simon went to bed that evening in the squadroom; all night long an indistinct pink light persisted on the far side of the casements. The squadroom woke at dawn with sighs and sounds of coughing. Simon's neighbour sat on his bed and from a piece of green baize took out an orchestral trumpet; he sounded an imaginary reveille, and played a waltz to which the men listened, dazed from sleep and lost beneath the squadroom's high ceiling. Simon told his neighbour that he played well; the soldier, who had a friendly manner, replied that he was called Di Maio and that he was soloist in a jazz band, and he took from his wallet a photo in which three young men and a woman grouped around a jazz drum-kit stared fixedly ahead of them; the skin of the bass drum bore this inscription, under a painted garland: 'The Select's Jazz'.

— That's my brothers and a girl friend, said Di Maio. We do the dance-halls in the 13th. Do you know them?

Simon looked at the musicians' dinner-jackets and the beaded dress of the woman, who reminded him of Gladys.

— Yes, I know them, he said. Before going to gaol, I was at Lourcine, with the 23rd. That's my neighbourhood.

Thus it was that Simon, even before he was back among the men, had fallen once again among the ambiguous charms of the Gobelins district.

Simon went to see Rosenthal and told him of the tragic events regarding the defence plan. Bernard reproached him for not having taken more rigorous precautions.

— Your information was first class, he said. Now it's incomplete.

— Forgive me, replied Simon, I'm not cut out for plots.

— That's a pity, said Bernard.

X

Extracts from a Black Notebook

*   *   *

Saw Rosenthal and several of his friends. Unbearable, of course, givers of lessons. Growing old: I find all young people detestable. But I envy their sense of irresponsibility and improvisation. At their age, I was fighting a war, every instant of my time was taken up by the most absurd duties.

Idea that command was our absolute due. Our mistake. Wartime command never justifies the responsibilities of civilian command. Don't confuse command and government. Idiocy of the Horizon-Blue Chamber, Italians transforming regret for command into legitimation of government. Government is effected through politeness, flattery, knowledge of the private aspirations of the governed, persuasion. Because we believed in the rhetoric about efficiency, we all lost our bearings. Not our class. Escape from one's class is a phenomenon possible in peace-time. Little *normaliens* putting out journals are seeking their bearings too; they'll find them in the great disorders that are on the way. Not us, that's over.

Adventures. I've had them: Verdun, Gallipoli. It was war and its wonderful disorder, blood, hunger, women, states of consciousness almost unimaginable in peacetime, luck. P. said to me: 'Why on earth should surrealism interest me? I've had more violent spiritual experiences on the Somme.' I haven't the least idea what meaning our adventures had, all the keys are missing, but I've got a bad liver and rheumatism and, after all that stinking gelatinous mass of death, life is insipid. We've put the war behind us, we've put everything behind us. Yet we expect new fortunes. Or should we take refuge in discreetly metaphysical systems: radicalism, or the League of Nations, or nationalism? Weariness. We shall be pretty decrepit ten years from now.

*   *   *

Impossibility of leaving Simone, or even, for the moment, of deceiving her. Oh! to win women, as at the age of twenty-five, for the pleasure of prevailing; discovering the mechanisms that undo them all; being reborn. But those dances in front of the female, the warbling, the strutting, the conversations about them and about me, the fabrication of what they expect – it all bores me. I feel myself superior to all the versions of myself they might imagine. Simone would want to avenge herself – for the sake of dignity and a sense of justice, or retaliation – for the broken contracts. I'd lose her. But I've been living like this for seven years: I'd lose myself. No way out: deceiving a woman in order not to feel oneself grow old, in order to make a new start; fearing to do so, in order not to lose seven years, ten years of one's life. Love is like a career: once one has *arrived*, is one to serve apprenticeships again, start again from zero?

Write the story of a man faithful because he fears death, a man unfaithful for the same reason.

Women never give the men they love holidays. Where should we go, if houses of pleasure did not exist? Young people are really lucky.

*   *   *

89

For want of anything better, one can imagine remarkable destinies. For want of anything better: at thirty-five, one has only one destiny left. One is neither a phoenix, nor a snake that changes its skin. The great temptation is to translate these daydreams about possible worlds into reality, to orient lives, to propose examples, to have influence. I wonder whether Stendhal was tempted. He must have been far too tough. In any case, a virile man almost never writes to you – always adolescents, women, failures, as if the writer could tell the future, console, avenge. How wearisome when one is neither God nor priest, like that father confessor Duhamel or that pastor Gide. Nothing will replace real holds.

Nothing is a better preparation for literature than wars. All peaces are Stendhalian.

*   *   *

About young men, in Scheler's *Vom Umsturz der Werte*:
   In certain psychoses, for example in hysteria, a kind of altruism is found whereby the patient can no longer live or feel by himself and constructs his experience on the basis of another's, as a function of the perception, expectation or reaction which that other may have in any given circumstances . . . Sometimes a collective illusion even occurs, as in the pre-war Russian intelligentsia, particularly among the university youth, in whom thirst for sacrifice and flight from self, both of them morbid, by assuming a dimension of moral heroism inspired political or social goals.

*   *   *

Rosen tells me about his 'plan'. Stupid, ineffective, forever improvised, but how bored those young men must be! He'd like me to give him my blessing, it's very odd. He argues about espionage in general, about 'conspiratorial values', about the significance and the ambivalence of actions, he attempts to justify his undertaking instead of seeking out its real motives or consequences. Like everybody. Fear of motivation always did encourage justification. But these young men couldn't care less about the correctness, the *congruence* of their justifications. I tell Rosen:

— Your justification of this whole business strikes me as quite arbitrary.

He laughs, it's clear he thinks I'm a fool, and answers:

— Never mind that, we'll find you others! Our attitude to action is like that of Epicurus to celestial physics, we don't give a damn about hypotheses.

Since, however, he is exceedingly careful and timid, well brought up, he wants someone to tell him that such and such a piece of spying is not repugnant, but noble instead. Why not? He's pleased with me. Fortunately, I've nothing to worry about: they'll only dream.

Growing old means (among other things, all less serious) finding it indispensable to verify hypotheses: what then appears most worthy of oneself is a justification of action capable of surviving the man justified. Ill omen: you worry about the chances for eternity of the values for which you live, you're ripe for God. Or for the inevitability of communism's great future.

No one accepts his fate. But one makes shift.

Novel. How to describe a mutable man or world with means effective enough to give one's description a chance of durability? Let's give up writing. But one's not wise at all, one believes in books, in children, one lives as though the world didn't even have to come to an end.

What bothers me is not just having to die, but the idea that one day there will be *absolutely* no more men. Is it then necessary to come thus far in history only the better to leap into annihilation?

*   *   *

I seek to please young people as an ageing woman seeks to please men. Am I finally going to try to believe in myself in mirrors?

Rosen comes to visit me, tells me the story of his friend S. in his barracks and the defence plan. He looks strangely proud of it, like a man who has just discovered his sovereign power over a woman he did not even love, but who is ready for anything in order to follow him. I tell him:

— My dear fellow, you behaved like a swine, risking nothing as you did!

He explodes, telling me:

— Moral scruples! I thought such fetishes left you cold. That you were much less the black savage. You'll be telling me next that a person must be straight with his friends: whatever is this pimp ethics?

*   *   *

Lie. Through pretermission. How one does keep quiet with a good conscience! 'I've a perfect right to keep quiet: it's by reason of this silence that I shall some day be fruitful. I'm the sole judge.' Reserve for the future. In literature. In love.

I imagine a time when greatness will lie less in rejection than in joining, when there will be a certain glory about feeling one is conforming. All human greatness has hitherto been only negative. In hope. The spirit always says no only in the name of hope. Imagine the day when one will no longer hope.

*   *   *

These young people spend their time in a state of dreaming; they're quite satisfied by the manufacture of their symbols and signs. They're indifferent to the traces and effects of their action.

It's enough for them that one of the deeds they adumbrate bear a family likeness to their dreams; that they recognize themselves in it. Their actions do not have a very high coefficient of reality, that's why they're never afraid of causing suffering. I say to Rosen:

— After all, suppose everything had gone wrong, your friend had really gone to gaol, been court-martialled?

— What then? says he. He'd have finally understood it was serious, it wasn't a game.

— The gap between your speeches, your ambitions and your successes strikes me, all the same, as extremely comical.

— You don't understand a thing about it.

How serious we were at the Sorbonne, before the war, in the days of Alfred de Tarde and Massis! The war which took away their fathers has robbed this generation of every last whiff of responsibility.

Rosen is quite right! It's still a game for them, any little thing diverts them. They lack perseverance, they switch games with the versatility of children. They don't know how lucky they are.

*   *   *

The conformity of life would cease to be unintelligible and ignoble only if time could be reversed, and it were possible to change one's direction. There isn't any direction to be changed, there's just a single way, obligatory, *one-way* and *no way* . . .

The basic situation of life consists in never being able to return to a crossroads – always left behind and always imaginary – of possibilities and choices: all roads go the same way. This situation is not so much agonizing as absurd, it doesn't bear thinking about.

In an absurd spirit of punning on the word *way*, people have always tried to substitute a *solution* for a *direction*. But existence is unrelated to anything. All our intelligence fails to discover a dimension of meaning in life's one-way street to death.

May ONE perish! 'ONE' disguises everything, 'ONE' has no destiny.

Man has never produced anything that testified in his favour except acts of anger: his most remarkable dream is his principal greatness, to reverse the irreversible. All his physics, all his industry aim only to raise the energy that fails, to climb back up from its most degraded forms to its noblest forms, to delay its falls and dissipations. Whatever the losses and weaknesses of the yield may be.

To delay death by rage. In private life. In politics.

*   *   *

Read on a wall, opposite the Santé prison:
— The woman who whips her children inspires passion. Heard in Rue des Martyrs, in front of a shop window full of pink underwear and silk stockings, a man with a piece of green canvas under his arm. He was talking to himself and said:
— I want to speak about nature. I don't have horses, and you make tin contraptions and want to fly away!
Heard two months ago, a concierge chatting with a tenant, in front of her cubbyhole:
— It's not our fault, she was saying. It's all to do with Evolution . . .

*   *   *

I'm too lazy for anger.

Poe, in *The Domain of Arnheim*:
'. . . even now, in the present darkness and madness of all thought on the great question of the social condition, it is not impossible that man, the individual, under certain unusual and highly fortuitous conditions, may be happy.'

Still too ambitious. For fifty years perhaps or a hundred, it's going to be necessary to renounce happiness *absolutely*.

Luckily, I've no child: I don't see myself growing old. But each day I feel myself erased. The only hope would be to re-commence.

A man can scarcely re-commence other than by a woman. Or by war, revolution. Let's write books.

PART TWO

Catherine

XI

Since he spends almost all his days in Rue d'Ulm, or at the
Sorbonne, or on the streets and in cafés in the company of
comrades whom he thinks he has chosen freely, and since he
endeavours to organize a life that has little connection with
Avenue Mozart, Bernard Rosenthal has the illusion of remaining entirely outside the concerns and pleasures for which his
family live. How should a young man escape so agreeable an
illusion, which so swiftly discharges him from resolving the
difficult problems of class, complicity and blood?

But Bernard sees his family quite often for dinner, which he
takes with them four or five times a week in Avenue Mozart; he
spends part of his holidays with them; and the monthly allowance his father gives him allows him not to touch the money he
inherited from his paternal grandmother – he would, in any
case, have no need to seek ways of earning his studies or his
daily bread. It is all very well for him to refuse his father the least
gratitude, and conclude that this allowance is no more than what
is owed him – and always that much recaptured from the bourgeoisie on behalf of the Revolution. In fact, these financial
arrangements and these meetings maintain virtually all the links
he believes he has broken internally: how easy it is, an internal
break which no action certifies other than the heart's satisfaction!
To his mind, he is alone: nobody giving him details about the
time when he was a child, so serious and so much nicer than

now; nobody furnishing him with an opportunity to love himself through touching images of his life's beginnings, lost and eroded by time.

M. Edouard Rosenthal was a heavy man, with flabby cheeks on which razor nicks bled lengthily, notwithstanding all styptic pencils. With a kind of anger Bernard sometimes thought he recognized himself in him. He had only to look at his father to imagine the future of his own body with unbearable accuracy. This kind of living prophecy or incarnation of time to come is hard enough, when it reveals through her mother's features the physical future of a young woman you are beginning to love; still harder when it is a question of yourself. It is dreadful to resemble your father or your mother and foresee yourself. A person can consent to live only if he knows nothing about the style of his death and the forms of his ageing.

Bernard was a young man with a lean body which three or four women had chanced to find quite handsome: he had a slender nose, high forehead, sinuous mouth, a dark expression and pale skin; but he saw himself thirty years on, bald, the muscles of his face slackened, with a heart-sufferer's bags beneath his eyes, a blood-suffused nose drooping over his lip and a bilious complexion. When he thought about the family poisons that his liver and kidneys would not always eliminate, he no longer knew whether it was his father he hated or himself in his future form. His father was like a portent of what time would reveal to him, after a terrible metamorphosis which would extract from the young man of Asia Minor a fat, stooping man of Volhynia or Galicia.

— The East's one thing, he would say to himself, but the East will degenerate: I shall look like an old Rumanian.

M. Rosenthal lived as though the Bourse, where he had a certain importance, sufficed more or less to sustain a man's passions and energy; as though those business relations based on the manipulation of a few abstract signs and fleshless ideas had nourished him well enough. He amused himself seldom, and briefly, with a few games of bridge, which he liked and at which he excelled; with a few spring afternoons at Auteuil, Chantilly and Longchamp; with visits to the theatre; and with Sunday hunting trips to the Sologne, in autumn. He travelled little. He nursed the ambitions of becoming a syndic of the Company, and being promoted to Commander of the Légion d'Honneur. Then he would die. Death did not seem in the least frightening to him: he did not have the imagination needed to rebel against the paradoxes of nothingness; he merely wished not to suffer greatly, to pass away – perhaps die of an embolism or burst blood vessel – in his sleep.

His son had never enjoyed very warm or definite relations with him: they do not arise easily, out of that vague mistrust which almost always prevails between fathers and sons; out of that rivalry, that ambition to outstrip and that temptation to despise defeats which are engendered in sons when the age of imitation is over and they begin to tell themselves that fathers are always beaten.

Bernard had been such a brilliant pupil at the lycées first of Janson-de-Sailly, then of Louis-le-Grand, that M. Rosenthal, who had enough good sense to assess a stockbroker's role at its true spiritual worth, had never imagined his second son would ever succeed him in the offices on Rue Vivienne. Since the presence of an elder son ensured the survival of the firm, Bernard had been free to become, if he liked, an intellectual – or, as people began to say not long after nineteen hundred and twenty-seven, a *clerc*. Perhaps M. Rosenthal had vaguely had the feeling that Bernard's vocation would one day justify his relatives: that the Spirit would absolve Money. In just this way, in provincial families, there is no angry reaction at all when one of the sons becomes a priest, or a daughter a Carmelite: people have so much for which they need to be forgiven that it is quite useful to have a mediator who can one day intercede for kith and kin.

*　　*　　*

Madame Rosenthal had never been beautiful, but people had always found her distinguished.

— Berthe isn't pretty, people would say in about eighteen hundred and ninety or nineteen hundred, but she has a certain style.

Whereas her husband was growing old in the way of collapse and sluggishness, she was growing old in the way of dessiccation: tall and bony, she boldly supported the dewlaps of her neck with ribbons of grey moiré; in an evening dress, she was not afraid to display yellow collar-bones, or shoulder-blades that quivered beneath her skin. She had the authority conferred by command over a great house, a cook, a chambermaid, a chauffeur and a couple in Normandy; by the raising of three children; and by the management of considerable benevolent works in which she collaborated with eminent doctors and lower-ranking members of governments well known in Parisian charitable circles.

Berthe Rosenthal would sometimes speak of a fourth child she had lost through meningitis when it was three years old: nothing in the world was unknown to her, not even tears, not even grief. One had better not venture to speak in her presence about illnesses! It is not that she had experienced them – she had an iron constitution – but she was familiar with them: she overwhelmed everyone with the dreadful cases of peritonitis, the generalized cancers, the miraculous operations of her uncles and her cousins, with the ills that bore down on her family and over which it always triumphed. She came of stock where nothing could have been mediocre.

Mme Rosenthal had never sought to know whether her husband had sometimes found idleness, tenderness or merely pleasure with other women. She did not think so. Moreover, she was quite right to be sure of her husband: M. Rosenthal had had only fleeting escapades in houses of easy virtue, or with those artless whores who, as they undress, tell you how Gentlemen are ever so fond of stockings and lace – and you are always fed up with being first a Gentleman, and not a man.

*   *   *

Claude Rosenthal had read Law and Business Studies at the Ecole des Sciences Politiques. While at university he would assuredly have joined the ranks of the Camelots du Roi, if a certain sense of honour had not counselled him, all things considered, to reject a political organization inspired by the pamphlets of Drumont, and whose writers daily insulted the Jews. He had contented himself with the Jeunesses Patriotes, though they had struck him as far less exalted than Action Française, and M. Taittinger less important than Maurras, who had written poems and three newspaper columns every day. He consoled himself for this second-class membership after receiving some knocks in the Rue Damrémont clashes: he used to say he might have died, you never know. He was a reserve cavalry lieutenant, he went regularly on training, he had entered his father's practice, he would succeed him.

Claude was five years older than Bernard, but the Bourse ages its men: people never imagined that the two brothers both belonged essentially to the same generation of young men who had escaped the War; many people took Claude to be a war veteran, and he did nothing to dispel this error when it was made in his presence.

M. Rosenthal was sometimes frightened by the cold perfection of his elder son. He was a man who had a frivolous side to him, who liked wine, who was not afraid of the ribald stories the speculators used to tell the manicurists in the big barbers on Rue Réaumur. He read a few books, he thought he liked Marcel Proust because he had once met him in the company of Léon Brunschvicg under the trees in the Champs-Elysées, and because he remembered having once caught sight of the spitting image of Charles Swann: he used to calculate how old Gilberte de Saint-Loup would have been, and say how all this did not make him any younger. But Claude, who had been totally corrupted by Rue Saint-Guillaume, where he had heard people talking about the laws of the stock market and the Harvard economists' curves, believed only in the scientific theories of the Bourse. In M. Rosenthal's eyes, this was the very acme of credulity:

— Come on now, lad, he would exclaim, you know as well as I do the Bourse is purely a game. Rio moves because there's some great political operation under way, or because someone over dinner at Gallopin's or the Omnium has told a silly story about the rise in metals! Funds make themselves scarce because some idiot or other is full of secrets about the imminent fall of the government! The whole market is based on the tittle-tattle of concierges: how can you expect there to be a science of Conciergerie?

They rarely saw Marie-Anne, since her marriage to an industrialist who lived in Cairo. This marriage had really been quite an adventure – the family had not yet recovered from it, and did not know whether it was ultimately a pleasing, or merely a remarkable, event. Demetrios was Greek. Luckily, he was descended from one of those old French families which have not budged from the Cyclades since the great Mediterranean blendings of the Empire and the romantic wars for the independence of Greece; and he was related to those barons of Lastic whose last heirs still dwell, clad in eternal robes of black wool, beneath the cypresses and olive trees of Ariadne's island, waiting for their daughters, who learn French from the Ursuline sisters in Naxia, to complete their outmoded studies. Marie-Anne, who had married her husband because she loved him, came to Paris for two months in winter and spent the summer in the house Demetrios had bought on Naxos. This oriental escapade fired the imagination of the entire family.

Of all his family, Bernard really liked only his sister: no doubt she was the only one he sometimes had the impression of having chosen. His happiest memory was of the summer of '25, when he had travelled for the first time and spent his holidays on Naxos.

He had just discovered (as people on cruises say) Naples,

with its baroque quarters, its stone rosettes, its brass-collared horses, the erotic lamps of Pompeii, the sugar-and-nougat façades, the deep waters at the foot of Capri; and Athens, where like all well-brought-up young people he had taken a great deal of trouble – between the white bull of the Ceramicus and the Virgins of the Acropolis, whose smile and the tunic folds over whose breasts no one ever forgets – to imbue Athene's columns with a private meaning. He set sail for the Cyclades.

A little before dusk the boat left the Piraeus jetty, from which one weighs anchor for the most mythological destinations in the world, laden with travellers who vomited the minute they were on the open sea, uttering dreadful cries of agony.

As they emerged from Piraeus, the day ended in a brief firework display; the ships' riding lights, side lamps and lanterns came on; Salamis disappeared, then Aegina, then the last sounds from land – a dog's bark on the coast, a call, a motor horn. The captain began to pace the bridge; the bulb went out in the chart-room; sleepers turned over on their deck chairs or talked in their sleep; a voice said:

— There's Cape Sunium . . .

They put in to Syra in darkness, at an hour when all the island's young women were still promenading on marble flag-stones level with the black-and-green waves, between the tables of the restaurants, and past shops selling Turkish delight pack-aged in the style of steam roundabouts, pianola rolls or date boxes. He would have liked to lose himself in the lights scaling the Catholic hill and the Orthodox hill, but the siren blared and they set off again for the mills of Paros and the little cafés of Naxia. A feeling of great excitement engulfed Bernard; he told himself that Syra was a spot to which he would return; he was intoxicated by this blind commitment to the sea.

In the morning he disembarked, boatmen took possession of his cases and of his person. He let himself be guided, a driver who spoke English in the accents of New York, where he had lived, took him towards Potamia. Bernard already had no further thought of formulating ideas of his own on Greece, and he yielded himself up to the pure wind that blew in from the Aegean Sea at every turn in the road, and to the spun-glass light wreathing the marble mountains and the villages like thrown dice on the velvety slopes of valleys. After an hour the driver, who was called Dionysos, pointed towards a square crenellated tower rising above an olive grove divided by rows of cypresses: it was Marie-Anne's house, one of those ancient Venetian castles that could be bought twelve years ago for thirty thousand drachmas.

Marie-Anne heard the car's engine and came down the first steps of the stairway; she was expecting her brother only on the next day's packet and cried out before kissing him. She was alone on Naxos, Demetrios's business affairs had kept him in Cairo. Children with shaven heads ran up and watched them enter the house. Marie-Anne clapped her hands and a little maidservant arrived: Marie-Anne gave her orders in faltering Greek and the girl returned with a tray of lemons, grapes, apples, cups of coffee and glasses of water. In the window recesses there were stone benches cut into the thickness of the walls, and they sat down.

Bernard thought he was dreaming in that limestone fortress, that brittle confection of marble and whitewash, beneath that ceiling five metres above his head. He looked at crosses and dark portraits on the walls; the maidservant's bare feet slapped gently about them on the flags; from time to time she would look at Bernard, then lower her lids over her blue eyes. Marie-Anne said a few words to her and she went out blushing.

A great vertical landscape extended on the other side of the open window, whose starched muslin curtains stirred feebly. Gardens descended to the bottom of a valley which had that deep hue of green velvet which Bernard had seen on the Potamia road, and which is the hue of orange, lemon and pomegranate trees. Beyond a stream hidden by shrubs and trees, the ground sloped up between the olive trees, then terraced houses rose in tiers. Though they were quite far away in a blinding glitter, all the details of the village could be distinguished as though a storm were on the way: women in black chatted on their doorsteps; red-and-blue peasants drove donkeys before them. Above the village, olive trees in staggered rows climbed towards the heights, like motionless puffs of smoke and silver. Higher up, there was nothing but vertical sections, or sloping sections, of marble and scrub – and the sky, where birds of prey soared. It was already very warm on the heights, and the crests shimmered like white-and-blue flames.

Everything was entirely enclosed and distilled. It was one of those landscapes which possess in themselves all their reasons: where no vanishing line, no absence, no aspiration of the horizon reminds one of the terrible vastness of the earth. Nothing seemed to grow old, or change, within a world that was repeated from one second to the next, always identical to itself like a very great work perpetually invented. It was a sight to take your breath away, from surprise and happiness. You were put in your place, in that utterly self-sufficient world: you no longer had either past or future, time and death seemed suspended, you were caught up in the great imaginary adventure of repeating eternal moments.

— Wake up, Bernard, said Marie-Anne.

Bernard looked at his sister. As elsewhere in the world, time began to move again. Marie-Anne broke out laughing:

— It really hits you, doesn't it? she said. How do you like my fortress and my landscape?

— Marvellous, said Bernard. I was a bit doubtful.

— It's a place that's dreadfully hard to leave, said Marie-Anne. Do you want some more coffee?

— No, I'd just like to wash, said Bernard.

— Kal-lio-pi! shouted Marie-Anne.

The little maidservant came back.

It was really the first time that chance had brought Bernard and his sister so close together. Only at twenty did they come to know the childish complicities of which their childhood, cluttered with nannies, teachers and relatives, had scarcely had any suspicion twelve years before. They did not even have any books, saw only Greek newspapers: one would never have believed Europe existed. Games alone were left for them to share. They roamed the island: the marble tower with its battlements dominated Potamia in the centre of Naxos. Since the road from Naxia to Apiranthos was not yet built, it was almost always necessary to go on foot or by donkey.

It was then the season of festivals among the sad peasants of the Cyclades – at Aegares, at Tragaia, at Komiaki. At Apiranthos, the place of pilgrimage at the top of the island, the pigeon hunters told stories around tables in the open air, upon which the farmers ate dry cheese and drank the resinated wine of the mountains; girls in starched, white, scalloped dresses came to kiss the dirty hands of the drunken, long-haired pappas in greasy cassocks. On open spaces near the churches, above the terraced fields on the valley slopes, men danced gravely in the centre of a circle of grim-faced women, who spoke in low voices till the night turned cold, while the men danced; from time to time an onlooker would have a glass of wine or raki brought to a dancer, who would drink as he danced, saluting the giver with his eyes.

In Naxia, the doctor, the notary and a prince who was a typographer in Athens invited Marie-Anne and Bernard to banquets under the trees on the square near the sea; each male guest brought an oka of white Apiranthos wine; the serving-women arrived from the houses along the arched streets, laden with stuffed fishes, hares stewed in oil, vanilla preserves and crystallized mandarins. The doctor found these to be foodstuffs straight out of Aristophanes. There were also picnics and hunting parties organized in the mountains, from which they would return by moonlight walking along the dried-out beds of highland streams, between mastic bushes, oleanders and rushes: Marie-Anne, exhausted, would every now and then stretch out on the sand or on a patch of ice-cold marble and have to be woken before they set off again.

In a field at Komiaki, and at the far end of a little bay at Apollon, they went to see colossal recumbent statues of Phoebus, their backs still attached to the marble quarry: the face of one had been split in distant times by a thunderbolt. Bernard mused over these statues, abandoned before their solemn departure on ships bound for Delos, and he imagined great religious and wartime cataclysms which had dispersed both sculptors and priests. He felt himself veering towards a poetical enthusiasm for history: fortunately Marie-Anne stopped him. She preferred visiting her husband's female cousins at Tragaia, to hear the girls recounting over coffee, outside the little white castle dating from the time of King Otto, how people lived on the island – the stories of failed marriages, of great and violent love affairs, of disputes between the Orthodox believers of the lower town and the descendants of Venetian Catholics in the upper town – and talking about Athens, where they were waiting to go, as a girl in the French provinces will talk about Paris.

The rest of the time Bernard and his sister remained at Potamia, where a great terraced orchard of pomegranate, lemon and orange trees extended around the Venetian tower, with troughs of warm, green water to irrigate the gardens and rows of aloes and prickly pears on the dry stones of the little walls.

— What a pity it is, said Bernard, that I didn't get to know you earlier. All through our childhood, I was convinced you sided with the others against me.

— All I wanted was to be a nice sister, said Marie-Anne, I was fond of you, but you've always been about as approachable as a hedgehog or a cat . . . I used to call you the cat who walks by himself . . .

Bernard spoke of his friends, of their plans, of their dreams, of himself, as if in front of a mirror. Marie-Anne listened to him very patiently, although these stories and concerns appeared to her dreadfully exotic. She described the people of Cairo to him, the big red hotels at Heliopolis, holidays at the bathing resort of Helwan, walks in the ruins of the Hecatonpylus, the ibises, the boats on the Nile, the evenings under the trees of Mena House at the foot of the Pyramids when the fat Egyptian ladies laugh their cooing laughter, the dinners at the Gezira Club with the English from Asiatic Petroleum. She told him, for example:

— You'd find Cairo University extraordinarily amusing. You go there by car along the electric railway to Heliopolis, it's a new neighbourhood full of almond-paste villas, I always think of the marzipan from Hédiard's, with masses of gratings, street-lamps, rockeries and glass spheres. The University looks just like a casino; on the lawns and stairways, there are students wearing the tarboosh, all terribly elegant, perfumed and gazelle-eyed. And all of a sudden you see M. Lalande turn up. The French are marvellous, with their boaters and the frock-coats they trail around to all corners of the earth. M. Lalande has a frock-coat, he rushes up to you with his splendid beard like a king's from the Iliad, his pince-nez and his good manners, he tells you he remembers you very well from the Sorbonne, he clutches his briefcase to his heart and swings his umbrella, it's thirty-eight degrees in the shade . . .

Marie-Anne used to deliver these accounts with a great deal of frivolity, as she would have delivered accounts of Limoges and Bourg-en-Bresse if she had married in the French provinces. Bernard told her:

— You're utterly lacking in seriousness. I ought to abominate you . . .

But in fact, for all that Marie-Anne lived on another planet and understood nothing of what he used to explain to her about Revolution, she viewed him with affection, she laughed with him, he felt her very sympathetic and well equipped with pass-words on families. Bernard was at last discovering that he was capable of relaxing: he had never been so much loved.

Marie-Anne received a letter from Cairo, and informed Bernard that her husband was unable to join her and she must return to Egypt. She told him he could remain on Naxos for as long as he pleased. Bernard dreamed for a while about the solitude, and thought about Marie-Anne's little maidservant, but eventually he told his sister that Naxos would seem empty without her and that he preferred to go home: they took ship together on the *Adriaticos*.

At Athens, since it was the end of September, all the Egyptian Greeks were taking passages home. One evening Bernard accompanied his sister to the Piraeus jetty and was left feeling lonely. However, he remained for a few days in Athens, which he at last took in the proper way, accepting that he definitely had no liking for all that barren purity and those ruins stripped to the bone, those whitened skeletons. He no longer forced himself: he consented to like only the extravagant National Museum, with its wax Palikars with horsehair moustaches, its tattered flags, its hazy prints of assaults and naval battles, its long rifles, its Turkish scenes and the romantic mementoes of Byron, Miaoulis, Botzaris and Colocotronis; the most oriental streets of the city, round the Tower of the Winds; the Asiatic bad taste of the Erechtheum ceiling, with its hydras, its painted crabs and its blue-bearded storm god, sparks and birds in his hands, wings and snakes at his shoulders; and the Acropolis in the evening, at the hour when young recruits led by their sergeants make obligatory visits to glory, to Antiquity, and when the Acropolis becomes once more – just for these conscripts; just for the lovers kissing, turned towards the darkness rising behind Lycabettus and Hymettus, and attempting to recognize their street and their house in the forest of stone and lights – a tufa cliff sprinkled with marble aeroliths, a promenade, a sentimental, shrub-filled garden from which you can look towards the sea.

Had Marie-Anne, with her air of levity, taught him to yield only to himself? He told himself that this was perhaps true, and that in any case he liked only the Orient and arabesques; that he abominated reason, and that he was very happy finally to have found the climate of his race.

Yet Bernard was not entirely at peace. He still had that bad conscience which followed him everywhere, which he had barely lulled to sleep in the sloth of Potamia. He felt it was impossible for him to ignore the insolence of the cadets and police; the corrugated-iron and cardboard shacks along the road to the Stadium; the political prisoners; the pink-eyed children; and the excessively beautiful bourgeois ladies from Smyrna, emigrées from Asia Minor after the Greco-Turkish war, who would walk of an evening on Constitution Square and under the nightingale-filled trees of the Zappeion, their cheeks powdered, their arms bare, their bosoms insolent, and who would drive off, sprawling in the rear of big American cars, to dance under the Venetian lanterns of the seaside dance halls of Glyphada.

XII

They still did not know Claude's wife, Catherine, very well, since prior to her marriage, which had taken place in January '28, she had belonged to none of the little clans who made up the Rosenthals' milieu. Her father was a hospital surgeon: she had lived among the kind of doctors who concern themselves with fine arts or literature and look after the grippes and liver attacks of writers, seeming only as an afterthought to consent to heal the generality of patients. The fortunes of nautical Sundays in spring on the Meulan basin, where many marriages are made, had brought together this girl and Claude Rosenthal, who was out sailing on the Seine with some young speculators. It was a still outmoded world, where no one imagined girls had any other vocation than marriage: they would almost always seize the first opportunity that presented itself to become women. This stupefying obedience to the conventions of morality and money used to beget many subsequent catastrophes.

For a long while, perhaps four or five months, Bernard thought of his sister-in-law only as a chattel his family had acquired in the course of a ceremonial sale with flowers, a big lunch at Rebattet's in Avenue Mozart, a religious orchestra which played wedding marches and fragments of Rossini's *Moses*, children in brown velvet, cars all the way to the bottom of Rue de Villejust, and an amazing speech from the rabbi, seated behind the little stone dais of the Rue Copernic synagogue, on the virtues of the Rosenthals and the dignity of surgery.

It scarcely crossed Bernard's mind to look at Catherine as a woman.

Had she been a stranger, he would perhaps at once have desired that tall, blonde, rather bored young woman, not unlike the long-limbed girls on the Champs-Elysées who made his heart thump at fifteen when he saw them going into Fouquet's or Le Claridge. But the spell, the kind of aura, which protects women of the family from natural incest had fallen upon Catherine. When Bernard saw her cross her legs, he would automatically avert his gaze: Catherine was for him still only a woman of wax, whose hand or cheek he could kiss absent-mindedly but whose body inspired in him only a vague, holy revulsion.

He should, of course, from an early point have been surprised to be enjoying his sister-in-law's company. He would agree to escort her to the theatre or a concert, when Claude said he was overburdened by the imaginary tasks that made him appear important. The whole family wondered at his seeming to yield to what they termed Catherine's smile.

— Kate's taming our savage, Mme Rosenthal would say. I've never got that much out of him . . .

For they called Catherine Kate – it was a custom of the Rosenthals to Anglicize names. The mothers and elder sisters of the family, not all of whom knew English particularly well, would utter simple sentences to their sons and younger brothers:

— *Shut the window. Ring the bell. Go to bed. Eat your eggs . . .*

Every least dinner to which the children were admitted resembled an elementary lesson replete with textbook examples and commands, as though those children had still had only the intelligence of puppies.

For it was a family which, like every other, liked to compose reassuring images of its cohesion and permanence: stock-exchange prices that went up, brothers and sisters who got on well, patients who recovered, evenings by lamplight, children's schoolwork, marriages, births, engagements, funerals when the living assembled at the gates to the Montmartre or the Père-Lachaise cemetery, journeys, the furniture they changed round, the dinners they ate, the birthdays for which they gave greetings – everything seemed to protect the Rosenthals from misfortune, from fear and from death.

So they were not displeased to see the ungracious Bernard show himself less hard towards the latest arrival than towards his first cousins or his mother, telling one another that they had endured his worst years and the effects of the awkward age, but that he was fortunately going to change with maturity and become sociable.

Bernard was a bit cross with himself for agreeing to these expeditions, which in his eyes were the actions of a worldly dissipation of the kind he and his friends called complacency. They struck him as truly unworthy of himself; he would have blushed to have to describe them to his comrades and could just imagine how crudely they would scoff. But he ceased to feel guilty as soon as he saw Catherine appear, in readiness for their outing; or as soon as he heard her say, through the half-open door of her room in Avenue de Villiers:

— I hope I'm not taking up too much of your time?

When, on leaving a theatre and still immersed in that enchanted world of lights, music, red glints, warmth and perfume, he used to drape Catherine's coat over her shoulders again after the show, he would not know if for the first time he was yielding to the pleasures imparted by the company of women concerned only with their charm – their pearly lustre – or whether he was already wishing to be compared by Catherine with his brother, and to emerge victorious from that comparison.

One evening in June, Laforgue came to dine in Avenue Mozart. Laforgue was the only one of his comrades from Rue d'Ulm whom Rosenthal invited to his parents' house. He attempted to convince himself that all the others would have been embarrassed by the table and conversational customs of a world more devoted than their own to courtesy. He would never have admitted to himself that he was afraid of being laughed at by his father, by Catherine or by Claude – a vile jibe of whose he had never forgotten, one day when his brother had come to pick him up at the Rue d'Ulm gates after a lecture by Emile Bréhier:

— Your eminent fellow students really are ill dressed! I'm beginning to understand why, in the provinces, the more decent Prefects daren't receive teachers . . .

Perhaps Rosenthal was no less fearful of his friends (from whom he required constant approval) discovering contradictions between the ideas which he defended more intransigently than they did themselves and the family setting in which he was still lazy enough to live.

At the end of the evening, as Rosenthal was accompanying Laforgue to the terminus of the AX, Philippe told him:

— You and your lot are quite a family, I must say . . .

— Explain yourself, said Bernard, who could feel himself blushing.

— Another day, answered Laforgue. A day when you aren't so prickly . . . It's not so easy for people like us to do without Families – oh! you know, that kind of complicit warmth of *nursery*, drawing-room and stables . . . I feel it too . . . Do you remember that character from *The Power of a Lie*, the son who can't bring himself to testify against his father – who's done some rotten thing or other – simply because it's so warm in his parents' house in winter and everyone's so nice to him when his tonsils play up? We'll talk about it again. That said, you mustn't, for whatever obscure reason, drop everything else. It's been ten days since you set foot in Rue des Fossés-Saint-Jacques. I had to put through the last issue with Bloyé. I'm quite willing to be decent and handle things, but since we have to take up a position on lots of things in the next issue – on the strikes, on the

American debts, on Marty's conviction – I'd very much like to see you at the next editorial meeting.

— I'll come, said Bernard, I've had things to do.

— I'm not asking you what they were, said Philippe. Speaking of which, as usual I didn't catch the names very well when you were introducing me to the Family. So who was that ravishing girl sitting to the left of the Father, who had eyes for you alone and for whom, if you'll forgive my saying so, you spent your time showing off about Greece, Italy and everything in general?

— On my father's left? said Bernard. That was my sister-in-law Catherine.

— Have I put my foot in it? asked Laforgue. With respect to the Incest Prohibition?

— Of course not, you fool, said Rosenthal. You saw wrong. Look, there's your bus, have a safe journey home. I'll drop in to the editorial office tomorrow afternoon.

Bernard went back along Avenue Mozart. He hardly gave a moment's thought to Philippe's reproaches: he was carried away by a surprising surge of happiness. He could not care less at that moment about the Revolution, he was in the state when a person says: 'To hell with people!' He walked for ten minutes in the deserted Rue de l'Assomption, then went home. In the drawing-room, he looked round for Catherine; she was playing bridge and, since she did not like to risk her partner's reproaches, she did not raise her head when Bernard closed the door again.

A short while later, the game ended.

— I owe you twelve francs fifty, M. Rosenthal said to his daughter-in-law. A ruinous evening.

Claude and his wife left.

Bernard, who could not get to sleep, was turning over in bed and wondering agonizingly if Laforgue had seen right.

Catherine, however, was not a woman whom a boy like Bernard would have thought he could ever love. There is a wide gap between desire, the pleasures of vanity afforded by familiarity with a woman, and love – a wide gap and a grand scenario that Bernard had not yet composed. He had always hated those women with flowers in their cheeks, of the dahlia or camellia variety, whom he had been accustomed to meet for the past ten years in his family and whom his sister-in-law resembled: with her perpetual presence of mind; that careless guard whose weaknesses were impossible to envisage; her hardness of decision; her sureness of judgement; that perfect knowledge of rituals, gestures and phrases; her voice and her laughter, as studied as a song; her adorned, prepared body which appeared exempt from illness or old age; her flesh invulnerable to fever; her incorruptible skin.

'Couldn't she just once have a migraine, then?' Bernard wondered. 'Or a liver attack? Won't I ever catch her off guard, then, saying: Don't look at me! I feel a fright today.'

Some of his friends might have looked upon Catherine as an admirable opportunity to slake repressed desires for vengeance, domination or revenge – resentment rather than the hope of pleasure. But for him, to be enjoying the company and the small talk of one of those unbearable, hard heroines of the world of ostentation for whose end he so passionately longed! He could not get over it.

'We won't go any further,' he said to himself. 'I'm wasting my time playing the beau.'

The oldest magic spells – even those which shackle savages and stockbrokers' sons with the same iron – never last more than a season.

Though regarding himself as a coward, Bernard continued to go out with Catherine. It was, in any case, a time of year to go out with a young woman: the end of spring – which passed. In April and May they had been to explore it far from Paris, in those peaceful *départements* environing the city where the seasons wax and wane unrestrainedly. The first wasps were buzzing, the first swallows uttering their cries: there were months of relief from the earth's silence. In village lanes, they encountered mother cats which had given birth in a field and were carrying their young in their jaws towards the farms. Swarms of midges or winged ants struck you in the face, and there were days when the surface of a road would be covered in a pollen of dead insects lifted by the wind. The clouds vanished. Steeples and castle towers pierced the earth like shoots. Every ear of corn emerged from its furrow, every snake, every dormouse from its sleep, and last perhaps among creatures that hibernate – the hearts of men.

It was really no time for prudence or calculation. Bernard shut his eyes to his pleasure and its consequences, telling himself that nothing would happen: these outings, this ambiguous companionship, would not last for ever.

'I really needed', he thought, 'to relax in the company of a young woman. A person is hardened by such indulgences.'

When summer came, Bernard agreed to follow his parents to La Vicomté. It was the first time for two years that he had not insisted on spending his holidays alone.

Catherine, too, was leaving for Normandy with her parents-in-law: he could no longer do without her – the sound of her dresses, her even voice, her look of boredom.

— You can't imagine how pleased I am, said Mme Rosenthal, who had the impression she was in the process of regaining the most fugitive of her children.

Claude was to stay in Paris until M. Rosenthal returned to Rue Vivienne towards the middle of September.

XIII

Around Neufchâtel, the Pays de Bray is a vast, sad, green region, swept in mid-season by salt winds from the Channel coming up the open valleys behind Dieppe and Le Tréport. Dominating the maze of fields and quickset hedges, the swirl of streams through orchards and the hamlets of wood and red-and-white brick, the high chalk cliffs have the solemn, dreamy immensity of coastal cliffs and, on the road from Neufchâtel to the sea, at each turn you expect the waves to make their sparkling appearance. Great edifices of cloud pile up over this whole region: above the forests, the pastures where half-wild herds of colts gallop and the bare ridges where the form of some abandoned plough or sowing-machine will sometimes appear against the sky like a huge insect – a harvestman or grasshopper of iron . . .

La Vicomté is situated a mile away from the village of Grand-court. It is a long Norman villa of pink brick with ashlar string-courses, built onto the former main building of a sixteenth century hunting-lodge: on the mantelpiece in the dining-room, one can still make out the blurred arms of the Guises. La Vicomté possesses lawns of a velvet less smooth than in the days when M. Rosenthal's mother used to order rye-grass seed from Oxford; festoons of rose-bushes along the paths; a dovecote where bats make their abode; a river; white-painted wooden fences; a warden's lodge; and over-large stables, inhabited only by two horses, Bois-Belleau and Urania, barely roused from their slumber by a few holiday outings, and six Harlequin Great Danes.

Behind La Vicomté, on the far side of the main road, the valley rose towards the edge of the Forêt d'Eu, breaking the horizon with its storm-tossed crown.

No type of landscape weighs upon the leisure of townsfolk with a more intense tedium than these stifling pasture regions, which have nothing to show for themselves but a few sublime lines and some charms of detail, and which are metamorphosed only by dawn's scarves upon the meadows or the theatrical onset of night. The inhabitants of the châteaux would attempt to escape from those leagues of faultless greenery by prolonging throughout the summer the social diversions of the winter in Paris. The holiday weeks would be spent in conversation, in continual communication between one estate and another, in visits, in urban ceremonies that were termed neighbourly relations. No one yielded to a natural indolence scarcely imposed other than by sea or snow. Least of all the bourgeois, conscious as they were of an old provincial society of landowners living above them, bound by inimitable exchanges of still feudal forms of homage. Those noble families of the Bray region, who lived for six months of the year in melancholy apartments round the church of Sainte-Clotilde where their daughters would be married, in the fine season used to do the rounds of their farmers, who would really be in need of advice from the tall vicomtesses with manly voices and big feet, on account of their daughters, who used to conceive children by unknown farm-hands, and their last-born infants, whose bottles spiked with cider spirit used sometimes to kill them off a bit early. In the meantime, the head of the family would go off with his steward and farm manager, to haggle over cows and horses and drink with copers and land agents at the fairs which used to be held all along the borders of Picardy – at Envermeu, at Londinières, at Gamaches and at Foucarmont. Courtesy visits would be made to the Château d'Eu, where the

Princesse d'Orléans used to spend her holidays amid ebony and tortoiseshell mementoes of La Grande Mademoiselle and Lauzun, and whose green-latticed rooms – filled with primitive weapons, and with macaws and lizards stuffed by Don Pedro I, Emperor of Brazil – she would partially open for her guests. In autumn, packs still used to hunt in the Forêt d'Eu and in a theatrical manner slay the noble beasts who know how to die sobbing by torchlight: stags, does, or wild boars which defend themselves to the last against the hounds on a bloody bed of dead leaves and clay. The bourgeois lords of the manor, meanwhile, who would sometimes hear a horn sound in a wood or beneath the trees of a park, hesitated to get up little packs to course hares and used to regret not being English – citizens of a country where the fox is consigned to the blows of nobles and commoners alike.

The Rosenthals used to receive guests almost every year. Some would make a detour on their way to Deauville or Le Touquet, others would come down from Paris for a few days.

Guests not travelling by road would, as of old, arrive on the nine thirty-six train at the station of Blangy-sur-Bresle. They would leave the waiting-room, they would glance round the dark, hostile square illuminated only by the distant lights of a bar, and they would remark to one another that it wasn't going to be much fun. But Jules the chauffeur would emerge from the shadows to save them and they would set off for La Vicomté in the old nineteen hundred and eighteen Panhard, which had belonged to M. Rosenthal's mother and in which, in nineteen hundred and twenty-two, as a last journey before her death she had gone on a tour of the Scottish lakes. La Vicomté would be floating like a ship in the depths of the night, all its lights ablaze. The Rosenthals would be sitting in the small drawing-room: they would barely stir to welcome their guests, the conversation would resume, the maidservant would take the cases up to the rooms and Mme Rosenthal would say:

— You have the yellow room – or the blue room.

She would also say:

— Well, as you can see, I'm not putting myself out for you, family life goes on. I want guests at La Vicomté to feel entirely *at home* from the first evening; to understand that there'll be no fuss made, no great to-do in their honour, and that everybody's absolutely free and among friends . . . I'm for British hospitality, there's nobody like the English for putting you at your ease . . .

On the first evening, the guests would report the latest news from Paris, where, they would say, nothing was going on, where there was nobody left – apart from the two and a half million Parisians who were not going away on holiday. At around eleven, the conversation would begin to flag.

— I think, M. Rosenthal would then say, that the moment has come to sound lights out . . .

Someone would reply:

— These first hours in the country really knock you out . . .

— Don't they just! Mme Rosenthal would exclaim in a triumphant tone, as though she had been expecting this avowal of La Vicomté's irresistible power over city-dwellers. Don't they just! One feels slightly tipsy . . .

When there was a moon, before putting the guests to bed they would shepherd them out onto the terrace of the large drawing-room, to show them the pearly wraiths of mist floating above the lawns. Naturally, they would always sigh, and murmur:

— How peaceful!

Or:

— You don't know how lucky you are . . .

Like everybody else, however, they would feel a vague unease confronted by all this whispering vegetation, all these expanses of darkness, and would not be displeased to find themselves back in the protective light of the lamps. They would also be shown, on the far side of the meadows, the lowering woods of a large park.

— That's the estate of our friends the Besnards, M. Rosenthal used to say.

— Would that be the family of the weaving Besnards? the guests used to ask.

— They're the weaving Besnards, the refining Besnards, the paper Besnards and I don't know what else, M. Rosenthal used to reply modestly.

The stockbroker would pronounce this name Besnard in the very tone adopted by the local nobility when speaking – from the abyss of their two or three hundred hectares of wheat fields and meadows – about the Polignacs, whom they would see in August in the stands at Dieppe racecourse, or about the Bertiers de Sauvigny. No one has more respect for the big producers, or the captains of industry as people call them, than the men who play the roles of brokers and tragedy confidants in Capital's game of pass-the-parcel. M. Rosenthal, in spite of the pride he felt at belonging to the Company of Stockbrokers, was impressed by a big industrialist or a big steward of industry – a director of the Transatlantique or the Nord. He placed nobody higher than the Besnards, who in fact headed one of those awesome dynasties from the Nord who rule over spinning-mills, cloth-works, carding-factories and sugar refineries: people spoke of them in Lille – at the *Bellevue* or the *Huîtrière* – as they did of the Prouvosts or the Mathons.

The Besnards lived in a little pink-and-white Directoire château, delicate in style. 'Old' Besnard had hair so white it made him look at first like a good-hearted man: he still wielded absolute power over his wife, his sons and his daughters-in-law. The 'young' Besnards, who were thirty-four and thirty-five years old, scarcely dared open their mouths at table, except when their father was questioning them or catching his breath. All the Besnards were tall women and tall men, fair-haired and dressed in black since, like members of a princely family, they were always in mourning for some uncle or cousin. Mme Besnard wore lisle stockings and her daughters-in-law stockings of silk. On Sundays, the Grandcourt village priest used to feel none too easy when he sensed those six unmoving archangels behind him in their churchwardens' pew, overseeing the conduct of the children in the choir and the speed of the Mass – like the output of a loom.

Once or twice in a season, the Rosenthals would go and have lunch with the Besnards. This year, 'Old' Besnard told them:

— You'd never guess where I've just got back from this evening? From Roubaix. I drove my car myself, there and back again. There was a by-election at home. A person must be capable of making an effort, so I went to vote against my workers.

— If only all big industrialists had your conscience, my dear, sighed Mme Besnard.

— It's foolish anyway, said Alain Besnard, to think that Father's vote has exactly the same value as the ballot cast by the lowest of his hands.

Bernard did not attend the lunch with the Besnards, whom since his childhood he had dubbed the Ogres – or, since reading Gobineau, Kings' Sons. When his mother told him all about it, however, he regretted not going.

There was much to be said about the summer '29 visitors to La Vicomté. Where now were the days of Mme Rosenthal Senior, between nineteen hundred and the War, when – in a La Vicomté then full of plush furniture and family photos and with an Easter-egg collection in the children's room – old ladies in white dresses trimmed with guipure and embroidery used to parade their flounced parasols along the paths and the river, and maintain the rules of high bourgeois ritual with regal strictness?

Nothing, perhaps, better illustrates the destructive march of time than the disappearance from the estate at Grand-court of those former guests of honour the great Dreyfusard professors: friends of Mme Rosenthal and her sister Clotilde, after having been the same to M. Charles Rosenthal, founder of the practice and childhood friend of Scheurer-Kestner. That was the period when Edouard Rosenthal dared bring to visit his mother only those of his friends who had just discovered Wagner, published their first book, or were just back from a journey to Persia or

Egypt, or a mission to Italy – who were really 'interesting'. Money then seemed only the temporal condition of a life dedicated to noble concerns, to knowledge of the world: they would have blushed to seem to raise it above culture, music, ideas. But during the summer of '29, at La Vicomté there were only Adrien Plessis and spouse, Henry Lyons and spouse, and Comtesse Kamenskaia: the Lyons were bankers, the Plessis brokers, and Comtesse Kamenskaia a comtesse.

— What a crew! Bernard would say to himself. These people are impossible. The Lyons are pigs, the Plessis fools, the White Russian lady has walked the streets in Bucharest and Pera. Let's get the hell out of here!

Bernard would drag Catherine – who, after all, was only twenty-two and had not yet entirely lost the ability to laugh at people – into playing the giddy goat.

They would go swimming at Criel, Dieppe or Le Tréport, or buying novels at Neufchâtel-en-Bray. In the morning they would set off, mounted upon Urania and Bois-Belleau, whom Bernard had five or six years earlier rechristened The Muse and The Unknown Horse. Two or three Great Danes would follow them or bound ahead at the nostrils of the horses, who would toss their heads and make their bits and curb-chains jingle. The Forêt d'Eu was no less damp and rotten than all other forests in rich and fertile regions; but they appeared to savour the pleasure of emerging blindly onto a windswept scarp gleaming like a horse's flank in the sun, or of galloping, without a thought for the animals' fragile legs, along a main road between two rows of trees. Bernard would then go so far as to call Catherine *Diana of the Crossways*, because of the excitement of the race and the wind – and because it is easier to love women of flesh and blood through great replicas from novels.

One always tells the woman one is destined to love about one's childhood. You tell yourself you might have played with her when she had bare knees and wore short skirts revealing the long white scars of her scratches – and that all that lost time must be recovered, but you won't manage to do it. You are in despair, you would need to have a whole lifetime of fond chatter before you. Bernard was still mistrustful. He scarcely spoke to Catherine except about the fine weather, the sea, horses, a few journeys he had made, and the singular buffoonery of adults. In order to establish complicity with a woman, it is quite enough to teach her a few passwords and think one understands her at a glance.

One day he took Catherine to have lunch with the regional councillor for Martin-Eglise, whom he had known for fifteen years: they ate a never-ending prosperous farmer's repast, in a dining-room that smelled of mould, dust and carbolic acid. In the glass cases, there were stuffed monsters – five-legged calves, two-headed sheep, a foetus – the councillor's collection. The councillor's wife wore a dress with a bertha, and an amazing auburn-and-grey false bun.

— Why did you bring me to this Punch-and-Judy show? asked Catherine as they left.

— To amuse you, said Bernard with that little derisive laugh of his – which resembled the loud derisive laugh of his brother more than he would have wished. But the finest piece in the collection was missing: that's the son of the house. Young Victor is thirteen, he's got a thyroid deficiency, he's apt to dribble, he has frog's eyes and a Mongoloid complexion. It's due to Calvados in his ancestry, and collateral marriages to round out the estates. But he will inherit the councillor's two million and the paternal seat: the elector won't look all that closely. The priest at Martin-Eglise, who gave me a few Latin lessons ten years ago, says he's a good boy: he'll vote in the senatorial elections for M. Thureau-Dangin, who'll still be alive, praise the Lord. Senators live to a ripe old age in these parts. Doesn't it make you laugh, that future Norman bourgeois grandee with a calf's head?

— No, said Catherine, it doesn't make me laugh. It's quite sad, and I find you disgusting.

*   *   *

On that day, Bernard and Catherine came home quite late from Neufchâtel-en-Bray. Bernard brought the car to a halt in front of La Vicomté's white front gate. Catherine, who to go out for lunch at Martin-Eglise had put on town clothes again, gathered up her handbag and gloves: a movement she made revealed her leg, right up to the cruel swell of the thigh over her stocking-top. Bernard blushed, and felt his heart thump, at this discovery of so much nakedness in the confused clouds of silk and wool.

After perhaps a second, Catherine finally realized from Bernard's total immobility that she was in danger – that a catastrophic event was taking place. She saw her knee, pulled down her dress with a reaction of modesty as violent as a gesture of anger. She looked to her left, she met Bernard's eyes. It was over, the family magic was dead. Getting out of the car, Bernard took Catherine's arm above the elbow and squeezed it with such violence that she gave a sigh and said plaintively:

— You hurt me!

— I beg your pardon, he said, but he did not release his sister-in-law's arm throughout the unending time they took to walk from the front gate to the perron. M. Rosenthal was reading in the drawing-room – it was still broad daylight. He asked them:

— Did you have a good outing?

— Excellent, replied Catherine, but your son took me to visit some impossible people.

— The Burels, I'll warrant, said M. Rosenthal. Bernard has always had an inexplicable soft spot for those people.

That evening, when dinner was over, Catherine came up to Bernard and lifted the sleeve of her dress: her skin still bore the marks of his fingers. Without a word, he took her arm again with the same force. She did not free herself, merely said to him in a low voice:

— I'll have bruises tomorrow . . . What shall I look like for the next two or three days, with long sleeves in the middle of August?

XIV

How few authentic actions exist – couplings, murders, building monuments, opening roads, capturing a large body of troops, risking one's life! Almost everything one does is but a dream. For Bernard, love was perhaps merely the entrance of reality upon the scene, Catherine his first chance – because the occasion of his first clash and the pretext for his first action.

'Well now,' Bernard told himself one evening, 'no more games! A victory to be won, defences to be overcome.'

But everything was too easy. What Bernard doubtless needed was a woman hard to conquer, a mistress whose capitulation would have been the outcome of a battle and a surrender. Catherine did not resist, she was a woman who knew she wished to yield . . .

For five days, Bernard lived as in a dream. He spent his days extracting from his nights all that they contained. He no longer even needed Catherine's company: he fled it to walk alone or stretch out in a meadow, listening to Mme Lyons, Mme Plessis and Comtesse Kamenskaia twitter like birds in an aviary.

When everyone was asleep and he could no longer hear anything on the first-floor landing but his father's little nocturnal rale, which since childhood had made him think of final agony and death, he would go to join Catherine in her room.

An overwhelming silence would reign there, scarcely broken by the plaintive hoots of night-birds or by the rustle of a bird or cat on the tiles of the roof. Through the window, which looked out over the lawns, there would sometimes enter an insect to buzz and blunder into the walls, or a hesitant wisp of mist.

For five nights, within that cold and velvety darkness, that gloomy solitude of a countryside which speaks to men only of heavenly bodies and death, Bernard and Catherine shared the terrible secrets of pleasure: its alternations of self-oblivion, sacrifice, patience, indolence and slumber; its sighs, from fighters conspiring in a rigged fight; its miraculous oblivion of the disgust a body inspires in a body; its indulgence, its exaltation and its degradation. How could Bernard fail to confuse with love: flashes of happiness; the death of time; the company of that tall girl, moist and naked; and the connivance which, at times, made them long remain motionless because they had heard something creak, with the sound of blood in their ears covering everything like a sea? On the sixth day, Claude came.

He arrived in his car as he did every Saturday, at about five in the afternoon. Bernard was flabbergasted: he had entirely forgotten his brother.

Claude took a bath, came down from his room again in a tweed suit, with stockings and white spats reaching halfway up the calf. Catherine smiled, Bernard felt like laughing.

The dinner hour came. The chambermaid came into the drawing-room and said everything was ready for Madame. The whole machinery of La Vicomté continued to function perfectly. At table, Mme Lyons asked Claude:

— What was the weather like in Paris?

Mme Lyons was a very fat lady who wore gold-framed spectacles and a pearl necklace: she had no concerns in the world except the dishes she ate and the temperature – since great heat used to give her palpitations. However, she would sometimes come out with a cruel witticism, which everyone would find admirably accurate but surprising on those soft lips.

— Abominable, Claude replied. It's getting warmer by the

day. Yesterday we had thirty-two in the shade, and when I got into the car this morning on Place de la Bourse it was already thirty-three . . .

— You'll see, said Mme Lyons, today or tomorrow we'll have a dreadful storm. I'm sure of it, I only have to listen to the palpitations of my poor heart . . .

— Thank the Lord, said Mme Plessis, at least you can breathe in the country, where a nice big storm is not all that disagreeable.

— Speaking of the Bourse, asked M. Rosenthal, how's it doing?

— Haven't you heard? said Claude.

— No, replied M. Rosenthal, come now, you know very well that holidays are sacrosanct and I never open a paper when I'm at La Vicomté.

— I always forget that you're a broker with principles, said Claude. Well, the market's pretty fair. Suez ended up around 23,000 and a bit over, and Royal Dutch at 43-44,000. Norvégienne went up 95 points . . .

— That's not bad, said M. Rosenthal. What was it? The celebrated confidence of those fools in the Palais-Bourbon?

— I think, said Claude in what Bernard used to call his Rue Saint-Guillaume tone of voice, it's the international situation. The Hague agreements were signed only yesterday, but since the signature had been anticipated since Wednesday speculation got under way at once, with provincial customers following suit . . . The trend's just beginning: the Young Plan and the Bank for International Settlements – that could be quite good for the European markets. As always, people are asking only to be reassured. If it wasn't for the trouble in Palestine, which is causing London such a lot of nuisance . . .

There had, in fact, just been six hundred deaths in Palestine. Such carnage was still a surprise to men who, seven or eight years later, were to accustom themselves with terrifying adaptability to the incredible massacres in Abyssinia, China and Spain.

— I'd have given something, said Bernard, to be present at the final farce in The Hague, when Henderson was so overcome he put the gold fountain pen he'd just presented to Jaspar back into his pocket. All those characters must have had a proper laugh, apart from Chéron, who still can't stand Snowden. Well, at any rate the French Army's going to evacuate the Rhineland. That's at least one rotten business coming to an end. A bit late.

— Let's discuss that, exclaimed M. Lyons, who was almost as fat as his wife and had not yet said anything because he had been eating. Let's discuss that! It's the last guarantee we held against Germany. Oh! they've wasted no time in taking advantage of Poincaré's exhaustion to demolish his work! There's going to be some fine goings-on, with that gangster Briand . . .

— It's not the first time, said M. Rosenthal, that a bad prostate will have had historic consequences.

— Edouard! said Mme Rosenthal.

— You're quite right, said M. Plessis, looking fixedly at M. Lyons. The Boches only understand firm methods. This Bank for International Settlements and this Young Plan are going to be just one more swindle. They'll have managed to nibble away at our Victory all right . . .

— It's perhaps not all that bad financially, said Claude. The occupation of the Rhineland wasn't always good for business.

— Enough figures, Gentlemen. *Never talk shop* as they say across the Channel, exclaimed Mme Rosenthal, diverting the conversation with authority. They spoke about the countryside: Mme Lyons said that even with excellent friends it wasn't fun every day, and that so far as she was concerned she missed her little Paris habits 'cruelly'. But Mme Plessis, who was younger and more aware of what is due to one's hosts, found that it was splendidly restful and 'so much less enervating than the seaside' for people with sensitive nerves.

There is no better subject than health, and Mme Rosenthal explained their constitutions to her guests, whereupon they sang the praises of doctors, of whom people always speak ironically when they are healthy, but whom they are very glad to summon as soon as their temperature reaches thirty-seven point nine. Then it was time to go and take coffee and herbal infusions in the small drawing-room and elevate one's mind before going to sleep.

Comtesse Kamenskaia, who like many Muscovite women was rather short but whose flaming auburn hair had its admirers, went to look through the French windows leading to the terrace and exclaimed that she liked nothing in the world except great plains, so she 'adored' this region, because the patches of steppe interspersed with copses where Picardy began reminded her of the surroundings of Zagorsk, where she had been brought up, and the time when she used to go and visit the abbot of the Convent of the Trinity, in his little Louis XV office with its Chinese screens. All the guests were familiar with the Comtesse's adventures – apart from the life she had really led after the evacuation of Baron Wrangel's army from the Crimea – but they always used to feel a certain pleasure in hearing a few accounts of atrocities from the mouth of *la petite comtesse*, who had such a ravishing accent. So she spoke once more:

— Well, on the evening of my wedding, my husband took me to one of his villages, which was in the *guberniya* of Kiev. It was terrible, the peasants insulted us and someone threw an axe at the head of one of the horses. At daybreak we escaped through the back gate of the park, and the four-horse carriage that had brought us to Kiev remained behind in the stables. At Kiev I lost my husband and it was two years before I saw him again. The Bolsheviks arrested me, but a little Jewish student of seventeen or eighteen, who was sitting as a judge in their court and who was perhaps in love with me, saved my life, and then somebody remembered that I used to sing before the Revolution and they made me act parts in their ridiculous propaganda films. Then they arrested me again. I was in a horrible green building where there were fourteen of us women. I used to hear gunshots being fired outside my window and it was certainly people being killed, but I couldn't see anything because they'd nailed planks across the panes, I could see only a snow-covered roof high up, and in the morning, when the red sun of Kiev was shining, the crows used to let themselves roll down the snow as far as the gutter. How cold we were! And hungry! But we always managed somehow to get hold of cocaine, through a woman who was called Marusha. What a life that was! My God, what a life that was! Then one day the Whites released us. For thirteen months we'd been so accustomed to dread, the streets scared us. Friends fed me and handed me some pearls my mother had given them to keep safe for me, and, of course, in all that misfortune my poor mother had died . . .

Mme Rosenthal patted Mme Kamenskaia's hand, and Mme Lyons said the Comtesse ought to sing something Russian to take her mind off it. She made them entreat her, then promised she would sing the Tsarina's Song. M. Rosenthal suddenly recalled the Easter-egg collection which had been at La Vicomté in his mother's lifetime, and which reminded him of Nicholas II – he really wondered why.

Mme Plessis asked Claude if he didn't get too bored in Paris:
— It's pretty deadly, he answered. Everybody has left and one can't even play bridge. There's absolutely nothing to see at the theatre. When I tell you that on Wednesday I went to the Concert Mayol!
— Aren't you worried, Kate dear, asked Mme Lyons. All those naked women . . . You know how holidays are the ruin of husbands . . .
— I'm not worried, said Catherine. With Claude . . .
'This life can't go on,' thought Bernard. 'What are we doing, she and I, among all these hateful phantoms?'

Later, after other phrases by lamplight in the small drawing-room and after the Tsarina's Song on the terrace (someone, as always, finding that Boris Godunov was definitely superior to Prince Igor), when Mme Plessis had declared that women would be plump next winter and at last one would be able to have one's waist in the proper place, and when Mme Rosenthal had stowed away in her work-table the beige garments – beige like all garments for the poor – that she was knitting for the poor, Bernard suddenly heard his brother say to Catherine:

— Shall we go up, if you're ready, Kate?

That 'we' struck Bernard as horrible: it coupled Catherine. He felt indignant that, after those five nights, she should still be his brother's wife.

'I'd be a coward to put up with this sharing any longer,' he thought. 'It's nothing to have slept with Catherine. He has too. It's me alone she must accept into her bed . . .'

Next morning Bernard – who had not slept; who had been walking for two hours along the road, right on past the barking of the dogs into a slumbering Grandcourt – scrutinized Catherine's lips and cheeks for Heaven knows what marks of happiness he was terrified he might discern there. At one moment during the morning she smiled at him, but he saw in this smile only the evidence of a hateful complicity: the mark of a whore's familiarity. It was enough to destroy the childlike plenitude of the first moments of love – to make Bernard forget their recent walks, their recent nights. He told himself that Catherine must be torn away from her husband completely, that this was even his sole duty.

At table, over lunch, Claude spoke of going that afternoon to the races at Dieppe.

— The meeting seems decent enough, he said. It's the day of the Grand Steeplechase, obviously it won't be quite Auteuil or Deauville, but the horses aren't bad in these provincial races.

— How about pushing on to Deauville? said M. Plessis.

— Do you think that's really a good idea in this heat? asked Claude. And it must be a hundred and fifty or two hundred kilometres via Rouen, you know, we'd just get there for the last race.

— Anyway the roads are impossible on Sundays, said Mme Plessis. Now that everybody drives a car!

Claude said to Bernard:

— Will you come along? Unless such capitalist amusements are in contradiction with the demands of the Revolution?

How could he abandon Catherine, in God knows what dark though sunlit void?

— Idiot, replied Bernard. I'll come.

M. Rosenthal said:

— Would this be the beginning of infidelities to your principles?

— You're extraordinary, said Bernard. Anyone would think revolutionaries were all priests. You're as surprised at a communist taking a bath as at a priest smoking a cigar! Traps like that are childish.

Mme Rosenthal smiled: Bernard was going to the races, he wasn't angry. What a happy family they made!

A little before their departure, Bernard spied Catherine putting on lipstick, alone in the big drawing-room. He entered and went over to her:

— How was your husband last night? he said.

— Dreadful, said Catherine, closing her eyes.

It was a reply which clearly hinted at everything Bernard had to fear. Yet he breathed again, as though accepting his brother's exercise of his husbandly function at the weekend – for he felt himself preferred. He had a reaction of pride: a desire to strut, to run outside with Catherine and cleanse her of her husband's body in the wind.

'That brute doubtless thought only of himself,' he told himself, thinking of his nights of patience when he would sacrifice his own pleasure to Catherine's.

Catherine reopened her eyes and looked at Bernard, then continued spreading lipstick on her lower lip with her little finger.

They left. On the Dieppe road he mused in the back of the car beside Comtesse Kamenskaia, who was perhaps not a comtesse he said to himself; it's hard to tell, with her white breasts set high – they haven't made them like that for three hundred years

– and her cooing. He imagined himself alone in the company of Catherine, of an escaped Catherine, finally stripped of every-thing, carried away on an impulse so passionate she would no longer recognize herself, in Italy or on Naxos. For every man there exists a place where he imagines love: for Bernard, since '25, it had been the Greek islands.

'Naxos,' he thought, 'I was happy there with a sister. What happiness to live there with a woman I loved, who'd sleep in my bed and not leave me alone at night!'

At the races he remembered Anna Karenina: he saw himself running, jumping and finally falling from his horse like Vronsky. Would Catherine utter a cry similar to Anna's cry, which would reveal all? Would she have the icy courage not even to blush?

On the way back Claude was not happy. In the Prix d'Elbeuf he had backed Theocritus to win, but Theocritus had paid out only 8.50 francs for a place, behind Dragonfly. In the Prix de Clôture, Lady of the Parish had paid out 97.50 francs and, of course, he had not backed her. One winner out of five races, which had paid nine francs – he had nothing to be pleased about.

— It's not the money, he said, but I detest losing.

He complained about provincial meetings and about the idiotic names of the horses. The Comtesse, who was sitting next to him, without hearing what he said answered him with accounts of races at Tsarskoe Selo. The weather was perfect, the heat was diminishing, the storms forecast by Mme Lyons had not broken out. Bernard caressed Catherine's wrist and the wind on the road eventually lulled her to sleep. Bernard did not like to see a woman he thought he loved sleeping: he was afraid a hateful woman – and one who would hate him – might take her place while she slept, at the very moment when nothing but death could take her body from him. He woke Catherine.

— Why did you wake me? she said.

— So that I wouldn't lose you, Bernard replied.

How romantic!

*   *   *

That evening, while they were all talking in the small drawing-room, Bernard and Catherine left and went to stretch out side by side on the lawn, out of range of the rectangles of light from the windows and the hum of voices in the house. Bernard looked at the sky and said:

— When we were sixteen, Laforgue and I, we had a soft spot for a star called Aldebaran; we thought it was that star over there, just below the Great Bear to the left. Perhaps that's not really Aldebaran but Cassiopeia, or Betelgeuse, or some other Greek or Arab lady, but it was Aldebaran for whom we had a liking.

— Yes, Catherine said.

— Catherine, said Bernard. Leave everything, let's go away, all this can't go on. These compromises will become vile. People like me can't be content with complicity.

— Let me breathe, said Catherine. You really do have to bring things to a head right away! Don't you understand the pleasure of hesitating? Aren't we happy?

— No, Bernard said, people aren't happy when they're split in two. I don't want you to hesitate, I don't even want you to breathe, I want to take you away.

Bernard undid Catherine's blouse, kissed her breasts. She pushed him away, covered her bosom.

— You're utterly crazy, Bernard, she said.

— Thank God! said Bernard. And I don't even have the excuse of the moon, as somebody else said, you know, *It is the very error of the moon; She comes more near the earth than she was wont, And makes men mad* . . . The first quarter will appear only in two days' time, close to the earth, just above the elms in the Besnards' place . . .

— You're a fifteen-year-old, she said, you're a schoolboy.

— Catherine, said Bernard, there are too many people round us, we can't hear each other any more. What we need is great expanses of stone or water, a desert, the sea, or mountains with lakes, slopes covered with barren snow the colour of hyacinths or forget-me-nots . . .

Catherine rose to her knees and bent over Bernard to kiss him, then they returned to the drawing-room.

— Why don't you all go outside? asked Catherine. It's one of those nights . . .

They all went out onto the terrace and, of course, everybody exclaimed at all those stars. Mme Plessis, who loved nature, said it was a sin to stay cooped up indoors when the weather was like this, Catherine was quite right.

— In days gone by, said M. Rosenthal, I was very strong on cosmography. But now, if my life depended on it, you couldn't get me to say where the Pole Star was . . .

XV

Claude went off again on Monday morning at first light. It was 2 September: like every other day, it was going to be fine. Bernard, still in bed, heard the car's engine turn in the dawn silence and – far away across the fields, on the farms – the last cockcrows greeting the break of day.

— Everything's going to start all over again, he said to himself. We'll be doing this for ever.

Down below, the engine roared: automatically Bernard counted the successive gear changes. Claude drove away, Bernard went back to sleep.

Everything should have started all over again, if Bernard had been capable of rediscovering the careless ardour of those first days; living only for his sleepless nights at the summit of La Vicomté; being, from one day to the next, only remembrance and anticipation of the dark. But he lapsed into endless reflections upon existence and fate. He no longer thought about anything but saving Catherine, forcing her to be happy in accordance with the idea he had of bliss. All men are like this – but they rarely find women to put up with imposed bliss of this kind. If Bernard was already thinking about organizing the future, he was going to lose everything: you can preserve love only by welcoming it with your eyes shut.

That evening, he once more joined Catherine in her room.

She was waiting for him, stretched out on her bed: she was telling herself how pleasure was about to be reborn for a further night. When Bernard entered she jumped from the bed and ran to kiss him, but he told her they must talk. Catherine sighed, knelt on her bed or went to lean out of the window, above the dark, moist countryside lit up nightly by summer lightning.

Pacing up and down the room bare-footed, Bernard explained to Catherine in a low voice how he wanted to rescue her from complacency and death, and how one could accept life only by laying down conditions for it – by dominating it with the most exigent demands. Catherine finally asked him what he expected of her:

— Absolutely everything, he said. At once. Why do you resist?

Catherine resisted like life, passively.

Was she then just a woman equipped for pleasure, but dying of love for the world, money, consideration and respect? Bernard was frightened by the thought that perhaps Catherine was stupid, for one can triumph over everything but not over foolishness. Or that she had no desire to leave her husband; that she found him bearable now that another man loved her and was avenging her for Claude's existence; and that she was in fact capable, like most women, of enjoying a revenge in falsehood and secrecy.

— I want you to have nothing left but me, Bernard said. I want you to start everything all over again. We'll go away, I have a bit of money, we won't even be very poor . . . Nothing keeps us apart – not even a child, not even responsibilities. You're free: free as a barren woman, free as an orphan. You don't owe them anything . . . After a few months of idleness and love, we shall have become companions, accomplices, we'll be able to communicate by half-spoken hints and allusions, we shall return. I'll begin the struggle and the anger once again . . . You'll see, eventually you'll follow me – it's a life that offers joy. You'll be released entirely from your first and second lives . . .

— Don't tempt me, Catherine answered. I don't know where you're dragging me, let me wait a while longer . . .

— No, Bernard said, the holidays have lasted long enough. It's time for you to abandon everything.

Ten years later, Bernard would not have made plans – he would doubtless have felt confident of carrying the day through patience. But a young man believes himself so insecurely established in his life that he wants forcibly to chain the future, to obtain pledges and promises. He is the only creature who has the heart to demand everything, and think he has been cheated if he does not have everything. Later, nothing will be left but contracts and exchanges.

Everything, it seemed, was owed to Bernard – though he would one day restore all that he now asked should be bestowed upon him. It was necessary for Catherine to commit herself for her whole life. Might he add that he wished his victory over his brother and parents not to be a clandestine victory, of which the vanquished would be unaware, but a scandal – a rupture – that would make Catherine the public, radiant, shocking witness of his triumph? He still barely suspected this secret. He said merely:

— You cannot remain on the side of this angerless world, where everything's settled peaceably. Where money alone must remain undivided, while hearts are parcelled out . . .

He sensed that Catherine was fleeing; that each renewal of love into which she drew him dispensed her from answering everything; and that she kissed him so fiercely only in order to have a reason not to speak.

— No, Bernard would answer.

These new sleepless nights were full of bitterness and time lost.

Then Bernard received a letter from Laforgue, who was now far from his thoughts. Philippe wrote:

Dear old Rosen,

you will find enclosed with this letter my modest contribution to the Conspiracy: the plans, which will surely appear just as obscure to you as sketches of flying machines by Leonardo da Vinci, are elucidated by a number of typewritten sheets and some blueprints. Our friends will understand these technical arabesques. The plans are of a model boilerworks they have just completed at the railway workshops which, as you know, my father runs.

I have just returned from England, where I spent six weeks and where I explored the Lake District on foot. There is a great deal to be said about Great Britain and the Englanders – if you like, it could be for the journal.

Family life lacks fire, and lamplit dinners with the maid in felt slippers in a corner lack passion. My father is becoming more and more reduced to his condition as an engineer and product of the Polytechnique – and I know nothing about him: he would doubtless have to be ill, or suddenly struck down by some social cataclysm, for the shells to crack and the man living inside them to make his appearance. In the meantime, he displays an unbearable self-satisfaction and professional pride which overwhelm me. The evenings are full of speeches about the manufacture of machines, the management of firms and the sly vices of the working class. These meals would dismay the members of your family, where the mistress of the house never fails to exclaim in English, when a guest begins talking about contangos and settlements: Don't talk shop! My mother is a decorative, frivolous person, who spends her time seeing ladies of her own station and who lives in pretty well exactly the same manner as the wife of a high official in Hanoi or Casablanca, who does not mix at all with the natives. She has moments of affection when I will suddenly see her come into my room, where she likes to tuck me up in bed just as she used to when I was ten years old: this action, which for years never failed to touch me, impresses me much less today. All this lacks reality, and it is difficult to be passionately fond of phantoms; but they inspire in me a kind of pity, which my father repays with affection and with scorn.

So I gave some thought to our projects and, since my father was talking with pride about the boilerworks constructed from his plans which he says is the most modern in Europe, I said to myself that perhaps there was here a subject for research that might be of interest to *us. No one is more open to flattery than men like my father, and when I told him I should like to visit the new installations, he was astonished to see an abstract and light-minded intellectual like me being interested in the virile exactitudes of technology. I sensed the rebirth in his breast of a hope he entertained, for a time, of seeing me, after my* agrégation, *become an expert in rationalization and Taylorism – somebody like M. de Fréminville or M. le Châtelier – although I explained to him a dozen times that I had no taste for that kind of sophisticated spying and grassing, with chronometer and slide-rule. I do not have to tell you that my father is one of those stewards of capitalism who, after the War, were dazzled by the neo-Saint-Simonians, and that he views Ford as the greatest man of the twentieth century.*

I visited the factory and the new boilerworks, which struck me as clean and sensible. My father showed me blueprints indicating the location of the machines, the order of operations and standard diagrams for the total overhaul of locomotives – he talked to me at great length about tubes, lagging sheets and struts. All this was at the back of a filing-cabinet and already gathering dust. Since the cabinet had no key, I wonder if these papers are really very sensational. But I reckoned I owed our project at least a symbolic collaboration, so I took advantage of a fresh visit to the factory to remain there alone in my father's office and take the plans and diagrams. This act – contrary to all filial values – struck me as entirely natural. Here are the results. I entrust them to you. Give me some news of yourself. I suppose La Vicomté, where you are browsing, is not much more fun than the villa at Grafenstaden and the streets of Strasburg. Yours.

Bernard was surprised to discover that this letter did not have the least effect on him. He was a bit alarmed, however, to think that an idea he had launched with enthusiasm, but which he had ceased to care about, could still produce consequences and lead a kind of autonomous existence. He told himself that he would have to reflect, but there were other things to be done and Catherine's love was more important than all the plots of youth. He reread Laforgue's letter and found that it had a childish ring

– for a woman had just abruptly given him man's estate. He put Laforgue's papers away in a drawer and endeavoured to forget them. However, since he felt a vague unease each time he thought that he ought to have answered his friend but the answer was still not forthcoming, he eventually went to send off a telegram from the post office at Grandcourt:

'Letter received safely. Thanks. So long.'

This missive set him at peace with himself. Laforgue wondered what the telegram hid. He could not yet guess that Rosenthal wished to make a new start, accepted that his friends might think he had betrayed them, and was already exclaiming – with an inner impulse of defiance:

'So what? They can't imagine what strength a person derives from the carefree state born of love. I'm ready to renounce everything, even the pleasure of influence. They'll have to grow up without me!'

A week went by in this manner. Claude was about to return to La Vicomté for a month, M. Rosenthal was already packing his bags to go back to Paris. Bernard divined that he would never endure for thirty days what he had barely stood without exploding for a weekend. So he resolved to leave and give Catherine a further month's respite to make up her mind to choose his bed. He was counting on the fact that she would find her husband's company hard to put up with, and that the pleasure he was at least sure of having given her granted him a power over her which absence would cause to grow: she had made him a party to many humiliated confidences concerning Claude.

But Catherine lacked imagination – and her body memory. Bernard never suspected that she had welcomed the contractions and releases of pleasure only as pieces of good fortune, as delicious accidents: she did not say she would no longer be able to live without them. She was a woman who, in love, was like those people whom music overwhelms at the time they hear it, but who cannot remember a tune.

XVI

Back in Paris, a Paris where none of his friends was there to distract his thoughts from himself and where he would dine tête-à-tête with his father in Avenue Mozart or alone in restaurants, Bernard began to invent a great love.

Nothing is more dangerous than these times spent in solitude or unfamiliar surroundings – these refuges for the heart. Bernard built systems, analysed his senses and his pride. He never even noticed that he had forgotten everything about Catherine's face and that she was simply an absence, like a persistent ache: such forgetfulness has never prevented anyone from constructing – around a few symptoms, a few snatches of remembrance and a few wakeful nights – the great fables of love. He did not write a single line to La Vicomté, and Catherine like him remained silent. She was a woman who used to say:

— I don't like writing . . . And, besides, I don't know how . . .

Bernard was not worried. One has to be twenty to believe in the virtues of such silent interludes, and to convince oneself that courtesy and words are not the food of love.

So he busied himself with preparing for a new life. He informed his father one evening that he was going to look for a small apartment close to the Latin Quarter, since the year of his *agrégation* was about to begin and he did not want, as in previous years, to waste a huge amount of time shuttling back and forth between the Sorbonne, the Ecole Normale and Avenue Mozart – and there was certainly no question of his deciding to room at Rue d'Ulm. M. Rosenthal winked, did not say no and offered his son the money for his future rent: Bernard accepted the cheque.

After roaming about for a few days between the Observatory and the river, he found an apartment on the sixth floor of a building on Place Edmond Rostand. Beneath his windows he saw the rolling green billows of the trees in the Luxembourg. He imagined Catherine there with him. He brought workmen in, telling himself that when she returned the apartment would smell dreadfully of paint.

The summer ended badly: that year, September was the season of storms.

Bernard would sleep till late. In the evenings he would go and prowl about Paris, reflecting how everything was in suspense and he had absolutely nothing to do except wait for the moment when Catherine would be there – and he would wager his life.

At around six o'clock, when people had had time to forget entirely Paris's crystal guises, great copper monuments would start to arise in the sky to the west. The pigeons would hobble down the steps in the Tuileries and the Luxembourg and colourless men with secret obsessions, spinsters, and children encouraged to pity animals so that they would have no pity for men, would continue to throw bread feebly to these repulsive birds. Passers-by, sticky with sweat, would lift their heads and sigh with an air of lassitude and impatience. At last, towards evening, the storms would break: open windows would bang in violent draughts, curtains would fly out and flap like captive ghosts, showers of glass would rain down and the swallows would twitter as they wheeled, skimming the earth. Huddled for shelter in doorways, the passers-by would shake themselves and gaze up like dogs at the curdled sky and the loosed arrows of the rain. Everyone would feel that desire to laugh, run and shout which takes hold of men confronted by great atmospheric phenomena. Anguish would evaporate and a limpid sky be reborn.

But the sky used to contain such ample reserves of anger that fresh clouds would form in the depths of the stifling night. Across the city, sleepers would awake with a start from their first sleep. Not a leaf would be stirring on the trees by now. Along the streets, after midnight, there would still be people sitting on their doorsteps, who would spread their thighs and open their mouths like fish. Atop the canals, on their barges, the watermen would sleep stretched out on the deck.

Bernard, suffocating in this Paris of impatience, had the impression it would never end. He came within an ace of yielding, taking the train to Blangy: Catherine was only a few hours away from him. However, he managed to be faithful to his self-imposed constraints and did not budge.

Catherine came back at last, much earlier than he had expected: Claude, who was bored at La Vicomté, had decided to take a fortnight's winter holiday at Davos and cut short his summer holiday. The bags were unpacked in Avenue Mozart and Avenue de Villiers. Bernard telephoned Catherine to say he wished first to see her elsewhere than beneath the family roof: he asked her to meet him at eleven the following morning, in front of the Triumphal Arch in the Place du Carrousel.

Bernard did not like the dresses and hats women were beginning to wear in that late autumn season. As he paced along the Carrousel balustrades, he told himself Catherine was perhaps going to have a hat that would crush her hair, or a dress that would make him die of shame: the least flaw could ruin this meeting. He looked from afar at all the women arriving, and thought he recognized Catherine in each of them. At last she appeared: she emerged from the gloomy entrance to the Carrousel on the Palais-Royal side, wearing a pink-and-black crêpe-de-Chine dress and holding her hat in her hand. Her dress fell free, at each step revealing the firm, glossy surface of her legs. Bernard told himself she was more ravishing than ever, more sparkling than he had dared hope. He walked towards her as though her reappearance were a kind of miracle: a victory over time, distance and the great pitiless flywheels of life. All his plans, his hopes, his projects for immediately organizing his existence with her were forgotten. He thought he had been mad to live, like all men, only for long waits: not to be capable of an artless presence in the world.

'I want nothing more,' he told himself. 'Everything's being settled precisely at this very moment, when I'm about to touch Catherine's bare hand. She's taking off her gloves, she's quickening her pace, she's smiling – I've never known such happiness . . .'

There is no happiness like that of people who expect nothing, who have no more future because everything has been called into question: like people who love one another on the eve of a battle, or of death. Bernard was making this discovery for the first time.

— Where are we going? asked Catherine. My whole day is yours.

It was the first day of autumn. The weather was wonderful, the kind of weather that made you want to get away from Paris, where it was pleasant to live only in the evening when the moon's last quarters rose over the city. Catherine said she would like to go to Trianon. They took the tram near the Louvre and lunched at Versailles, beside the gravel incline that slopes up to the gates of the château. Later, after walking across the park – down avenues that vanished amid great architectural compositions of stone, statuary and expanses of water, and along weathered walls covered with the last roses of September – they stretched out behind Trianon in a wilderness of tall weeds, upon a world of cool velvet: wild tufts idly flattened by vague gusts of wind from the open country, from the plains of Saint-Cyr and Saint-Nom. Suddenly Bernard said to Catherine:

— My autumn rose . . .

She raised herself on one elbow and began to laugh:

— That's the first word of love I've ever heard from you, she said. Do you realize what's happening?

Bernard kissed her, thinking that he was completely stupid

and engaged in a dialogue in abominably bad taste – but that he was still perfectly happy. Hours later when they stood up, they noticed two men who were looking at them from some distance away: one was holding his bicycle propped against him, and Bernard and Catherine heard him exclaim:

— Pity they didn't go all the way!

Catherine blushed. Bernard, who was trembling a little after all those hours of happiness and half-pleasure, told her:

— I wish there'd been ten thousand people – the crowd you get on a Sunday when the fountains are working!

— We're terribly imprudent, said-Catherine.

This happiness lasted only for a day. Bernard at once lapsed back into his ambitions of absolute conquest. He had had time to prepare his home and his heart: Catherine found a lover full of tricks.

Bernard, who had practised on himself a great deal during the September storms, tried out on Catherine his dramatization of weakness and leisure, and the great fable of the woman who takes the warrior's mind off things – the fable few women can resist.

'She must pity me,' he said to himself, 'believe that I'm overwhelmed by work and anguish, doomed to an early death, engaged in a struggle, destined for the violent fate of revolutions. War itself may break out tomorrow.'

He let himself appear weakened, said to Catherine:

— You're my idleness . . .

He believed himself sincere then, released from a hardness that had been only a disguise – but he was merely natural. He did not perceive that nothing is more artificial than sincerity, and that nature is the realm of mimicry: of the infinite lies of plants and insects. He was simply seeking the image of himself that might finally, out of all possible variants, enchain Catherine for ever and persuade her to face scandal.

But everything slid off this over-smooth woman, including

the very idea which undoes so many women, that she is necessary to a life – that she can save a man who loves her.

— How pessimistic you are, she said, stroking his hair.

— I'm not pessimistic, he replied. I simply think everything is a threat to flashes of happiness. Joy is the most tragic thing in the world, it always springs from misfortune overcome.

Catherine never said to him what he was waiting for her to say: 'I don't want you to die, I shall pluck you from misfortune, I shall remain beside you to protect you.'

Nothing would bind her for ever. No great role tied her down. She was merely a perpetual reluctance, a tender refusal. Everything was a failure.

Bernard sometimes wondered if she doubted him and doubted what he would become; if she feared she would never find in him the reasons for pride that women need. He told her one day:

— You really are a woman, Catherine. Old like all women, cautious, horrible! You never judge a man on his promises, only on his successes ... How is it you can't understand that I'm living only for a great future which is still entirely unknown to me?

— You're like a child, Catherine replied, who tells one, with tears in its eyes: 'When I grow up, you'll see what I can do.' But I'm neither old nor cautious, I love you just as you are ...

The trouble was that Catherine had never thought about these things; she did not understand a word of what Bernard was saying to her; her responses were dictated only by the easy grace young women possess. Bernard was simply speaking to a deaf person. He never suspected that Catherine was a perfect match, as they say, for Claude.

XVII

— It's going to be a nice little awakening for him, said one of the superintendents.

— He'll have nothing to complain about, answered a detective-sergeant. He'll have had more sleep than us.

The policemen laughed.

They were in high spirits because they were about to arrest a man they had been looking for, after all, ever since the Public Prosecutor's office issued a charge right back on 5 July. Also because the weather was still summery, though they were well into October. At least the weather would have been summery if there had not been one of those mists over the Seine valley which herald the frosts and lurid sunrises of winter; but that year they were living in the strange suspension of death which recurs every three or four years, during which the trees retain their leafy crowns until some gust of wind or frosty night that suddenly strips away all the cargoes from their branches.

The plain-clothes policemen down from Paris and the Saint-Germain gendarmes watched the sleeping house. The drivers of the Prefecture vehicles had climbed down from their seats. The officer commanding the investigation said it was time and walked towards the gate. He rang the bell. Since the boundless silence of morning reigned all about them, every noise being entirely muffled over the river by the wreaths of fog, the ringing reverberated to quite a distance across the countryside. The commander pushed open the gate and a spray of fine droplets fell on him from the leaves of the wisteria. The superintendents followed him. On the first floor, a window opened. Régnier leant out, running his fingers through his hair.

— Police, said the commander.

— No! Régnier said.

The door opened. The commander and the superintendents disappeared.

The detectives and gendarmes continued to watch the house, guessing at a great to-do within.

— It's all going to go off nicely, said one of the detectives.

— Political arrests, said one of his companions, aren't always easy to bring off; but once you've got your man, they're usually peaceful enough.

They had to wait. Perhaps twenty-five minutes or half an hour. The policemen smoked and looked at the landscape, trying to make out in the distance Le Vésinet, Bezons, Sannois, Rueil and Nanterre. The weather brightened, the fog lifted.

— They're taking long enough in there, said a gendarme.

— The gentleman's taking his bath, a detective replied. Or he's learning the Writ of Summons by heart.

Eventually the door of the house opened. The prisoner appeared first, the commander followed; then the two superintendents. From the door to the gate, a cobbled path ran between the two borders. They started out on the round cemented stones. The commander was walking behind the prisoner and, since he considered it humiliating not to be walking at least abreast of him, he effected a little change of step and plunged into the soft earth of a geranium-bed. The prisoner was much taller than the commander. Régnier ran down the last three steps of the perron: he had slipped on an overcoat over his pyjamas, and across his shoulders thrown the plaid for which he had asked his wife on the day of Rosenthal's visit. He reached the cars and caught the prisoner's arm.

— I shall never forgive myself for this arrest, he said.

— Oh, it's not your fault at all, my dear fellow, the other replied. It's not the end of the world. And he started to laugh, not restraining his guffaws.

— Get in, said a superintendent.

Finally a detective emerged from the house with the suitcase of the man they had just arrested. He came and threw it into the car at the feet of the commander, who told him to be careful. The cars drove off in the direction of Saint-Germain.

— Where are we going? asked the prisoner. If it's not a violation of professional secrecy.

— Versailles first, the Public Prosecutor's office in Paris next, and ending up at Rue de la Santé.

— It'll be a very pleasant trip today, said the prisoner. Do you like the country?

— No, said the policeman.

— And do you believe in the conspiracy for which you're arresting me? asked Régnier's guest.

— If I didn't believe in it, I wouldn't be here, said the commander.

— You amaze me, said the prisoner.

In front of the gate, on the road, Régnier was by now just a little man clumsily waving his arm.

The commander was quite pleased with himself. He was telling himself that the indictment issued by the Public Prosecutor's office to the investigating magistrate on 5 July had contained one hundred and twenty-two names, and the supplementary indictment of 18 October thirty-two; and that, after Vaillant-Couturier's arrest at Voulangis on 14 September and Monmousseau's in Place Clichy on the fifteenth, only the man he could hear breathing gently at his side – who was Carré, member of the Central Committee of the Communist Party, charged with conspiring against the

154

external security of the State – had remained at liberty. Carré sighed and said:

— One never gets up early enough in the morning . . .

The cars vanished into the forest of Saint-Germain.

It had been not quite a month that Carré had been living in François Régnier's house, where he had arrived one morning with his suitcase to ask Régnier if he would have him: Régnier had simply told him to move in. So ready a response can surprise only those who know nothing about male relationships. Among the bonds that bind men, those of war are strong. Régnier could ask Carré:

— Do you remember 20 October '17, in front of Perthes-lès-Hurlus?

Carré would answer that he remembered. With Régnier he enjoyed a less close relationship than with his party comrades – party loyalties are more powerful than the loyalties of death and blood – but he nevertheless knew he could ask of Régnier what a person has the right to demand from a man he has witnessed in a war.

Carré had been wandering all over France since the July arrests and his entry into the difficult but exhilarating world of clandestinity. He had thought of Régnier by chance, on a street in Marseilles, when he saw in a shop window his Somme companion's latest book, at a moment when the party was asking him to return to the Paris region. Since his arrival, Carré and Régnier – who had seen each other seven or eight times since '18 – had renewed their acquaintance, by talking: they were men who had things to talk about.

Communism for Carré was not just the form he had given to his action, but the very consciousness he had of himself and his life. His meeting with Régnier gave him the opportunity to express personal values so deep that he no more thought of calling them into question than he did his heartbeats. Nothing disturbed Régnier more deeply than this coincidence between a politics and a destiny – this harmony he despaired of ever achieving between history and the individual. He asked questions.

These conversations took place under apple trees in the garden, when Carré had completed his day's work: at a time when he was relaxed, when he smoked and talked, continually running his hand through the beard he had allowed to grow and in which grey hairs were already visible. Régnier asked him:

— I don't understand, the world you come from seems pretty impenetrable to me. Explain yourself.

— It's not simple, Carré answered. People like you, who think they've read everything, can't see communism as anything other than one system of ideas among all the rest. As though there were boxes with labels on – the socialism box, the fascism box, the communism box – among which you choose for reasons of affinity, aesthetics, elegance or logical coherence. Communism is a politics, but it's also a style of life. That's why the Church fears us and is for ever sizing us up, even though we're not anti-clerical and have nothing in common with M. Combes. It knows that communism, like itself, is wagering on the certainty of an absolutely total victory. No doctrine's less pluralist than Marxism.

— But how about yourself? asked Régnier. General ideas don't tell me anything.

— I've been a communist since the Tours Congress, for a whole number of reasons, but none is more important than having been able to answer the following question: with whom can I live? I can live with the communists. Not with the socialists. The socialists meet and discuss politics, elections – and afterwards it's all over: it doesn't govern their every breath, their private lives, their personal loyalties, their idea of death or the future. They're citizens. They're not men. Albeit clumsily, albeit gropingly, albeit sometimes lapsing, the communist has the ambition to be a man, absolutely . . . The best time of my life was perhaps the period I spent as an activist in the provinces, where

I was a branch secretary. Everything had to be done, it was a region that was being born – or reborn. The branch committee toiled away like Balzac's Country Doctor. But for serious! A communist has nothing. But he wants to be and to do . . .

— I don't see how you, an intellectual, someone of critical descent, said Régnier, can accept a discipline that extends to thought. That's always been the stumbling-block for me.

— Inveterate liberal! Carré replied. Disloyal to man! You put everything on the same plane. You're consumed with pride, you want to have the right to be free against yourself, against even your loves. You see every participation as a limitation. You immediately want to revoke your decision, in order to show yourself you're free to reject what you've just embraced. And proud to boot, and Goethean: 'I am the Spirit that negates all . . .' When will people stop living with the idea that there's no greatness except in refusal? That negation alone does not dishonour? Greatness for me lies only in affirmation . . . It's true that on certain nights, and certain days, I may have told myself: 'The party's wrong, its evaluation's not correct.' I've said it out loud. They replied that I was wrong – and perhaps I was right. Was I supposed, in the name of freedom to criticize, to rise up against myself? Loyalty has always struck me as of more pressing importance than the victory – won at the price of a rupture – of one of my ephemeral political inflections. It's not by little daily truths that we live, but by a total relationship with other men . . .

They pursued these dialogues at length. By the time a fortnight had gone by, Régnier was beginning to form an idea of a hard, enviable world which it still did not seem possible for him to enter.

Not long after Carré's arrest, Régnier wrote to Rosenthal that he wished to see him, and that it involved a serious matter concerning one of his visitors at the beginning of April. Rosenthal, who had just been reunited with Catherine and was struggling with her, felt a spurt of impatience as he read Régnier's letter. This sudden return of everything he had so passionately embraced six months earlier seemed a hateful distraction from what was essential. However, he thought there was no question of escaping, without incurring pangs of remorse that would be abhorrent to him. So he apprized Laforgue – whom he had greatly neglected throughout his stay at La Vicomté, and who had just announced his imminent return to Paris – telling himself he would be satisfying simultaneously the commands of duty and those of friendship, thus killing two birds with one stone.

— Do you remember, Laforgue said in the electric train taking them to Maisons-Laffitte, our arrival at Mesnil-le-Roi seven months ago? I've a vague sort of idea we haven't made fantastic progress towards getting the conspiracy under way. For, leaving aside the Simon escapade and the paternal boilerworks . . .

— We're wasting a terrible amount of time, Bernard replied. There've been these three holiday months holding everything up. We're going to have to get down to it again. And perhaps revise the actual principle of the conspiracy, as you say . . . It's lucky the journal has only nine issues a year . . .

— Speaking of conspiracy, said Laforgue, have you at least transmitted the first stuff to the appropriate party?

— Oh, for Heaven's sake! said Rosenthal.

— Good, said Laforgue.

François Régnier gave them a brief account of Carré's arrival, sojourn and arrest, which had just bowled him over: he would have liked his house to be an inviolable sanctuary. It struck him as intolerable that the outside world should not expire at the edge of his burrow. There was a fire in the grate, as in April, and the plain was equally grey over towards Le Vésinet. Laforgue said to himself: 'It's terrible. We've not moved a step forward in seven months. Everything's still asleep. Nothing has happened.'

Rosenthal, who was thinking only of Catherine, looked at the dining-room as though it were a scene forgotten for years, the ruins of a former life. Everything seemed strange to him. He felt himself the child of a new – and far less dusty – universe: a world of crystal.

François Régnier then explained that he must share with them a suspicion he was unable to keep to himself, even though the whole affair was none of his concern – or concerned him only as the offended master of a place of refuge. He told them that during the entire time of his stay, Carré – who had really taken all the precautions that his situation as an outlaw imposed – had been seen by nobody except himself and Simone (whom he doubted as little as himself), until a strange visit by Serge Pluvinage a few days before Carré's arrest.

— So one afternoon I saw your friend Pluvinage arrive. I should draw no conclusion from this visit, whose motives I am absolutely unable to see but which was perhaps inspired by one of those inexplicable romantic impulses that move people of your age, if Pluvinage – since there really is a Pluvinage – had not had a very odd look about him – much odder even than his pluvious plover and Alfred Jarry monkey of a name. You'll tell me this suspicion doesn't hold water from the novelist's point of view, since it's basically tantamount to judging the man by his demeanour, and his heart by his external marks of virtue, which is unserious. But all the same, to an unprejudiced mind your comrade's got the perfect mug for a perjurer and double agent, one that would immediately inspire mistrust in friends less ardent than you . . . I had the impression he had things to tell me and was awaiting the delivery of a manuscript or the confidences that I expected, but that were still not forthcoming. At which point, Carré came down from his room. Your Pluvinage cried out that it was Carré, who seemed pretty annoyed at being recognized by this individual. Ten minutes later Pluvinage left, after a good deal of stammering . . . So that I'm wondering . . . You understand, perhaps there was nothing in it and Pluvinage is a good and honest fellow, but all the same there's a singular coincidence between that pretty shady young man's visit and the arrest of my friend Carré, which I can't get over . . . Perhaps it's just a matter of loose talk or carelessness, I shall always hesitate to believe a man capable of informing on someone . . . You'll find me naive, but informers will always strike me as so much rarer than murderers that I should never get over having come close to one . . . But since this visit is the only suspicious fact, the possible occasion . . . The confidence of the police was too apparent for them not to have been sure of their facts; and their look of infallible and triumphant modesty, which made one want to slap someone, spoke of people who were well briefed by an informer . . . Well, that's all I wanted to say to you . . . You must be far more familiar than I am with such matters. In your place, I should make some discreet inquiries . . .

Rosenthal and Laforgue reflected how they had not seen Pluvinage since their return to Paris, but how this absence on Serge's part was not mysterious, since the holidays were not over and Serge did not necessarily know they had come back before the reopening of the Sorbonne and the resumption of lectures at Rue d'Ulm. However, they were surprised to discover that Régnier's suspicion did not strike them a priori as monstrous.

— Let's be careful, said Bernard. We've never had anything against Pluvinage up to now except his mug, and a kind of vague and rather disagreeable servility towards us – his toadying, over-obliging side . . .

— It mustn't be forgotten either, said Laforgue, that Serge is a member of the party . . . He must have joined in about May . . . Do you remember, we were flabbergasted that the first of us to take the plunge was precisely the one who seemed the least certain, the most ambiguous . . . After all, it strikes me as a pretty serious thing to suspect someone of treachery who had the courage to commit himself, make the jump, before we did . . .

But at that age nothing surprises. The most violent revelations about a man's character appear natural. One has a weak spot for monsters who confirm a theatrical idea of life: plain beings seem humdrum and false. Moreover, these suspicions, if they were confirmed, promised opportunities for Bernard and

Philippe to speak as judges and find themselves pure. For three days they drove Catherine from Bernard's thoughts.

They summoned Pluvinage to the Ecole Normale, where Laforgue had ensconced himself in a wilderness of silent corridors, halls and dormitories. On the appointed day, while awaiting Pluvinage, they talked about him.

— It would be dreadful, all the same, Laforgue said.

— I'm afraid the tone of our letter may have been rather hard, said Rosenthal. He'll be on his guard, if there is anything.

The door opened. Pluvinage came in like a cat. Rosenthal and Laforgue fell abruptly silent and wondered if he had been listening to them through the door before coming in. But a strange incident gave them the courage to plunge in almost immediately. For as soon as Pluvinage was in the room, he abruptly turned and bolted the door. Bernard asked him why he was shooting the bolt. Pluvinage denied having done so – and was doubtless not lying: he had not been aware of his action.

— Very well, said Laforgue. Odd for an unconscious slip! Are you being followed?

The conversation got off to a bad start, dragged. Were they going to talk about the weather they were having? Rosenthal made up his mind, he believed in the virtues of brutality.

— Let's not beat about the bush, he said. Neither Laforgue nor I has asked you here for an exchange of views on the holidays, the rain or German phenomenology. Here's what it's all about. Do you know about the arrest of Carré, the CP Central Committee activist, in Mesnil-le-Roy, at Régnier's place?

Pluvinage looked towards the window, outside which the black tops of the trees bordering Rue Rataud were swaying, and said that he had learned of the arrest from the newspapers, a short while after those of Vaillant-Couturier and Monmousseau.

— All right, said Rosenthal. Régnier, who has told us about an odd visit you paid him just before the arrest, suspects you of bearing responsibility for the police action – whether inadvertently or by design. What do you say?

Serge at first said nothing and went to lean out of the window. A pigeon was walking along the gutter. Eventually Serge said in a low voice:

— So you reckoned that swine's suspicion was well founded?

— We didn't reckon anything, said Laforgue. We're asking you.

— Didn't you tell yourselves that you've known me for years, that you know how I live, that I'm a member of the party? Didn't you burst out laughing in the Great Author's face?

Rosenthal replied that it was necessary to examine every least ground for suspicion thoroughly; that no friendship is above the Revolution; and that there really was a coincidental connection between the visit to Carrières and the arrest, which obliged him at least to pose the question. He had Stuart Mill's precepts at the tip of his tongue, but thought the reference would be distasteful in such solemn circumstances. Pluvinage told him he had always been a moralist, and was still ignoble in the way moralists are. He even pronounced the word Pharisee, which seemed in extremely bad taste to Rosenthal and Laforgue, who came within an ace of speaking derisively about whited sepulchres. They pressed Serge further, without provoking anything but his anger. Serge told them, with manifest good sense, that there can be no proof of negative things, and that he could only say no and cast doubt on their suspicions. He added that he would give them his word of honour, if they wished; but that a word of honour is no better at establishing proof than a simple denial, and he could see they were determined to refuse him their trust.

— But we must know! exclaimed Rosenthal.

— No chance, said Laforgue. Pluvinage is right. We believe or don't believe, but we'll never have anything but moral certainties.

Pluvinage left slamming the door, after fumbling with the bolt which he had closed at the start of the meeting.

*　　*　　*

Rosenthal and Laforgue waited for several days for him to reappear, but he did not come back or give any sign of life. As time passed, they assembled memories that justified every suspicion. The accusation took shape, gradually came to seem obvious: innocent, Serge would have come back to them. This continuing absence, this silence, slowly reassured them. Eventually they wondered what they ought to do, without any shadow of real proof but with strong emotive presumptions. They hesitated to attempt an approach to the party.

— What would we look like? asked Laforgue. One doesn't turn up at the house of people one barely knows and tell them: 'You know, your son's probably a thief, or a swindler . . .'

They did decide, however, to write to the party secretariat, reporting on the conversation with Régnier, their suspicions and Pluvinage's denials. When they had completed the letter, they found it fitting and suddenly felt their consciences at rest. Nothing in the world weighs heavier than the need to judge – they were finally relieved of that burden.

— When one comes to think of it, Rosenthal said one day, it seemed strange to us that Pluvinage should have informed only because we were thinking about his phenomenal character; but there's doubtless a great deal to be said about his intelligible character. Who is not twofold?

Laforgue found this fairground display revolting, and told his friend:

— No Kantism, I beg of you! Perhaps we've behaved like swine . . .

XVIII

No one dared look Bernard in the face.

'The family council's a flop,' he said to himself. 'They're afraid of me. They're still wondering if they're going to eliminate me or devour me. Shall I be too tough for my carnivores?'

He looked at them, ensconced in their judicial poses. Mme Rosenthal seated – her hands flat on her knees, motionless – in a Louis XV armchair, in front of the little marquetry bureau on which she wrote her letters and checked the accounts of her charities and her cook. M. Rosenthal standing behind the rampart of the piano, his torso illuminated by a large lamp, his face in shadow. Claude behind his mother, his hands on the back of her chair, like a squire. The circumstances smacked too much of tragedy for all the lamps to have been lit: the large drawing-room was submerged in twilight, as though there had been a local supply breakdown and just one lamp had been brought from the pantry. And in the depths of this domestic semi-darkness where the radiators knocked, like an exile from youth and summer, sat Catherine in a pale blue dress, her neck resting against the fluted wood of the settee: she had crossed her legs, her stockings gleamed, she was smoking.

Never had Bernard experienced such a sense of triumph. The evening before, Claude – wishing to 'see over the property' at the apartment on Place Edmond Rostand, which he did not know – had arrived at his brother's place. He had entered

Bernard's bedroom where Catherine, who had fallen asleep there an hour earlier, had just woken up. He had paled, he had not said a word, he had simply fled. Catherine had sprung up and in turn taken flight ten minutes later. Since five in the afternoon on the preceding day – for twenty-five hours – Bernard had remained alone, waiting.

'Thank God,' he thought, 'the time for deception is over. Events have taken a dramatic turn. They're going to have to find a way out . . .'

His mother had asked him on the telephone to come to Avenue Mozart. She had said, in her toneless voice:

— Your father, your brother and I have to talk to you.

Bernard was playing his first big game. Catherine was the stake – and, with her, childhood, the future, love, hope.

He came of a generation in which successes in love were almost always confused with those of an insurrection. All women conquered, all scandals, seemed victories over the bourgeoisie: it was eighteen thirty! Bernard was convinced that love was an act of revolt – he never suspected it was complicity, friendship or idleness.

'If I tear Catherine from their clutches,' he told himself, 'I'm definitively saved. If they keep her, what shall I do with my defeat?'

Catherine still did not move. Perhaps she was dreaming; perhaps she was trembling with impatience or dread; perhaps she was simply waiting for this ceremonial to come to an end.

'All her strength lies in her boredom,' thought Bernard. 'Even against me. Is she going to abandon me? Go over to the enemy? When she fled last evening, was she making her choice?'

He wanted to think only about fighting: a fighter is always delivered. He looked at his brother, perhaps for the first time in twenty years without hatred. The unease, the strange anguish he had always felt in his presence had just evaporated. He had finally been cured of his family by scandal, by daylight. He had finally forced them to enter with him the world without lies: the unpolished world of Cain and Abel, Eteocles and Polynices, the Seven against Thebes – the world of tragedy. Claude was crushed and certainly looked it: everything was about to collapse – family tradition, primogeniture, brotherly love. The irruption of the unforeseen into the Rosenthal order was making him doubt his reason and his eyes.

'Who'll dare to speak?' Bernard wondered. 'They'd be wrong to think I'm going to begin . . . My mother, no doubt – the woman for big occasions.'

Bernard sat down. The silence, of course, was unbearable. From time to time the sound of glassware could be heard coming from the dining-room: the housemaid was setting the table. Even if there is a dead person in the house, one has to eat. Mme Rosenthal said, quite quietly:

— Bernard . . .

'Here we go, then,' he said to himself. 'I knew it . . .'

— Bernard, you know no doubt that we know. Claude has told us everything. Catherine has confessed. We wanted to talk to you, in front of her.

Bernard looked at Catherine, who still did not move, who was no longer even smoking. The smoke from her cigarette climbed straight, then trembled at a distant eddy of Mme Rosenthal's voice.

— I suppose, she said, that it's no use reading you a sermon.

— No, it isn't, Bernard said.

— Be quiet, said Mme Rosenthal. You're a kind of monster. You fill me with horror. And please don't defy us.

— Oh, of course, said Bernard.

Mme Rosenthal burst out sobbing. She lost face at the thought that she must renounce all power over her son. When she was able to speak, she sighed:

— And I almost hoped that when you saw us, you'd understand the horror of your behaviour . . . that you'd at least have some good impulse, some cry of regret. From you, my poor child, there's nothing more we can look for . . .

— Look for what? said Bernard, casting another glance in Catherine's direction, catching the ghost of a smile which she suppressed and telling himself: 'She still sees them with my eyes!' What good impulse? Ought I to throw myself at Claude's knees? Since I didn't imagine he could ever forgive me, I don't really see what we could do in the way of tender feelings, morals and collective tears . . . And since I regret precisely nothing . . .

— Swine! exclaimed Claude, tensing and gripping the back of his mother's chair.

— Claude, said Mme Rosenthal.

M. Rosenthal, who could stand no more, left abruptly slamming the door. His wife shrugged her shoulders.

— So, we have very little to say to one another, said Mme Rosenthal. No one must know anything about our troubles. Catherine will remain with her husband . . .

She looked towards Catherine, who gave a slight nod. Bernard thought it was impossible, they were all crazy and this family tribunal was vile.

— You'll live on your own, his mother continued, as you've begun to do. Your father will pay you your monthly allowance. If you want to, you may come here whenever you wish – you're our child. I shall make arrangements so that you don't meet either your brother or his wife here. There will be no public rupture: I won't tolerate a scandal. Later, we shall see . . .

— Time doesn't solve anything, said Bernard. Let's make no plans. Is that all?

Was it all? He still waited. Was no one shouting? Was no one hurling themselves at him? He had had a moment of hope, when Claude had called him a swine. It was over, they were all silent now, they were curling up like hedgehogs, softening the impact of the blow.

'Are they hoping I'll roll at their feet, or weep? I look a fool, nothing's happening. No tragedy. No sentimental drama. At most a bourgeois piece, second-rate Diderot, that middle course . . .'

Bernard stood up and walked to the far end of the room,

towards Catherine. Catherine's cigarette, almost completely burnt down, was still smoking in the ashtray. It was the time for decision. Catherine watched him coming, she straightened her body, crossed her fingers. Mme Rosenthal stood up. Claude held his breath.

— Let's go, Catherine, Bernard said. Come and put your coat on . . .

Catherine raised her eyes and looked at Bernard.

— Go away, she said.

— Yes, go away, said Mme Rosenthal.

Everyone began to move. Catherine uncrossed her legs and her fingers, leant back on the settee, closed her eyes. Claude kissed his mother, Bernard left.

XIX

The days went by. Bernard did not go back to Avenue Mozart, where no doubt, he thought, they were all saying that the hardest moment was long past and, after an ambiguous stifling of passions, life would begin again.

Precautions were taken against him. He did not manage to see Catherine again, or speak with her. He came up against the dreadful barrier of the housemaids' furtive glances – Catherine was never there. He wrote letters without expecting any great result from them – wasted messages – telling himself that a letter is torn up or forgotten: that what was needed was his voice, his anger, the heart's eloquence, his presence, his body. With what terrifying ease, then, was she complying with the conditions of her pardon? Was she simply saying that she had got off lightly?

Bernard felt that a kind of great machine had begun to operate – at the very moment when he had let Claude enter the room on Place Edmond Rostand – and that, strive as he might to arrest its driving-rods, he would not stop it turning now.

How powerful and inflexible a family is! It is as peaceful as a body or an organ that barely stirs, that breathes dreamily until the moment of danger – yet it is full of secrets, hidden counterstrokes, a biological fury and swiftness, like a sea anemone in the recesses of a fold of granite, peaceful, inattentive, unaware as a flower, which lets its dapple-grey tentacles drift as it waits to close them upon a crab, a shrimp, a sinking shell.

At last Bernard received a letter from Catherine, in November. She entreated him not to write any more, not to seek any further meetings.

'Understand,' Catherine wrote, 'that I simply do not want to see you any more. My poor Bernard, I am not cut out for your challenges and your love of storms: you demanded too much of a woman like any other.

'You are terrible, you want everything from a woman, you will never have anything. For weeks you blinded me to yourself, to myself, to your mother, to my husband – and it is over, that is all, I have woken up, I can see clearly again. They have been simply perfect: how could I have guessed that Claude was capable of dignity?

'Your terrible pride is your undoing – you, who are worth no more than others, who are merely a little different. This tragedy happened because you wanted it. I have wondered – I still wonder – whether you had not warned my husband yourself. If you did not bring him deliberately to the room where I was sleeping . . . I do not know how I resisted you so feebly. How I did not understand, even during that summer, that you believed you loved me, whereas I was only the opportunity for you to revenge yourself on your family. How easily you breathe in the midst of scandal! Not I. I feel as though I were convalescing . . .

'Perhaps we shall see each other again one day. In the end everything is forgotten. Forget me too, think of yourself.'

Bernard told himself furiously that Catherine had aligned herself with the party of order against him. What a capacity to retreat and forget!

'As for me,' he thought, 'I forget nothing of her body . . . And there's no other truth than a body.'

It is hard to accept despair, or recognize that matters are closed. Love is as tenacious as life itself. This letter, arriving out of the blue, re-established a kind of link. Catherine's farewells seemed less cruel than her silence. Perhaps she had forgotten nothing – perhaps she had just been lazy, cowardly, duped. Bernard had to believe that Catherine was lying: for he could overcome lies, but not oblivion. One can defeat sicknesses, but not death. He pictured Avenue Mozart, Avenue de Villiers, big emotional scenes, heartfelt phrases, a comedy of generosity and affliction, Catherine's tears, his mother's open arms, his brother drowning his humiliation in the charms of magnanimity. The idea that they had triumphed over his Catherine only by under-hand means gave him the courage to hurry round once more to Avenue de Villiers, in order to say to Catherine: 'Do you remember?' For an hour he thought himself omnipotent, still capable of saving her.

The housemaid told him that Madame had not come home, and had said nothing about when she would be back. This lie seemed insulting to Bernard, who from the pavement had seen a light in Catherine's room. He went away. In Rue Jouffroy he entered the post office and wrote an express message, in which he told Catherine that he did not believe her and that the hardest words in her letter had been dictated to her.

'I want a reply from you,' he went on to say, 'which has the same tone that was ours during our Grandcourt nights, when the bats used to come and dash themselves against the walls of your room and I would restrain your cries; the tone of Trianon; the tone of our mornings in the Forêt d'Eu. Will you not have the courage to break with their appalling life? Do not write, I no longer even have the courage to wait. Do not be sensible, speak to me across the frontiers of Paris and your heart, telephone me. I shall wait at home this evening for your telephone call. Or yourself. Everything is still possible. Even the happiness that can spring up again at the limits of despair. You have no idea what love's fury is capable of . . .'

XX

Bernard returned to Place Edmond Rostand. It was five o'clock.
As in September, there was nothing more in the world to do but
wait. He had issued his final appeal. Nothing protected him any
longer except the hope of a telephone call, or the entrance of
Catherine – which suddenly struck him as inevitable.

At eleven o'clock Catherine had not come, the telephone had
not rung. He called the Avenue de Villiers apartment. The
housemaid told him that Madame had come home and gone out
again, and that she had doubtless gone to dine at the house of
Monsieur's mother. Bernard asked for Catherine at Avenue
Mozart, telling the housemaid that it was M. Adrien Plessis who
wished to speak to Mme Claude Rosenthal. Catherine came to
the telephone:

— Did you receive my express letter? he asked.

— Oh! so it's you? exclaimed Catherine. Yes, I received your
letter.

— What's your answer?

— Nothing, said Catherine, I've nothing more to say to you.
Catherine hung up.

Bernard pictured the little scene at Avenue Mozart, the
conversations interrupted while Catherine was on the telephone
in the small drawing-room, Catherine's return. Mme Rosenthal
must be saying to her daughter-in-law, in her voice for big occasions:

— It was that unfortunate child, wasn't it?

For them, he was no doubt that unfortunate child, against whom it was necessary to have so much courage and who was so dangerous – and what a good thing it was that Catherine had once again become as hard as the moral code of the Rosenthals required.

'They're sure I'm going to surrender,' he thought. 'That I'll implore their forgiveness.'

A Rosenthal could not be eternally guilty, eternally an enemy to his clan. The excuses they invented, with the blind skill of instinct, to explain their mistakes, failures and weaknesses – how should they not have manufactured them even for him? Wise as spiders, they were preparing the revival of life from afar. They must already be practising for him the parable of the prodigal child, as though they knew that everything would lapse back into the Rosenthal order. That in three months or six, the crisis suppressed and his repentance over, he would reappear with the modest air of a prodigal son, a disloyal brother, a consoled lover and a pardoned offender. That he would agree to pose for the family portrait gallery, following Claude the magnanimous elder brother and Catherine the wayward child. That he would act the young romantic placated, with the aureole of bygone storms like the glory of an illness from which he had almost died. And that of an evening he would have games of bridge with his father and with Claude – who, to the very end, would have displayed so much kindness and understanding of human passion.

Bernard was less moved by despair than by anger at all these soft walls that were not collapsing. He no longer knew whether he was rebelling against Catherine's disappearance, or against the victory of his relatives. It simply struck him as shameful, impossible, to live any longer defeated, despoiled, forgiven and without Catherine, once captured from the enemy and whom the enemy had now retaken: whose hair, naked back, knees, he would never again touch; whom he would have to watch walking amid the smug looks of the Family – promoted eventually, no doubt, to the tender dignity of young motherhood.

'It's a sure thing,' Bernard told himself. 'These family reconciliations and grand healings always end up with a pregnancy. That fool must already have given her a child . . .'

Bernard went out. It was late and the Luxembourg had long been closed, abandoned behind its railings to a nocturnal life full of mystery. He visited a number of cafés and the bars of the Latin Quarter. He drank a number of brandies, and some whores who felt like dancing accosted him. When he had no money left, he returned to his apartment. He felt really drunk and went to vomit in the bathroom. Coming back to his bedroom, he knocked over a desk lamp, whose bulb shattered with a sound like torn paper. He burnt some letters and some pictures of Catherine, telling himself this adventure had been enough for her: she had taken her revenge on Claude and could now be faithful to him for the rest of her life.

'Is this really where the tragedy begins?' Bernard wondered. 'They've defeated me . . .'

He convinced himself that the purity of passion had come up against the omnipotence of myths, society and fate. But the passion he still at this moment believed he had felt for Catherine was less pure than he thought: it was mingled with jealousy, anger, old childhood resentments; it lacked strength and freedom from guile. No one was there to wake him up and tell him that he had himself manufactured an irreplaceable woman. He was incapable of comparisons. Incapable of saying to himself that, at his age, he could still survive on women unknown to him – and that he had been mad to gamble everything on Catherine. He was blinded. He no longer knew anything of love but the obstinacy that survived it. He was never going to admit he had been mistaken in imagining that, in the whole world, he possessed only one protection against death, only one fortune. But he was standing at the furthest limit of rage, at a point from which he could discern no possible revenge; no undertaking that could touch his relatives; no way of regaining Catherine. He took for despair the impotence of pride. It never even occurred to him that he might be able to win Catherine back by accepting, if need be, every compromise. For, in fact, he loved Catherine less than he thought ...

Bernard reflected, with that tottering solemnity of drunkenness, that all the motivating forces of tragedy were denied him, except the will to die.

'Death could be the affirmation against *them* which none of my actions has succeeded in being. Am I going to sacrifice to them even the freedom of my death, my sole action? ... Besides, they'll look pretty sick if I kill myself ... I've failed in everything, but at least I'll have been once to my uttermost limit. If love is lost, let's at least save tragedy!'

It was one of those days for him when any man will admit that his death would not be particularly important to him, when even fear no longer protects him. He did not suspect for an instant that this disastrous solution would be an excellent outcome for his relatives. Once they knew he was no longer there – that he was eternally inaccessible – how they would forget him!

When – towards the end of the night, after actions dictated to him only by rage, sloth and alcohol – Bernard had with two or three bouts of nausea swallowed a kind of white mash of Gardenal, he experienced his first respite for weeks, his first feeling of relaxation and almost happiness. Gardenal erases everything as a wind erases frost patterns: grief, anger, wakefulness, barriers, distances, the women one used to love and will see no more. Bernard then experienced indifference and, so to speak, a lazy dive into darkness. He was at last capable of judgement. Telling himself he had missed love – that complicity of laughter, eroticism, shared secrets, a past and hope; that union resembling a permitted incest; that bond, strong as a bond forged by childhood and blood – he recalled confusedly the gardens of Potamia, Marie-Anne, the day at Trianon, the moments when he had seen the portents of happiness appear. All that tempest and this final calm suddenly struck him as terribly absurd. He no longer even loved Catherine and he was going to die cheated. What madness! No, he must live!

Bernard sought to stand, run, rid himself of the poison, but he managed only to slide from his bed and – without ever getting to his feet or even to his knees – to reach the entrance to the bathroom, where he finally subsided into the oozy mires of sleep.

In the morning, the woman came in to clean as she did every day. She screamed when she saw Bernard lying there, half on the fitted carpet of his bedroom and half on the black-and-white tiles of the bathroom. She touched him and felt beneath her fingers the vile coldness of the dead. She was the concierge, she went down to her lodge, the running about and the drama began.

That afternoon, Catherine came to see Bernard's body. The room was already full of chrysanthemums and gladioli. Everything had settled into the order of death. Bernard was covered to the chin with his sheet, the white expanse lifted by his knees and the tips of his toes. Mme Rosenthal, seated at her son's bedside, was no longer weeping: but no one is a monster and she had sobbed for hours. When her daughter-in-law came silently in, she scrutinized her. Catherine was wearing a black suit, she approached the bed and looked at the body for an unbearable length of time, she made no movement: she was a young woman of great promise – or perhaps her self-control cost her no effort. Eventually she sighed and looked round her and – as if this sigh and this look had been signals bringing the paralysis of the alert to an end – Mme Rosenthal rose and came over to embrace her daughter-in-law: all was truly forgiven. When death has passed, the living all adapt. Mme Rosenthal then had the second surprise of her life in six months: Catherine, who had allowed herself to be embraced, violently repulsed her mother-in-law and burst out sobbing.

When she had left, Mme Rosenthal resumed her vigil and put her daughter-in-law out of her mind. Since the telephone had been in operation, people began to file past and console the mother. Claude came to join her and watched with her; he kissed his brother's forehead. M. Rosenthal, who was weeping as men do, had to be sent home to Avenue Mozart.

Two days after Bernard's death, Laforgue – who had read the news in *Le Temps* – arrived. Mme Rosenthal was still there. Laforgue in turn looked at the body, in which he scarcely recognized his friend: no dead person resembles the living person he has replaced, during that period separating decomposition from life. Everything about that yellow mask, that neck dark with blood beneath waxen ears, was foreign to Bernard. Laforgue found only the hair familiar, like the natural hair implanted on Chinese papier-mâché masks. Like most dead people, Bernard had that distant serenity which the rigidity of corpses creates. People were doubtless telling Mme Rosenthal, in order to cheer her up, that her son was so handsome in death he seemed to be asleep: but, as always, it was a lie – all dead bodies are horrible. Laforgue was not taken in by the myths of consolation. Anger suffocated him: they were all affected. He felt his throat constrict and his eyes fill with tears, which comforted him a little. What young man does not breathe easier when he suddenly sees himself less hard than he had expected? This softening gave him the strength to go and greet Rosenthal's mother: she refused his hand, drew herself up and said to him, very quietly, in a tone of confidential fury:

— You can be proud of your handiwork, you and your friends!

Mme Rosenthal, in a flash of inspiration as she saw Laforgue enter, had just discovered the family version that would once and for all save the honour of the Rosenthals: the version which explained the taste for Revolution, the seduction of Catherine, the death. The fable of influences, the legend of evil friends, were going to find a new lease of life in the tragic folklore of Avenue Mozart – since Bernard had died of an illness, a deadly germ that had come from outside, and the Rosenthals knew they did not themselves manufacture the poisons that killed him. Laforgue looked at Mme Rosenthal's heavy theatrical mourning and told himself that he understood almost everything. He felt like striking that long lugubrious face like the dried-out muzzle of a horse – but a person must be polite, after all, so he simply said:

— Come now, Madame.

The morning of the funeral arrived. It was high up in the Père-Lachaise, above the Mur des Fédérés. Laforgue, Bloyé and a few others had arrived by the Place Gambetta gate and were waiting behind a tomb, in the strong damp wind that was blowing. The procession finally emerged round a bend in one of the avenues. They were the last to file past the vault. One of those officiating, who had spots on his black tailcoat, proffered them a little shovel that appeared to be made of silver and a vessel full of earth and grit. None of them took the shovel, but all bent over the coffin whose brass plaque was already disappearing under the shovel-fuls of ritual earth. Philippe went by last and dropped onto the bier an aggressive sheaf of red flowers. Then they went off without greeting anyone, casting insolent looks in the direction of the family: Bernard's father was weeping as he clasped people's hands, his shoulders shook with his sobs; Mme Rosenthal and Claude responded to the young men with curt glances of anger. Bloyé said between his teeth that it was good theatre, something which death never escapes. Catherine was not there. Mme Rosenthal told herself that her daughter-in-law had perhaps loved Bernard after all. Laforgue and the others went down towards the cemetery gates, past ruined tombs and worn statues from the days of the Restoration, after pausing to muse for a few moments in front of the Mur des Fédérés.

*   *   *

Two days after the burial, M. Rosenthal received a letter from Philippe Laforgue:

'Although we know,' he said, 'that friendship has never conferred any right upon anybody and are ready to bow to whatever refusal you may make, we have nevertheless decided to ask your authorization to extract from among the papers our friend Bernard Rosenthal left the articles he had completed and the notes he had prepared.

'We think the funeral tribute that he would have placed above all others would have been the publication of these writings in the journal he had himself founded and whose prime mover he was to the end.

'We should be deeply grateful to you for allowing us to examine your son's texts and agreeing to their publication.'

Several days passed. Laforgue said to Bloyé:

— You'll see they'll refuse. They're upstanding people. Their sense of private ownership must extend to corpses. Rosenthal's finally returned now to the Family bosom, they won't let go of anything.

— It's what's called the return of the Prodigal Son, said Bloyé. Anyway, I always told you that your letter to the Father was in the servile mould. One never gains anything by that. You should have insulted them.

Eventually M. Rosenthal replied to Laforgue that he would await his visit next day in the apartment on Place Edmond Rostand. He had said nothing to his wife about the letter from the young men. The fact was that he felt oddly guilty towards his son and wished to obtain his shade's forgiveness – for what enduring and fatal treachery he was not quite sure.

Laforgue came to the meeting, which was cool – or rather awkward. The broker and the young man intimidated one another dreadfully. And just you try talking about the rain and the bad weather and this gloomy season which seems as though it will never end – or about politics which isn't getting any better

– with a dead body full of bitterness between you. M. Rosenthal, sitting in an armchair, smoked and said nothing. One by one Laforgue opened Bernard's drawers, which were full of yellowing papers as though Rosenthal had been dead for ten years. He read pages more or less at random, and took manuscripts fairly indiscriminately because he could feel the father's gaze between his shoulder-blades. In the bottom drawer, he found two folders bearing the following inscriptions: Industry, Army. It was over. Laforgue straightened up, M. Rosenthal rose to his feet and coughed, suppressing the sound.

— This room is freezing, he said.

He opened the window to reclose the shutters, a gust of wind entered the room. Philippe turned the switch: the room was illuminated by the same light as on the night when Bernard died. As they left, M. Rosenthal said:

— I think we can turn out the light. You haven't forgotten anything?

Laforgue gave a clumsy bow. M. Rosenthal ushered him ahead. On the stairs, he suddenly asked him, in a timid voice:

— Did my son sometimes talk to you about me?

Laforgue was shattered by this admission of defeat, this sudden surrender – but he was not going to miss this first opportunity to avenge Rosenthal.

— Never, he said.

M. Rosenthal sighed.

Laforgue took a taxi to return to Rue d'Ulm, and the driver protested because it was only just up Rue Gay-Lussac. But Laforgue was impatient to sort out Rosenthal's secrets: to find among them Heaven knows what answers, what discoveries, what testament – and the least mendacious face of a dead man. At Rue d'Ulm, Bloyé was waiting for him. Without a word Laforgue threw him the two folders which he had had time to open in the taxi. Bloyé opened them in turn.

— Do you recognize them? Laforgue asked.

— I recognize them, said Bloyé. What a strange business!

They were André Simon's interrupted notes and the plans for the boilerworks, all that remained of the great conspiracy of the previous spring.

— So he lied to us, said Bloyé, he hadn't done anything with them.

— I've always been certain of it, said Laforgue. Don't you recall his impatience, whenever we asked him what stage the business was at? He ended up telling me one day that it had all been handed over and that he was finalizing some other things. He was lying. But he'd lived for a month or two on the dreams of this venture . . .

— That's what he was like, said Bloyé.

Both of them mused for a while on the disparity, the remarkable gulf, that had always existed between their ambitions and what they had accomplished, and on the miscarriage of various undertakings.

— We're ridiculous, said Laforgue. Like paranoiacs. What a load of make-believe!

He added, however, that these setbacks were fairly irrelevant, that they should be taken merely for what they were, failed limbering-up exercises, and that life would not always be subject to the fluctuating rules of improvisation. They preferred no longer to think about Bernard, whom no life and no future would henceforth allow to make a new start, who was definitively a loser: it was essential for them to set aside death's entry into their ranks. A group of young men defends itself not much less skilfully than a family against death.

Later, between the sheets of a handwritten article, Laforgue found an envelope bearing the date of Bernard's death and addressed to Catherine. The envelope was not sealed, Laforgue opened it: it contained only an identity photograph of Rosenthal. The photograph was struck through with a big cross in blue pencil, and on the back it bore these lines:

Is it a sin to hurl oneself into Death's secret abode before he dares come for you?

Then Laforgue recalled the evening at the Rosenthals' place in June, just before the last summer holidays, and the way Catherine had looked at Bernard, and their conversation while waiting for the AX, and Rosenthal's evasive air for months past.

He wondered if he should send Catherine the photograph with an insulting letter. But when he had hesitated for two days and turned over in his head various aggressive formulae, he no longer knew what letter to write and was afraid that the duty of avenging his friend might be mixed up with a profane desire to humiliate so beautiful a woman. The photograph never went off, it remained among Laforgue's papers as the last appearance of a Rosenthal eternally young, eternally deceived, freed from time and the metamorphoses of life – for as long as a piece of paper and fixed impressions of light last . . .

Part Three

Serge

XXI

One can endure anything except a man's gaze: it is a kind of fixed star whose light no one succeeds for long in bearing.

When Pluvinage lowered his eyes, he knew they were look-ing at him by a warmth on his cheeks or on his forehead; he raised his head quickly, but the looks had already eluded him.

The comrades from his branch stared at the table in front of them or at their hands and fingernails, or allowed their eyes to roam through the wisps of smoke filling the air, but they did not let their gaze be caught. Ever since the beginning of the meeting, Serge had been playing this game. Ever since he had felt on arriving a kind of expectation and suspicion, which transformed the very air itself and in which he was the centre of a furtive but weighty scrutiny.

He did not usually seek to meet anyone's gaze, he was shifty. A man who has trouble controlling the muscles of his eyes does not seek the eyes of another: Pluvinage envied people with poor eyesight, who have only to remove their spectacles and they can stare at someone without seeing anything. No problem with his hands – they were good hands, which did not tremble or conceal themselves, which were not the damp, dissolving kind of hands people suspect. Serge would sometimes say to Marguerite, balancing a piece of cardboard on his nails:

— You see, Margot, they don't move at all . . . I could be a pilot . . .

In general, he was not all that embarrassed about his body; and his voice was as obedient as his hands – it did not choke, or suddenly shift into the wrong register. He could stop himself blushing, or turning pale. He just had those two treacherous eyes.

That was how it had been since the end of his childhood: since he no longer had to seek answers in people's eyes, but merely suspicions, judgements, questions, contempt, pride. What a life, living in a world of looks! All existence is like a courtroom full of judges, who turn you about, assess you, and there is no way of not feeling guilty. Ordinary people do not know the feeling of calm you experience in meeting the white eyes of a blind man, or the blank eyes of a whore – what confessions one would make to a deaf man! – or, more rarely, the eyes of men who share your secrets.

But on that particular evening, Pluvinage was seeking to meet someone's eye all the same, because he wanted to be sure. To breathe again he needed a verdict. He recalled his interview with Laforgue and Rosenthal, their questions:

'I gave myself away like an idiot,' he told himself. 'They must have reported me to the party.'

At last he knew the verdict, after which another dreadful life was going to begin. The others were speaking about the activities of the branch, and they were still discussing the 1 August arrests. Daniel, who was the branch secretary, spoke opposite him, fiddling with a very slender pencil in his large, scarred, metalworker's hands. . Daniel stopped speaking, then asked:

— Are there no other speakers? How about you, Pluvinage, you haven't said anything, do you agree with us?

At last Serge met some eyes, their gaze threatening and reflective. He shivered.

— No, he answered. I'm in agreement.

— Because if you had anything to add, I'd give you the floor, it's not all that late, said Daniel.

Those eyes were still not moving.

— No, said Serge, I'm in agreement.

— Quite sure?

— Yes, of course.

'Should I explode?' Serge asked himself. 'Take the initiative? Call them to account for their looks? Defend myself! But if, by any chance, they suspected nothing . . . Impossible. I know Laforgue. He's talked. He loathes me. They know. They're going to haul me up in front of the Control Commission, some frosty fellow will question me, he'll have that way of lowering his voice at the end of every sentence, that tone they use in the party, I'll deny it . . .'

It was over, neither he nor they would speak. If he had begun a single sentence, he would have told them everything: it was all useless after Daniel's looks. Serge knew that they knew everything. That they had no evidence, no witnesses, but they knew, because he was all of a sudden utterly transparent to them – to their instinct, which did not deceive them. Serge sighed, because the explosion was not for this evening. Perhaps it would never occur. Perhaps the Control Commission would not even summon him. Perhaps they were simply going to abandon him, quite alone, to his fate.

'It's all settled,' Pluvinage said to himself all at once. 'I'll never see them again.'

The meeting ended like this, in confusion, with the same hubbub and relaxation as every other week. All these men who had not moved from their chairs – who had spoken seriously, struggling with the words, about politics and the world – now felt like stretching and cracking their finger-joints. They went down the spiral staircase of the small café. On the threshold, a voice said:

— Hey, Pluvinage, you don't look quite up to the mark. Serge gestured vaguely.

— I must be coming down with 'flu, he said. What with this filthy weather . . .

*   *   *

187

At Place du Combat they walked towards another café that was still lit up, to have a drink at the bar before separating. Pluvinage said goodbye to them and crossed the roundabout in the centre of the square.

Running off Place du Combat are Rue Vellefaux, Avenue Mathurin-Moreau, Rue de Meaux, Rue Louis-Blanc and Rue de la Grange-aux-Belles. It forms a star of hot-tempered streets, despite the nearby oasis of the Buttes-Chaumont and the peaceful descent, between hauliers' yards and hospital walls, towards the watery expanses of the Saint-Martin Canal. Because there are almost always trade-union meetings in Avenue Mathurin-Moreau (at the top of the stairs in No. 8) and at the back of the courtyard at 33 Rue de la Grange-aux-Belles, and because – ever since the rifle-shots and cries of the Commune – these have been the frontiers of Paris's most passionate districts, you always find blue knots of policemen there, at the exit of the Combat Métro station, in front of the gates of the Bellevilloise, and at the small gate to the Saint-Louis Hospital, where they look as though they were watching out for the secret egress of the dead. It is a gloomy area, but inspiring for any man who can freely enter the Grange-aux-Belles courtyard and climb the concrete steps in Avenue Mathurin-Moreau. Serge reflected on how he would be able to do so no longer, and on how this was the last evening of his double nature. He hesitated at the edge of the roundabout, like a man embarking for another continent. He knew the others were still watching at him, and that they were talking about him. That they were saying, for example:

— Who would have believed, all the same, that he was a cop?

Pluvinage turned and saw them in the doorway of the café: he raised an arm as a sign of separation. Daniel lifted his right hand limply and at once let it drop back. Pluvinage went down the left-hand pavement of Rue de la Grange-aux-Belles, along the Saint-Louis Hospital wall. It was fairly cold, but there was no frost, the weather was simply damp and oppressive. On Quai des

Jemmapes, the wind blew through the branches of the trees beside the canal and the gleam of Paris illuminated the low canopy of clouds. Serge raised the collar of his overcoat and walked along the bank. Although it was November, there were still men and women sleeping in corners, and others who were talking or scratching so hard that Serge could hear their nails rasping on their skin. They had piles of newspapers in reserve for the cold of the night, to hold out until the hour when they would have to take flight and walk. In the glow of the streetlamps, the men had the beards of corpses. The women were buried under bundles of material. Serge thought about the tramps who shave in summer on the banks of Quai Notre-Dame, before a fragment of mirror stuck up on a wall or a tree. The destitution of the tramps, and the utter solitude he had just entered, were identical forms of pursuit and flight. A man as lost as he can always hope that one of these nocturnal characters – moving about on the utmost fringes of life, and to whom he feels appallingly similar – will help him escape the pit that engulfs him. But Pluvinage did not meet anyone. He merely stumbled against the legs of a recumbent woman who sat up and swore at him. He quickened his pace and the tramp shouted after him, in that pitchy, vault-like darkness:

— Bastard! Sod! Idiot!

Another voice shouted:

— Shut your face!

Round the Gare de l'Est, the whores who work near the stations were waiting for the last trains to arrive. Pluvinage was accosted by a woman with a white, puffy face and wearing a short skirt with laced ankle-boots. He went down Boulevard de Strasbourg and Boulevard Sébastopol. Les Halles were beginning to come to life, market-gardeners' cafés were opening. He crossed the bridges and arrived back in Rue Cujas at around two o'clock. Marguerite was asleep, in the stifling heat from the radiators; she was half naked, illuminated by the blazing sign of a bar. He stretched out beside her, as circumspectly as a cat. Marguerite barely awoke and sighed:

— How late you're back . . .

— Go to sleep, he said.

She went back to sleep. Serge kept his eyes open until morning. All the time he could see Daniel's thick fingers twirling the blue pencil, with a feigned distraction more menacing than any anger, and he wondered what the day would be like upon which dawn was about to break again. He was utterly without hope: he knew that treachery is as irremediable as death, and that, like death, it is never wiped away.

XXII

At eight o'clock Marguerite left for the office and Serge remained alone in the room. He decided he would first go to see Massart: he could speak to barely anyone now except the superintendent. He saw himself standing for this one last day upon a curious ridge-line or watershed from which he could survey his future and his life, the party and the police, anguish and hope. For this one last day.

Superintendent Massart was a man of fifty, who wore black suits and somewhat over-large detachable collars. He bit his nails, which was the only sign of nervousness this official had ever given. His shaven face, its cheeks scarcely grown fleshy at all, would have been admirably nondescript if he had not had pale blue eyes of a blind and unfathomable transparency. Pluvinage suddenly perceived that Massart had exactly the same eyes as François Régnier. As usual, the superintendent displayed the kind of oily affability some policemen possess. He had known Serge for twenty years and used the familiar mode of address with him. He launched into the chit-chat with which he used to overwhelm his friends and those he was interrogating: it was an even-toned chatter whose form Massart used to study with care. Serge postponed the moment of speaking. Through the superintendent's windows he could see the baroque roofs and the dormers of Quai Saint-Michel, the curve of the Seine's banks towards the Jardin des Plantes, and people wandering past the bouquinistes' stalls or beside the slow waters of the side stream. A procession of carriages, motor cars, buses and trucks flowed – and every now and again congealed – between the stalls of the booksellers and the stores devoted to occultism, Japanese curios and magic round Rue du Chat-qui-Pêche. Massart was saying:

— You see, Serge my boy, your father always used to say that only intellectuals can make good policemen. There's a great deal of truth in that. Fouché – an intellectual. That Raoul Rigault – an intellectual too, who deserved better than the Ex-Prefecture of the Paris Commune . . . It's a question of being nasty, I mean of knowing what men are like . . . I can't stand those idiots who mix up policemen with police administrators. Of course, there are simpletons who go into Administration just as they would into the Registry Office or the Customs bureaucracy: I was brought a new detective-sergeant yesterday, six months ago he was a corporal in the gendarmerie at Belle-Isle-en-Terre, I spoke to him in the proper fashion about Defending Society against Crime – and he believed in all those capital letters! What a laugh . . .

— I . . . began Pluvinage, who simply could not bear any longer the superintendent twiddling his pencil in just the same manner as Daniel the evening before.

— Perhaps you needed to talk to me about our little business? Massart asked. In a moment, there's no hurry . . . So a good policeman is not a bureaucrat, and the Defence of Society against Crime is a slogan for academic painters, or for the Prefect's speeches to the municipal council in honour of Officers now Departed. Thank God, Chiappe doesn't believe in it, because Chiappe, who's a scoundrel by the way, is a great police-man. Your true police is immune from all those suckers' tales. The fact is, the police has a secret . . .

Someone knocked at the glazed door to the corridor and a detective-sergeant came in; he was wearing black lutestring oversleeves and had inkspots on the index and middle fingers of his right hand. He placed a file on the table and said it needed signing; the superintendent replied that he would ring when he had finished and the detective went out.

— The police's secret, Massart resumed, is that *there is no history*. All the professors have lied, all of them! There are no forces working to make history. The academicians talk about spiritual forces, and the Marxists about the forces of the economy, there's no end to it, it's the battle between Bossuet and his opponents still going on. Others talk about Cleopatra and the role of chance: if her nose had been shorter, the face of the world would have been changed. Cleopatra's nose and the stone in Cromwell's bladder – that's much less stupid. Pascal was the first author who gave the outline of a police conception of the world . . . Little accidents and little men manufacture great events. The masses and the professors never see the true connections, because there's no visible relation between cause and effect and all tracks are muddied. Everybody's unaware of chance working away behind the scenes, and of the secret of little men . . .

The superintendent mused for an instant and Serge, who was wondering why Massart was making this long speech, did not yet stir.

— You can control chance. Not leave anything to nature. Operate in a carefully preserved silence, which no one can penetrate. Imagine faceless men, sitting in anonymous offices like mine, rather like spiders or calculators – and bearing no resemblance to the great detectives we dream up from time to time in order to be loved. They possess files which actually contain – allowing for a few exaggerations – more or less everything that needs to be known about our public figures: about their youth, their needs, their weaknesses, their rages, their erotic preferences, their ambitions. I know of no more powerful way of acting, or not acting, than this intense concentration of information and ammunition for political and private blackmail. That's when you hold true power, manufacture your historical events, shuffle the pack. A little push in the right direction changes everything, no one knows a thing about it. This great man, who presided over the affairs of France, presided over them only because we tolerated his power. This revolutionary leader was one of ours. Villiers de l'Isle-Adam used to say the Church's secret was that there's no purgatory. Ours is that there's no history. One needs to have been around quite a bit, to appreciate the full value of this secret. You're still rather young . . .

Pluvinage was relating it all to himself, he looked at the superintendent and asked him:

— M. Massart, why does a person join the police? . . .

— Don't you have any idea? asked Massart. You surprise me, for it must be said, between you and me . . . It's so simple, Serge my boy. Joining the police is like committing suicide. Our kind of power consoles a person for the visible power he doesn't have, and for the successes he's failed to achieve. A true policeman is a man who's failed in another life. One of my old bosses, the one who taught me the job, used to cry when he was drunk, which happened very frequently, because he'd like to have been a great criminal lawyer. What do you think of that! Defeats make people tough. Those who are not so tough drink . . . The public doesn't know that out of twenty district chiefs, twelve or fifteen drink – you'll be hearing about old Death-Dodger . . . You were one of ours from the outset. I've known you for so many years, you've always been a humiliated nobody. Tell me if I'm wrong . . .

— No, said Serge between his teeth.

— The hardest part's over, lad, said Massart . . . Speaking of which, you had something to tell me.

Pluvinage raised his head and looked at the superintendent. He told him he was sure they suspected him in the party of having informed on Carré.

— I'm well acquainted with the atmosphere in the party, he said, I'm sure they know. Neither Rosenthal nor Laforgue were deceived when they questioned me. I shouldn't have blushed, for the first time in my life perhaps – or I should have looked them in the eye.

He gave an account of the branch meeting the evening before, which had confirmed his feeling. The superintendent rose to his feet and walked over to the window, then came back towards Pluvinage:

— And you let me carry on talking, you little fool, he said.

— I made a mistake, said Serge. I don't have enough self-control.

— Really! said Massart. You made a mistake! The young gentleman thought he was already the Duke of Otranto, and he was just an informer, a tiny little informer. And not very bright. You gave me some hope and I wanted to do something for Pluvinage's boy. And right away, you're rumbled. What on earth am I supposed to do with you? Drop dead!

— Anyone can be unlucky, breathed Serge.

— No philosophy, said Massart. And this is the simpleton I was already talking to like an equal! The Special Intelligence Branch has no use for clumsy fools. I'll think it over. For the time being, get out of here, I've seen enough of you. You can come back the day after tomorrow, in the morning . . .

Pluvinage left, white with anger, and went and hung about on the Marché aux Oiseaux and along the Quai aux Fleurs, looking at the fir-trees packed in straw, the plant cuttings, the animals, the hyacinths with their stench of death, and thinking less about his own fate than about Massart's words. Now that the break had come, he suddenly saw once more the faces of Laforgue, Rosenthal and Daniel with intense surges of hatred: he was already revenging himself upon them for having betrayed them. The superintendent had employed the words most calculated to strike home. A young man like Pluvinage, who has decided he is already a failure, is too fearful of the public encounters with men that all forms of activity involve not to be excited by the depiction of a world governed by secret motivations. What had attracted him about communism was less the future than its illegal existence, the hidden game. Impossible to doubt so intense a vocation for mystery! He suddenly saw himself destined for the religion of police work.

— The discipline of the Special Branch, he told himself, is quite as good as that of the Spiritual Exercises of Saint Ignatius. And Hérault de Séchelles . . . If they'd recognized what I was worth, I wouldn't be where I am. They'll all pay.

Carried away by a spirit of defiance, Pluvinage went off to tell Marguerite everything and break with her, as with all the rest of his life. He hastened to Rue Cujas. Marguerite had not arrived. She came home for lunch an hour after his return. As she was taking her hat off, he said to her:

— Margot, I've got something to say to you.

He began to tell her everything, without justifying himself, with an overwhelming desire to break off and destroy: the meetings with Massart, the arrest at Mesnil-le-Roi, the role he had played, the suspicions of his comrades, the interview that morning. It was a recital as dry as a report containing only deeds and dates and interpreting nothing. Marguerite heard him out and when Serge had finished she rose to her feet from the couch where she had been sitting and took a step towards him. She was pale: Serge saw in close-up the grain of her skin and the somewhat dilated pores on the flare of her nostrils, the lipstick that had smudged onto the down on her upper lip:

— You've put your lipstick on crooked, he said, as if everything was just continuing, as if the world had not been transformed by the terrible revelation of his falsehood.

Marguerite still said nothing, but she raised her hand. A little taller than Pluvinage, she appeared to him a very tall woman.

'How could I have loved such a tall woman?' he thought, 'She's built like a horse.'

Marguerite struck him twice across the face with all her strength and ran towards the door. The door closed behind her. On the table she had left her hat and her handbag. Serge went to the window and waited until Marguerite emerged onto the pavement. Rue Cujas was almost empty. There were just two passers-by, walking towards each other from opposite ends of the street – a woman and a Chinaman.

— You forgot your bag, Serge shouted, and he threw it down to her.

The bag emptied over the pavement and Marguerite knelt down to collect her money, her comb and her lipstick.

The hard thing then for Pluvinage was no longer the feeling of his treachery: that had been consummated, his decision had been made, Marguerite had fled as though she had discovered she had been sleeping for months with a sick man – Serge had the transparent ecstasy of fever, of irrevocable departures.

No, what was suffocating him was the feeling that henceforward he would be condemned to silence; that in speaking to Margot he had spoken for the last time; that no one would ever again hear the truth about his life; that nothing would define him any longer except the solitude he had just entered, where he would never again have anyone but accomplices. He remembered Massart.

'I must cling on', he told himself. 'I've only them left!'

It was one o'clock, but he had no thought of going down for lunch. He stretched out on the couch and almost at once fell asleep, worn out by his metamorphosis. Marguerite's hat had fallen to the floor.

XXIII

Pluvinage's Story

In the middle of December, Laforgue, who was feeling none too cheerful and getting ready to go off to Alsace, received at Rue d'Ulm a bundle of typed sheets without any accompanying letter. The last sheet simply bore Serge's signature. This is what Pluvinage had written:

Basically, if my father had not had the job he did, perhaps nothing at all would have happened . . .

My father was a civil servant in the Seine Prefecture: that seems insignificant enough, he had visiting-cards engraved with his title as head of section, but he was not responsible for such acceptable things as street-lighting, or transport, or public thoroughfares, or quarries; he did not have one of those rustic and celestial functions, like the upkeep of footpaths, or the special sub-division of clocks and lightning conductors; he was not even in charge of the department that maintains stoves, in Rue d'Ulm opposite the Ecole Normale – no, when I was twelve years old he became head of the Interment Section, under the auspices of Municipal Affairs and the Legal Department. In his office beneath the rafters of the Prefecture, in the Rue Lobau annexe, sedate water-colours were hung against the yellowish-green wallpaper with its dark-green stripes: they were views of cemeteries and chapels, generally depicted beneath an autumn sky with dead leaves in every corner. Like those sons of industrialists or engineers who make their first cut-outs from machine-tool brochures, in my early childhood I cut out models of catafalques, hearses and funerary vaults.

I think my father was fond of me. He used sometimes to take me for walks, which is a good sign – because men are ashamed to go out with a child who makes childish remarks, who talks loudly on buses, and who, in the eyes of the women you meet, is the visible evidence of your growing old. But he had odd destinations. I can still remember the Sunday morning when he took me to visit the Rue d'Aubervilliers depot. The Rue d'Aubervilliers is a strange street: it contains haulage firms and freight companies, the State Railways, the Customs Head Office and the City of Paris Funerals Department – in short, it is almost entirely given over to transportation of the living and the dead. Along with the Gas Company and the Bonded Warehouses, that meant an enormous quantity of cartage all day long, a shifting of straw and boxes and a great stamping of horses: there were not yet many cars in those days just before the War – or rather in its first year, since my father left in '15. The weather was perfect, it was spring I expect. The courtyard of the depot was full of sunlight, with great echoing spaces which, since that time, I have rediscovered only on the parade grounds of barracks. A man in his shirt-sleeves was watering the cobbles, and I can still see the falling mist of droplets which traced a little, shimmering rainbow. There were plumed hearses, which had just been washed and were drying in front of the sheds, their shafts pointing skywards like fine country wagons. Black horses straight out of Hades were stamping their hoofs on the cobbles. My father's profession, I said to myself, was truly a remarkable profession.

I know today that it is dangerous to live a life that unfolds behind the scenes of life. Ordinary people grow old without knowing those obscure margins, but what has struck me most is the family of clandestine worlds that gravitate around the obvious world where one spends one's life. In Paris there is a district which brings together in an extraordinary way and with style some of their monuments: it begins at the Place Dauphine and ends at the Ile Saint-Louis; in it you will find the Palais de Justice, the Hôtel-Dieu, the Conciergerie, the Prefecture of Police, the Seine Prefecture, the Hôtel de Ville and, to cap it all, the flower market and the Noyau de Poissy store; it imposes its glacial atmosphere upon Notre-Dame and the Sainte-Chapelle; in my teenage years a few curious people still used to visit, as Hector Berlioz had, the unidentified bodies in the Morgue, on whose site of an evening I now encounter couples kissing, and reduced by the public nature of their amours to sighing on benches. I know no other grouping of the same quality as this, although the 14th arrondissement too has some formidable locations around Sainte-Anne and the Santé prison, while the 20th near the Père-Lachaise is not bad either. These islands of death are reserved for the poor neighbourhoods, whose inhabitants will always have particular acquaintanceship with visions of misfortune and fate. Consideration is shown for wealthy people, who pay too much in taxes not to be protected against even the slightest allusion to prosecution, denouncement and death.

Close correspondences may be established among these various domains, which are namely those of sickness, policing and death: these terrible places where the mysteries of birth, marriage and death are played out. I would add to them the incinerator plants for household waste, if I did not yield to the prejudice that still solidly maintains the prestige of the dead – and if I were not thinking above all of places where it is essentially the ruin of the *soul* that is accomplished. I should like to make it clear, however, that I grew up in the world dedicated to the elimination of urban waste and the registration of personal catastrophes. Men are unaware of its byways. They enter it, in fact, only by accident: to ask for a passport, or to report a death, or to see a patient – for irremediable events. As for us, we lived there. All the time. My father's friends and colleagues lived there like us. I always tell myself that embalmers, makers of mummies, must have lived in this same way, among themselves; and that this is the destiny of those who work among impure things – of spies, policemen, the functionaries of death and dying. I felt this at fifteen, and I was quite right to believe I should not recover from it. There is nothing more shameful than death, and men are wise to hide it from themselves, like Noah's sons their father's nakedness. I have never met anyone except doctors who were capable of passing continually from the world of the scrap-heap to the world where existence has some pride. And even then, there are forensic doctors, medical registrars and those vile experts in mental health . . .

One of my father's best friends was a little old man who had the post of chief surveyor for cemeteries. I suppose he is dead now: the man I knew cannot have survived the disappearance of undertakers' horses and the motorization of hearses. He must have been pretty crazy – indeed, you have to be crazy to get so passionately excited about the cleaning of tombs and the alignment of the dead – but in our house we used to see such bizarre individuals that no one round me ever dreamed of finding him peculiar. Another friend of my father's was a police superintendent in charge of the Special Intelligence Branch: he was called Eugène Massart, and we used to read his name quite often in the newspapers. My parents must have been quite proud of him, because when he came to dinner there would always be a bottle of Moulin-à-Vent on the table. But I shall have occasion to speak again of Massart . . .

My mother was one of those women who overwhelm their husband and their sons with tearful, demanding, flabby affection. She poisoned my childhood. I noticed only very belatedly how ugly she was, at the same time as I found out that she had probably become, two or three years after being widowed, the mistress of Superintendent Massart.

My sister Cécile, who is fifteen years older than me, when she was thirty or so was a fat woman who would overrun us almost every Sunday with her husband and her two children, and who would talk in a high plaintive voice about her servant problems and about cooking recipes. My brother-in-law ran quite a large garage in the 12th, near Boulevard Diderot. He was as fat as his wife and I used to wonder how this couple, who represented so powerful a volume of muscle and blubber, so ample a circulation of lymph and blood, had been able to create offspring as thin and ill-favoured as my nephew and niece. Despite the kind of horror they inspired in me, I felt a certain pity for those nervous, slapped children; but I never think of Cécile's large breasts without a thrill of revulsion, and have always been unable to kiss the woman without holding my breath and closing my eyes.

We had peasant kinsfolk in the Massif Central, with whom, like many migrants to Paris, we no longer maintained any relations. My grandfather was in fact a sheep-farmer somewhere near Nasbinals. Two years ago, on my way back from the Midi, I crossed those black-and-yellow plateaux where, in autumn, contemptuous eagles can be seen perching on the stones in the grazing grounds. I love that region, but I do not know much about my Auvergne kinsfolk or my father's arrival in Paris.

My parents used to see a lot of a sister of my mother's, who was called Antoinette. My aunt, who seemed old to me, although she can hardly have been more than fifty, was paralysed and almost totally blind. As in all petty-bourgeois families, her disability was spoken of only with considerable circumspection that failed to conceal a kind of sly pride. When I was with Rosenthal and you at Sainte-Anne, working on a neuro-psychiatric ward, I realized that my aunt was simply suffering from Parkinson's disease and there was nothing to be so conceited about. As she lived on the western outskirts of Paris, at Le Vésinet – have I told you that we had a little bungalow at Neuilly? – we used to go and visit her every once in a while. My mother used to say she only had her sister left, so she must make haste to visit her, take advantage of her presence on earth, before she died. But Aunt Antoinette was taking a long time to die.

*   *   *

She had the honed malice of the seriously ill. She spent her interminable final struggle against paralysis and death preying on the existence of her daughter Jeanne, who looked after her and would not leave her. She had two other daughters, who were married and lived in the provinces; they came rarely to Paris and shut their eyes to the appalling life their sister was leading. Jeanne, who five years ago was fifteen and by now must have grown very beautiful – if her mother, before dying, has not succeeded in driving her mad – was totally uneducated, since she had left school at twelve to take care of her mother and now scarcely ever left the gloomy precincts of the Le Vésinet villa. She grew up simply in the company of my aunt, who all day long would look straight ahead with her blind eyes and tell interminable stories about the days of her youth: tales full of resentment and questions of precedence and respect. As Jeanne grew into a woman, her mother became increasingly fearful lest one day, like her 'two sisters, she fall in love with someone and go away. Little by little, with a patient, predatory skill, she inspired her with an unconquerable fear of the world. Jeanne had never come into contact with anything but works of piety: she believed in Saint Theresa of Lisieux and her miraculous rose-leaves; religious renunciation of the world seemed to her the one true happiness. I suppose my aunt – with that deep, calculating instinct of the dying who manage to hang on – thought that in this way she would shackle her at least until her death; and Jeanne used indeed to say that once her mother was no longer there she would go into a convent. I cannot really see how a girl as defenceless, frightened and ignorant as a country orphan could escape religion by any other means than what my mother calls 'going to the bad' – which is nothing but a passion for freedom and leisure.

Our visits to Le Vésinet were perhaps Jeanne's only holidays, since I would be allowed to take her for walks; and her mother used to say, raising the lids over her unmoving eyes, that it was quite right that the poor little girl, who didn't have much fun forever closeted with a sick woman, should at least get a breath of fresh air when the opportunity came her way. We would take the bus that goes up from Rueil to the station at Saint-Germain, and would go walking along the terrace as far as the last roundabout, where there are some old and rather weird houses. I was not ashamed to go out with this little girl, who was still virtually in short skirts, because people found her beautiful and men used to turn their heads after her.

She was too splendid for the idea of seeing her shut herself up some day in a cloister not to strike me as repugnant: I used to tell her she was, like all women, made to live. I was eighteen – it was the same year that I met you at Louis-le-Grand – how should I not have dreamed of playing the role of a tempter and a saviour? But at that time I had not known any woman: they filled me with a terrible dread. When I told myself it was necessary to save this child, I cannot have been thinking of anything but sleeping with her. She was the only woman to whom I was able to feel superior.

On one of those Sundays at Saint-Germain, we had gone quite a long way into the forest, in order to feel totally alone there: there were far fewer cars then than now, and the woods round Paris were not invaded by revolting groups of weekend trippers – those men in shirt-sleeves and those women sitting beside them with no shoes on, their ankles swollen by the heat and their toes cramped inside their stockings. We had sat down on a pile of dry bracken. That whole ceremonial army of trees about us hummed in the dry air. It was a time for forgetting everything, and I did forget everything – as though I had been stretched out beside a real woman who loved me, and not beside a little girl who said her rosary and wore a silver-gilt medallion from Lourdes between her breasts. I leaned towards Jeanne and I kissed her: she was half asleep, half dreaming, she scarcely put up any more resistance than a bird being choked. All my life I shall remember those moist, fumbling, cool lips. I was not much more skilled than she, but I felt as intoxicated as if I had carried off a great victory. Jeanne, with a shiver, told me we must leave and asked me whether what we had just done was very bad; but we stayed on for a long while in that warm place and she let me caress her breasts through the silk of her bodice. I did not go further, but I was still naive enough for this adventure to strike me as wonderfully sacrilegious.

I did not go back to Le Vésinet until three weeks later. I think we must have been studying for one of our degree examinations, and I must have been working on Sundays. That day Jeanne refused to go out, so we spent the afternoon in my aunt's little sitting-room. Shortly before we left, she signalled to me to leave the room with her and led me to the corridor where she kissed me: both of us had imagined a great deal in three weeks.

I do not know why I am telling you this story, which ends there, since I have not been back to Le Vésinet and have not seen Jeanne for five years. My whole life is made up of such abortions. It is probably the only memory that still consoles me for my youth, even though it is slightly sordid and tainted by some humiliating details.

It is not necessary for me to dwell much on my memories of school. I should be lying if I said that I suffered much, up to the age of seventeen, from the secret shame my family inspired in me. There was play, the occupation of children: childhood is able to put the future tragedies of the man into abeyance. Everything came to a head when I encountered the two of you at Louis-le-Grand.

We had all just started our first preparatory year for the Ecole Normale entrance; we none of us knew one another, since we came from a dozen different lycées in Paris and the provinces; we were all the pride and joy of our schools; we all felt that stupid collective arrogance of candidates for the Grandes Ecoles. We were supposed to be seventy equals. I did not share these joys even for a fortnight.

*   *   *

I still find it hard to explain to myself why my meeting with the two of you should have had such a devastating side to it. Love at first sight is a well-worn cliché, but no one has ever said anything about envy at first sight. Rosenthal and you straight away inspired in me a passionate emotion, in which a blinding compulsion to imitate you was all mixed up with the need to hate you.

You struck me as inimitable, and had the same attraction for me that, in the Army, Parisian soldiers sometimes have for recruits from the back of beyond. You managed everything with a facility I found disconcerting. You were the type, people said, who could get into Rue d'Ulm at will. The teachers maintained an odious relationship of complicity with you. You used to produce the most brilliant philosophical dissertations. You read books that none of our schoolmates from the provinces had laid hands on, and that I barely knew of: Claudel, Rimbaud, Valéry, Proust. You were boarders – yet you looked clean, you shaved, you would reappear of a Monday talking to each other about the girls with whom you had danced on Sunday. I was concerned only with you. There was no question for me of making friends with our fellow students from schools at Bordeaux, Toulouse or Lyon: those sons of elementary schoolmasters and minor officials struck me as plodding and dull, destined for obscure careers as teachers in the provinces; one could see in advance their whole lives, which, like those of animals, would be punctuated only by illnesses, accidents, couplings and death. Yet I envied the facility with which you, nevertheless, had made friends with them: I was indignant about it on your behalf – it seemed to me you were wasting your time. I did everything to make you notice me, to make you realize that I was at a higher level than those solid but crude lads, yet I managed to extract nothing from you save an indifferent cordiality. I saw you alone as worthy of me, yet felt perpetually exasperated by you. I fought against this feeling, but it was like an external force dominating me. I had trouble knowing my own mind: I could no longer tell whether I hated you, or merely wished to be your equal. I would sometimes find myself defending you, when Brossard said you were poseurs; actually, I was defending in you the man I aspired to be. At other moments I felt longings for revenge against you take shape within me – yet there was nothing, nothing was happening, those longings for revenge were based on nothing, they had no motive, I could find no justification for them.

I was living in an extraordinary state of bitterness, as vague as one's first ruminations on love. I had been well brought up – the humanities are a noble education – and I felt my concealed hatred to be base. I vainly did everything to overcome my bitterness. But nothing ever liberated me from myself: neither work at the lycée – do you remember how hard I worked the year of the Ecole entrance? – nor later on (without your ever knowing anything about it) debauchery.

In country districts, old wives' tales are told about rickety children who cannot grow up straight: I was like them, I was stunted morally. And you, you were there, *unforgivable* and exceptional – like every object, like every creature. Your existence alone was enough for me to feel myself the victim of a generalized injustice that was gradually poisoning me. You never suspected the hate-filled admiration I felt for the two of you: perhaps you would have found it natural, or flattering.

It was no use my exclaiming to myself, alone, that I was just as good as you. That I would oblige you to consider me your equal. There was always an intolerable gap between what I felt myself capable of being and the value you put on me.

Then came the entrance competition for the Ecole Normale. You got in, as our teachers and schoolfellows had expected. I was fortieth, after the oral. I could not bear to think of myself, on a state grant, taking a degree in some provincial university; so I chose the Sorbonne, and gave up my grant and a second attempt at the Ecole. That failure separated me from the two of you. I was in despair. I did not know how to carry on that life in common with you which had given me so much pain – it never even occurred to me that I might be able to forget you. You were hateful, you tried to console me for my failure, you never saw more of me than during your first year at the Ecole. You used to tell me to come and work at Rue d'Ulm in your digs; you obtained private lessons on the side for me, to help my existence as an unassisted student and because you knew I was poor. I did not once cross your threshold without feeling sick with shame. I sometimes thought myself a monster, for seeing in your marks of friendship merely pity and casual kindness. Yet I know I was not mistaken, since my treachery two months ago at once struck you as natural; since you suspected me straight away.

God, how hard these last years have been! Success at the Ecole would have saved me – I needed only to prove myself, failure was a deadly humiliation. Well, I told myself it was in the nature of things: that I would go and rejoin my family in some damp, dark existence of the kind one associates with insects in rotting wood; that I would be cast back into its universe. Then I began to be ashamed of my body, about which I had scarcely thought up till then: I would look at myself in the mirror with disgust; I would see myself doomed – in the domain of the body as in all others – to Heaven knows what sort of inevitable defeat; I could not forgive myself for this detestable frizzy hair, this butcher's-boy charm attractive only to little factory girls, the awkwardness of my movements, the dark bristles that grew on my cheeks. I could no more forgive myself for being me than I could forgive you for being you.

I envied you your gifts, your money, your families. The mockery you heaped on your fathers was merely one further ornament of style: a sign of your bourgeois nature, like the suits you had made for yourselves in Boulevard Malesherbes, at a Scottish tailor's. The music and painting of which you spoke seemed to me nothing but subtle means of excluding me: as you know, the world of music is utterly closed to me, I might as well be deaf; and each time you mentioned the Uffizi, the Prado or the Terme, I was sure it was only an occasion to make me feel I knew nothing of travel – Florence, Madrid, Rome . . .

What was most unbearable of all was believing you to be happy – for I had no doubt about your happiness. Yet I would have held it against you had you bemoaned your fate: suffering, in you, would have been merely an attitude and, as it were, an additional talent or luxury. Even Rosen's suicide, which I heard about a few days ago, I saw as the last challenge that could reach me from you: the last inimitable act one of you could propose to me . . .

What a dazzling revelation, the day I grasped that I should never be able to assert myself, take my revenge or give my full measure except in fields other than those which you had chosen! We are not so far away now from this story . . .

When Rosen and you began to lean towards revolution, I followed you at once: it was at last a way of establishing a link between us. I could not complain, you accepted me as you had never previously done.

More than it did you, who came from far away, revolution struck me as easy. I saw it confusedly as the site of all possible opportunities for reparation and the slaking of resentment, and as a kind of paradise for the formerly defeated . . .

I was immediately more violent than yourselves. We were in a new set-up, where the old distinctions no longer obtained. I sensed *other dimensions*: the possibility of becoming your equal, in a world where only differences of intensity, speed and emphasis came into play, not those of social attitude . . .

I breathed easier for a few months; I was soothed; I was united with you by a complicity. I suddenly ceased to see everything as an opportunity for failure. Your tastes, your clothes, your successes, your attitudes, became failings rather than advantages; you were supposed to be ready to sacrifice them to a new loyalty, to which you could not refuse to admit me.

This respite did not last: I soon saw myself being reborn before my eyes; I stopped forgetting myself. I sensed that even amid our shared ambitions, you were marking out Heaven knows what new boundaries against me. When Rosen founded the journal, you allocated yourselves the big articles, the prophecies, the 'messages'. You never left for Jurien or me, whom you despised, anything except reviews and critical comments. I was still only in your retinue, beneath you: there were still different *levels*. Do you remember that time earlier this year, around Easter, when Rosen and you certainly concocted something from which I was excluded: more than once, when I entered your digs, I caught you falling suddenly silent or talking of what 'lovely weather' we were having. So I had been pushed aside again – admitted only to your half-secrets and your esoteric life; excluded from your most intimate passwords and your deepest complicities. Never did I hate you as much as then. I was brought down to earth. It was as if I had inspired you with a physical disgust, against which you were yourselves ceasing to struggle.

I had an idea, which might perhaps save me – remember that I did not accept my ailment, but tried persistently to be cured. I joined the party.

I shall always see before me your look of perplexity when I gave you this news, it was around the end of May. Joining the party had for a year played too big a role in our conversations, and in what you used to call our problems, for my decision not to touch you: I was the first of our group to take the plunge. You were flabbergasted, humbled. You at last had something to envy me for – an act you did not yet dare decide upon. You did not follow me, you wanted to remain free, you contented yourselves with getting excited over those who had died on 1 May in Berlin.

Once again, I thought I could forgive you. There was a domain of politics and of the mind in which I had outstripped you; in which I was six months, or two months, ahead of you – you could not get over it . . .

I shall always remember my entry into the party as one of my rare moments of relaxation and peace. By chance, I had ended up in the cell at a factory in the 20th, a firm producing machine tools not far from Place des Fêtes. There were not many of us, eleven or twelve, it was an organization in which you could get to know one another. I was the only member drafted in, or 'attached' as they used to say in the party. Those fellows were extremely fine and friendly people, they did everything to put me at my ease. It was a period when there was still a great deal of workerism in the party, but they never made any allusion to my status as an 'intellectual', other than through a sort of kindly irony at which it was impossible for me to take offence. That little group of men gave me the only idea I shall ever have of a human community: one does not recover from communism, once one has experienced it...

No one called me to account for my past life, or my family. If I had spoken to them about my father's profession, they would simply have remarked how there really are people doing some funny things that you never think about. Understand me clearly: the question of original social sin was absolutely never posed...

This kind of political friendship covered everything – but only in the present of each one of us. It concerned not merely action, the factory, war and peace, but personal problems, anxieties, our whole lives. Since the party was extremely isolated at that time – as it is again, since 1 August – the feeling of shared solitude created an extremely powerful bond: something like a carnal complicity, an almost biological consciousness of one's *species*. For the first time in my existence, I felt a great warmth surrounding me.

My comrades were cheerful, they knew how to laugh, they were far more human than you were – you who were forever mouthing the words Man and Humanism. They were utterly free from resentment, or hatred: they were healthy constructors. The meaning of life shone out beneath the awkwardness of their words. I must have watched them in the way a child who cannot run watches other children at play: never did I see myself as more of a failure than among them.

I kept the secrets of my new life to myself. I did not tell you anything, but I pretended to know a great deal. I had a moment of pride the day Rosen, almost timidly, asked me in connection with some question or other:

— What do they say about it in the party?

I was your superior, your judge, each time I told you:

— All the same, we should make up our minds to raise the question of party control over the journal . . .

— There's no hurry, you would say.

And I would reply:

— If we're consistent revolutionaries, the decision is obligatory. The CP is the only authentic force in the service of the revolution . . .

The July holidays arrived. At the end of June, after the examinations, Rosen and you went away. I stayed alone in Paris: I did not have enough money that year to go away anywhere. I did not even have Marguerite, who was with her family in Brittany.

I was staying at the hotel in Rue Cujas where I still live. It was dreadfully hot. So, in order to escape the molten asphalt, the petrol and tar fumes, the scorched trees and dust of the Luxembourg, the troops of children and squalid lovers of the Latin Quarter, and the whores with their dubious underwear at the Taverne du Panthéon, I was cowardly: I went to see my mother at Neuilly. Down towards the bottom end of Neuilly, there is a kind of village rusticity. My mother talked, moaned – I soon fled her voice. I went to loaf around on the lawns of Bagatelle, where women from Suresnes and Puteaux would sleep on the grass and reveal their over-white legs; where young people played ball while the cars buzzed past like bees. I would sometimes climb up on foot to Mont Valérien, above the reservoir, and I would look at Paris and its vast conurbation swarming like living vermin; or I would stretch out under a tree and sleep, in that military air traversed by the bugle calls of the soldiers of the 5th Infantry regiment at their drill, which came up from Courbevoie. Not once did I think of going on to Le Vésinet, to see Jeanne again. I knew my aunt was still alive, and that Jeanne was looking after her. My mother said that her niece was fading away: the thought of her inspired in me not so much regret as a kind of strange revulsion . . .

Can you imagine the dinners with my mother: those tête-à-têtes under the sticky light of the pendant; the slithering of the maid's slippers; the drone of my mother's voice, as she talked to me about her youth in the 15th, about my father's friends, my sister and her children? I was caught again in the spider-webs of my childhood. On Sundays I would take flight altogether, to avoid my sister and her troop.

That loneliness was dreadful. I wrote to Marguerite that I loved her, and I convinced myself of it for a quarter of an hour – although for that big, simple girl, to whom making love came as easily as breathing, I never felt anything but a fairly strong sensual attraction. Well, one has to live.

I regularly attended party meetings, which were not always very cheering. As you doubtless know, in spite of your journey (to England I believe), that whole holiday period was extremely tense and the CP, which was organizing a big campaign against war, came in for some harshly repressive treatment. In the last week of July, incidents multiplied. The worker and peasant congress, which was being held at Villeneuve-Saint-Georges after having been banned at Clichy, was broken up and ninety-six delegates were charged with conspiring against State security. Searches were carried out everywhere – in trade-union offices, at *Secours Rouge*, at *L'Humanité*, and more or less throughout France. By about the 31st, there must have been two hundred political prisoners at the Santé, the Petite Roquette and Saint-Lazare, or in the provinces. Then came 1 August. The day before, Briand – who had just taken over the premiership – had a majority of almost two hundred votes in the Chamber. During the evening, *L'Humanité's* printshop was ransacked by the police. I was at Rue du Croissant, the whole place was black with cops, they were arresting printworkers at random. The unrest lasted until four in the morning, until the break of day. During the day, Paris was in a state of siege, police cars prowled about, horse-guards wheeled gently over the sanded macadam of the boulevards. In August and September the arrests continued. It was a vast conspiracy – the communists were accused of having planned for 1 August a 'concerted revolution with the aim of overthrowing the government'. The strength of this accusation lay in its absurdity. In October, new indictments spoke of espionage, because *L'Humanité* had published letters from workers in the war industries. Almost all the leaders of the party and unions were arrested: Cachin, Barbusse and Vaillant-Couturier were charged with espionage; Doriot, Marty, Duclos and Thorez with conspiracy. After that, at the beginning of November we got a Tardieu cabinet and you must know about the subsequent course of events.

I have recounted all these developments only because they affected me deeply. The ease with which the government and police had smashed the party apparatus; the species of disarray that prevailed in many branches, where quite a few members were echoing rumours being put about by people like Joly and Gélis (the municipal councillors who had resigned) about the presence of police agents in the party; the departure of the opportunists; the hail of convictions – everything convinced me that the party had just suffered a defeat from which it would not recover. I had joined an organization destined for victory; it seemed impossible to me to associate myself with a defeat. People like me must be capable of loyalty only to winners. I was already drawing political conclusions from my personal deviation: the discouragement I felt suddenly seemed to me susceptible to *generalization* . . .

One afternoon when I was reading in the sun in the damp little garden of the bungalow at Neuilly, beneath an apartment building with closed shutters, my mother told me that Massart was expected for dinner and asked me to stay in. I do not know why I accepted. I rarely saw Massart, but I knew, with that intuitive certainty that sometimes survives childhood, that he had been – that he perhaps still was – my mother's old lover. The images I conceived of that liaison were as repugnant to me as mouldy food. But Massart left me almost totally indifferent. I merely had an abstract contempt for him when I reminded myself that he was in the police . . .

It was so warm that evening, I doubtless lacked the energy to go out in order to avoid the meeting. Massart rang the bell at about eight. I saw him enter the hall, he was holding his hat in his hand and wiping its leather band, the maid said to him:

— How are you, Monsieur Massart?

— Warm, my dear, the superintendent replied, very warm . . .

I went into the sitting-room where my mother used to sew or knit all day long. Massart offered me his hand and I took it, it was damp.

— It looks as though the boy's grown even more, he said. Actually, Marie, it's been an age since I last saw your son.

We dined. We all three ate without enthusiasm, and my mother sent the maid to fetch lumps of ice from a cafe in Avenue du Roule: the ice melted at once, the red wine became lukewarm again.

— What a scorcher! said Massart.

I shuddered, it was just the kind of expression that caused the stifling, vile recollections of my childhood to erupt to the surface of my memory. The dinner ended and we went down into the garden, where the may-bugs came to dash themselves against the silk of the awning. My mother went back into the house to give the maid a hand. When we were alone, the superintendent told me:

— D'you know, I'm not at all sorry to see you, Serge, my boy? I can still speak to you without standing on ceremony, can't I? You won't object to such familiarity from an old friend? . . . I almost saw you born . . .

I assented, though I was rigid with anger and would have liked to make my escape. The superintendent smoked for a moment in silence.

— So we're dabbling in communism, he said. It seems we're collaborating in new subversive journals, alongside bankers' sons? . . . Member of the Communist Party?

Aggressively I assented, and Massart began to laugh and mumble something about the malady of youth. He told me he had experienced all those fevers of growth and, in his adolescence, while he was doing his first year of law, had attended a number of anarchist meetings. He added that those diversions, which had no great consequences for the sons of bankers and industrialists, who could always return to the embrace of their class, might involve serious repercussions for a petty bourgeois with neither fortune nor backing. He also said he would have understood my joining the Socialist Party, in which it was possible to make a career and which had prospects of power; but that it was absurd to take one's place in a party doomed to impotence, and which had just been severely defeated by a few police operations. I said nothing. Massart continued in a meditative tone:

— What are you going to do with yourself if you don't pass your *agrégation*? Your poor mother tells me you've let things slide since your failure in the Normale exam, and that you didn't even feel up to finishing your degree this year . . . She isn't wealthy, she won't offer you the luxury of two or three additional years of study . . . What's the matter? Your politics? Girls? . . . Oh! I'm not asking for any confidences. Let's never offend the modesty of a young male! We'll talk again about all that . . . But I wanted to tell you . . . If you have any real troubles, Massart's a friend. Have you never thought about the civil service? . . .

I leapt to my feet, I made no answer, I ran to the kitchen. In front of the sink, my mother was still wiping the plates which the maid was handing her. I said to her, in a strangled voice – I was beside myself:

— Was it you who asked that swine to offer me a position in his police force?

— Whatever's got into you? she said. Yes, it was me . . . What about it? What if you ended up failing? A person has to keep his weather eye open, my poor child. Your poor father was in the civil service, after all . . .

— Neither cop nor supplier of coffins! I cried. I'd rather die first. Go and tell your superintendent that!

With that, I left the house and went to sleep at Rue Cujas. Since then my mother has been writing me tearful letters, which I do not answer.

I no longer know how I whiled the time away until the end of September. Marguerite came and installed herself once more in Rue Cujas; I saw her reappear with a relief that she took for happiness at seeing her again. I did not know whom to talk to. One day I remembered Régnier, whom I had visited with all of you in the spring. I made up my mind to go and see him, in order to talk about myself, ask him for advice, tell him about plans for books and essays: literature struck me as being a way out. I still believed in givers of advice, in priests.

One afternoon I arrived at Mesnil-le-Roi and rang the bell. Régnier, who seemed quite put out at seeing me, opened the door. I was afraid he had forgotten who I was, but he remembered me. The conversation went badly. All of a sudden, footsteps crunched on a gravelled path. A man appeared: he was in shirt-sleeves and had bare feet in leather sandals; he saw me and said to Régnier:

— Oh, you've got company, forgive me . . .

— You won't be in the way, said Régnier.

— No, no, said the newcomer, I'll leave you to your company, I'm going back upstairs to work.

The face seemed familiar, but I was paralysed by the effort I was making to put a name to it. Suddenly it came back to me and I exclaimed:

— Of course, it's Carré!

In spite of a pointed beard which transformed him, I had just recognized Carré whom I had heard two or three times at meetings, and whose picture *L'Humanité* had published at the time of the conspiracy.

— That's right, said Régnier, looking embarrassed. You won't say anything?

— Have no fear, I said. I'm in the party. Tell him that ... Forgive me for coming. But I was out walking at Maisons-Laffitte, I thought I'd just come and pay my respects ...

— You're very kind, said Régnier.

There was nothing more for me to do there, I was in the way, I awkwardly took my leave of your friend.

Several days went by. I had forgotten the encounter. One morning I woke from a dream: I had just disclosed Carré's hiding-place to a man who at times had my father's features, at times my own face. I had to touch Marguerite's hip to assure myself I was no longer dreaming. How we laughed at psychoanalysis, when we were working at Sainte-Anne under Dumas!

When an idea makes its appearance, it has already in fact come a long way. It arrives perfectly formed and full-grown, it is too late to kill it. You cannot imagine how resilient an idea is, it must be harder to destroy than a man. This one haunted me for days. There would be whole mornings or afternoons when I would forget it – just as each time one thinks one is happy one forgets the anguish of death, the descent into the void – and then suddenly it would reappear. It was terribly hard and sardonic, as if all the time it had been playing hide-and-seek with me. It was like a motionless, sharply defined scene standing between myself and the world. I recall one of the last days: I was walking along the embankment, I was thinking about nothing – or vaguely about my body, my skin – I was looking at the Louvre windows opposite me and telling myself they reminded me of a memory that I would not be able to track down. It made its reappearance, just above and to the right of my head, with a stony glitter. Each time it grew, like a tic or an obsession, imperious as a gesture.

I attempted to shake myself out of it. I resorted to whores, to whom I have always been partial. I had a weak spot for the Faubourg Montmartre district. Perhaps because of its smells. The daytime does not really suit it, its climate is one of Paris's climates of the dark. Great lorries, which have navigated for hours on the ocean of the dark countryside, draw up all covered with dew before the lighted bistros of Les Halles. The newspaper windows shine out in Rue du Croissant. Between Rue du Quatre-Septembre and Boulevard Poissonnière you hear the clickety-clack of the linotype machines, which is exactly the same sound you hear high up in the Croix-Rousse district, when the silk-weavers' looms have not been halted by the fall of night. When the wind comes from the north, the smell of paper mingles with the fruit smells coming along Rue Montmartre from the Pointe Saint-Eustache: it is reminiscent of a faintly rotting countryside, overlaid by the freshness of ether. For eight or ten days, I went in search of women from the far side of the Boulevard. In the unlit alleyways, or on the pavement seats of the cafés, they would wait, while their men friends drank at neighbouring cafés or played cards, with their hats on, in the little bars of the Faubourg Montmartre. The girls were almost all tall and dressed to the nines, they would lazily turn their heads towards the passers-by and reveal their knees or the fold between calf and thigh. They were as ornamental as male birds. Each evening I would hesitate for a long while, and used sometimes to return to Rue Cujas without having chosen any of them. It would be enough for me to turn towards a girl, to walk slowly, for her to follow me to a deserted corner of Rue de Richelieu or Rue Vivienne and accost me: that was enough, I had drawn her far away from the fiery circle of the boulevards into the darkness which belonged to her and to me; I would tell her I had no need of her, that she had made a mistake, she would set off again listlessly in the direction of the Boulevard. On other evenings, I would follow a woman to her hotel and bed her in silence. But nothing check-ed the growing inevitability of my becoming an informer . . .

I knew Rosenthal had been back in Paris for weeks: I had seen him one morning when I was crossing Place du Carrousel; he was walking beside a tall young woman dressed in black and pink, who was looking at him the way a woman looks only at the man she loves. I passed within two metres of them, Rosenthal pretended not to see me. I felt you were all more distant, harder, more immersed in your lives than ever. Perhaps that was all it took to guide my steps towards Place du Parvis Notre-Dame. I was on my way that day to the Bibliothèque Nationale, but I did not cross Rue de Rivoli, I turned towards Châtelet, I arrived at the place where Superintendent Massart worked.

A policeman told me how to find the offices of the Special Branch. I lost myself in drab grey corridors that resembled the corridors of a hospital. I was rushing, eyes closed, into the depths of my childhood, my father was about to open the first of those glazed doors, I would see again his funerary water-colours on the walls. An office-boy finally announced me to Massart, who made me wait a long time. I went in, and the superintendent stood up and said:

— What brings you here?

— Are you still looking for Carré?

— Which Carré? asked Massart.

— The Carré from the Central Committee of the Commu-nist Party.

— Oh! Carré! he cried out. I should certainly think we are looking for him, the beggar! Would you happen to know where he's gone to ground?

— He's living at Mesnil-le-Roi, on the road to Saint-Germain-en-Laye, at the writer François Régnier's place.

The superintendent jotted down these names, looked at me and said:

— Sure?

— I saw him there, three weeks ago . . .

— And you waited all this time to tell me about it!

— What I'm doing isn't the easiest thing in the world to make up one's mind to.

— Of course, of course, said Massart. It all gets tangled up with honour . . . Does this little initiative mean that you've been thinking about our conversation, or rather my monologue, at Neuilly?

— I'm not one of yours, I said. Today I have – personal reasons . . .

The superintendent smiled, and gave me a gentle slap on the shoulder:

— There, there, he said. There's always some jibbing, at first.

I do not know what happened after that, in Massart's office. I recall only a vile photograph on the wall, under the family portraits of the heads of Special Branch – a photo showing the outer wall of the Santé, with a little man in an overcoat and top hat standing beneath the flintstone bulwark, and bearing the following dedication: 'To Massart. Short and sharp! Deibler.' Eventually I went down the grimy Prefecture stairs: it was done. I breathed again, as people say paranoiacs do who have long dreamed of murder.

Nothing was recognizable any longer in that world which had not moved. Informing on someone is nothing, it is just a phrase one uses, it is much less theatrical than a crime, it is neither a fragment from a thriller, nor a scene from a gloomy opera; but it is much more irreparable than a murder, much deeper, it is a metamorphosis in the depths, a leap, a break, a reincarnation: one is 'outside existence' as Montaigne says of the dead.

Shortly after that, our meeting at the Ecole Normale took place. As you waited for me, Rosen and you were talking about me; I had been listening to you from the other side of the door, I knew you suspected me. Those three months of holidays had taken you still further away. You had the skin of people who have experienced the sea, the sun, happiness. I shall always hear Rosen asking me in a vile, judge's tone, amid a horrible silence, when I had last been at Régnier's place and whom I had seen there. When I left your room, I was sure the two of you were going to reveal everything, and that I was going to be called up in front of the party Control Commission. I shammed dead, like those little hunted animals which flatten themselves on the ground and mimic the immobility of a corpse. I expected insults from all sides, like arrows. Perhaps I was at bottom hoping for the public exposure and the sentence; perhaps I was living only in the hope of some explosion that would deliver me for ever from you and from the party. I have never had the strength to be truly two-faced, even the intoxication of duplicity is not for me.

I tell myself today that some great idea must guide spies and informers, if they wish to survive. It is necessary for them to believe in the sacred character even of their treachery: man is decidedly too noble an animal for my taste. I do not feel myself justified. So here I am your enemy, the enemy of the communists: how am I to live without proving to myself the dignity of my treachery? Without forgetting that it was governed only by the hatred I felt for you, the desire to strike at you? Grudges lead to betrayal, but betrayal does not cure grudges. What was needed was an outburst, a discharge of resentment in hatred; but this explosive substance never explodes, all its bombs fail to go off . . .

Am I going to have to believe, in order not to despair of myself, that capitalism is an everlasting order, capable of sanctifying like a God all the treacheries one commits in its name? Am I going to have to believe in the filth of Order?

It is hard to think that the communists were right. That I have betrayed not just hated individuals, but truth and hope. You taught me everything about your truth, I can fight it. But I can no longer be taken in by the lies they marshal against it. The man who wants to trick history is always tricked, nothing can be changed by petty means. Revolution is the *opposite* of policing.

Basically, what took me to the superintendent was the suspicion you inflicted upon me from the first day. A desire to justify your mistrust: that accusing look in which my name, my face and my childhood all condemned me to live out the character you were never able to avoid suspecting me of being. The sense of my *difference*, of the impossibility of communion . . .

Massart told me one day that many policemen are workhouse boys, men without a name who were one day christened Faux-pasbidet or Peudepièce. I shall not escape those lost children. For twenty years I shall have eluded that universe of death where I was born – and which, for every man, forms only by degrees. A terrible inevitability is transporting me back to my father's environment. But only today, for the last time, do I admit that inevitability. Rosen is dead, so I shall hold you alone responsible for my fall, because you *existed* . . .

Pluvinage's story ended with these confused sentences. Serge had written another three words: 'It is useless . . .' but crossed them out.

XXIV

'How does a person leave their youth?' Laforgue wondered, on the platform of the Gare de l'Est, where he was pacing up and down outside the train that was about to take him to Strasburg and the snows of the Christmas holiday.

Many things had just ended.

Rosenthal was dead, which was after all more serious, more irreparable than all the rest. Pluvinage was an informer working for the Special Branch. His friendship with Bloyé and Jurien would last, as it was, till the end of the year, till the farewells – with no illusions or great hopes – after the *agrégation*, on the eve of their last long vacation, their military service, and travels that would scatter them for a long while. Philippe imagined they would see each other ten years on, their years of teaching in the provinces completed, with wives and children who would look askance at one another, and having only tepid memories of the École Normale and the Sorbonne to keep them from mutual silence.

'We'll not go very far,' he thought.

He suspected that some ordeal awaited him, because youth is always brought to an end by an ordeal and it is impossible to pass without a break from adolescence to manhood.

'Savages are really lucky,' he said to himself, 'with their initi-ation ceremonies ... There are great dances and there's drink. Lots of manly secrets are disclosed to them, under cover of a faked darkness and amid the bellowing of bull-roarers. One of their canines is broken, or they're circumcised. Rather elegant incisions are made in the skin of their backs . . . All the same, I'm not going to have myself circumcised, I'd lack faith . . . It's a quite simple matter of blood and erections, with suffering that comes from outside. But afterwards, just like with a beating up, it's settled. You're initiated. You've had your face smashed in, but you can have a chat with your ancestors and show off to women with a bit of white magic – you're a man . . . Whereas we don't have any medicine-men to make things easy for us . . . it's just love, death, filth, sicknesses of the mind . . .'

Philippe can sense that he is about to enter the age of ambiguity.

The young male is defined well enough in relation to his parents, about whom he thinks with a mixture of affection and rage – and a desire not to copy them. The man will be defined by rather more mysterious relations with his wife, his children and his job, whose various chains are perhaps subtler than those of a father or mother . . . Laforgue understands that, on his parents' side, everything is settled or is about to be; that within six months they will look upon him as a man, because he will have finished his studies, he will have letters after his name, and they will be able to file him away with his label in their herbarium of social conditions. But until such time as he finds himself manly bonds, he is afraid he will drift somewhat at random and, as he puts it, play the Cartesian diver . . .

When the express left, Laforgue stuck his head through the window. It was 22 December and freezing. Laforgue at once wept from the cold. But as he watched Paris disappear, giving way gradually to the black waves of the dark, he told himself that he would not escape: that things were going to happen . . .

Illness intervened in Laforgue's life and fulfilled for him the function of a sorcerer. One almost never thinks how illnesses sort everything out: how you are transformed, and how you meditate, during those flights and slumbers in which everything is suspended pending your return, your awakening.

Laforgue thought he was going to die. The doctors began to talk round his bed about blood poisoning, only too happy to have available an entity – microbes – to exorcise death. Laforgue, who had just been operated on in the usual way for one of those attacks of appendicitis which clearly play the same role among whites in the twentieth century as circumcisions do among negroes, two days after the operation had lapsed into the dizzy spells and nauseas symptomatic of serious infections.

Vaguely he would see his father, his mother or nurses bending over his bed; he was driven crazy by the injections, the thermometers in his rectum, the drips and probes; he would put his hand between his thighs and raise it slowly to his nostrils – and would find that he stank abominably. In the morning and again in the afternoon the doctors would reappear. One evening there was a consultation: one of the doctors had a long black beard and shook his head, another scratched the back of his neck.

'There are the sorcerers,' thought Philippe.

He existed feebly inside something hollow, which was at times a vast, yellowish thorax, at times a cellar lit by flickering lamps, and then sometimes a dazzling cell of a pure, cold, shiny blue that made him close his eyes – this meant there was sunlight on the snow in the clinic garden. He was not displeased by this existence as an irresponsible, feverish grub. He wanted nothing, he was filled with scornful indifference for everything that was happening, he was not even suffering; he merely felt vague, buzzing and sonorous. The action of the blood in his fever proceeded amid a deafening racket: the least external sound – a spoon knocking against a glass, a door closing – would reverberate with prolonged, lazy undulations and almost visible perturbations of the air. He was adrift on all that cotton wool: at moments he would recognize the whole wall facing his bed – it had a navy-blue door, a radiator and a blurred print – then it would all suddenly start to dwindle and vanish, and he would be surveying this whole universe from a great height and, as he mechanically repeated to himself that he was having Lilliputian hallucinations, he would have a stupid desire to laugh. Then he would lapse into the moist darkness of deep slumbers, where he had nightmares about his body of which he would remember nothing – it was what, in hushed voices, people were calling a coma. During a brief half-waking he heard the word, and told himself with stupefaction that he was in the process of dying; but he sank back, he no longer had the strength to brush away the luminous flies of the words or to fly into a rage because he was going to die.

Philippe did not die. There was an evening when he woke up again on this side of death's sandy frontiers: his room was in shadow, there was just a little electric night-lamp tinted blue that gave to his return the feel of a sleeping-car, of a nocturnal journey; on an armchair a night nurse was sleeping in her blankets and faintly snoring, her mouth half-open. He was transfixed by a surge of happiness, after which all his pleasures would never again seem to him anything more than shadows. He existed! Rising again from gloomy depths, he floated on his back upon the sparkling surface of his life. He smiled and went back to sleep as the living go back to sleep, to await the day.

In the morning, there was a great fuss around him; the doctors exclaimed that he was saved, congratulated him, and told him he must have an iron constitution; his mother wept, his father arrived from the factory and broke a glass on the night table – it was a great hurly-burly of resurrection. Laforgue closed his eyes on all that tumult: he was taking possession again of his long-lost body, giving orders to his limbs, clenching his toes under the sheet and feeling amazed that they should be obedient to the commands he was sending them from so far away. He was still empty and weak, but he felt upon himself an imperceptible breeze that no one could suspect, which passed over his chest, his forehead, his stomach: a breath from mountain and sea which flowed through the stifling heat of his room. His temperature was down to 38.2.

He could at last be moved back to his parents' house, in an ambulance which drove noiselessly over the snow in the garden. He continued his return to life alone.

That happiness of self-recovery absorbed him entirely, he was concerned with nothing in the world except his refound consciousness of existence: he would listen to himself breathe; he would lay an ear against his pillow to hear his blood. He did not speak, he asked for nothing, he would watch his nurse or his mother walk around and sit by his bed like shadows, he took no interest in anybody but himself, he was working at his return: the task diverted his attention from everything that was not himself. Every existence other than his own seemed to him inexplicable, indecent and full of cumbersome clowning.

He was allowed to get up, to look out through the open windows at the trees still covered in snow, the dazzling plain, the frozen ponds. He was more silent, more taciturn than ever. He reflected that he had just been born, that his illness had been his second birth. Everything had been consumed – his childhood, his adolescence. He existed; he had begun to exist for the first time at the very second when he had woken up in the darkness of the clinic under the blue light. And at the same time he had begun to walk towards his death, after the twenty-two-year reprieve that had stretched from his first birth to his great illness – after that parenthesis in which the time lost was of no consequence. He had been close enough to dying for even anguish not to be missing from his happiness at being alive; for it to give his every least thought or action an exhilarating character of defiance. This was one further similarity with his first appearance in the world, after the first anguish of taking breath.

'Was it then necessary to risk death in order to be a man?'

Everything was beginning, there was no longer a second to

lose before existing passionately. The great game of abortive attempts had come to an end, since it is really possible to die.

'I'm going to have to choose. Dreams about the duration of life have had their day . . . I'm going to have to look for intensity . . . Sacrifice what is of little consequence . . .'

What perhaps best gave Philippe the sense of the change that had just transformed his life was the dreadful debt of gratitude that his mother required him to pay off, once she could reckon he was out of danger. She harshly reproached him for his silence, his distance and his selfishness, and claimed from him the marks of gratitude he owed to the person who had watched over him for nights, who had no doubt torn him from death's clutches. He at once found himself back in that world where the people who love you best call you to account for your existence: do not forgive you for the solitary nature of happiness. Since he really had almost died, there were grounds for mistrust for the rest of his life. But he was still too weak to rebel, he could scarcely move. He began to weep silently. His mother thought these tears were signs of remorse.

But he was crying only for himself: everyone was mistaken.

Appendix:

WALTER BENJAMIN TO MAX HORKHEIMER

Paris XVe
10 rue Dombasle
24 January 1939

Dear Mr Horkheimer,

The main purpose of this letter is to present a politically oriented overview of a few of this winter's literary publications. It elucidates a package containing four new publications, which is making its way to you right now.

Before I start on this round-up, I'd like to thank you for your letter of 17 December, and also for sending the Institute's report.[1] It would seem that a fortunate coincidence has taken place between the publication of this report and

---

1   See *International Institute of Social Research. A Report of Its History, Aims and Activities, 1933–1938.* This report contained a short selected bibliography of works by Benjamin. Horkheimer wrote in his letter: 'In view of the fact that the Institute's funds are partly eroded and partly fixed, we are now reliant on gaining, in whatever ways we can, new endowments for individual members and, where possible, for the Institute as a whole. You can well imagine how hard this activity is for me, in the light of the peculiar nature of our work, which here, even more strongly than elsewhere, at any rate, is considered to be a luxury, plus through the medium of this language. As a part of this undertaking, a new brochure has recently appeared, which I enclose. May I request you do not make any use of what I have revealed above.'

Roosevelt's foreign political turn.[2] The report gives voice to the genuine solidarity that, apparently, exists at the moment between the Institute's future projects and those of American democracy. I don't need to tell you how much I hope that the agenda pursued with this publication will be broadly realized.

I was very glad to find in your report the first bibliographic survey of my things. Of the several publications that the Institute has announced for the spring, the theme explored by Kirchheimer is the one I particularly look forward to.[3] And it is also gratifying to see that the plan to do a philosophical primer, which I thought had been somewhat put in the shade, has stepped back out into the light.[4] It has come back to life for me in relation to something else. When the time comes, I hope to be able to hand you a few fine passages from Turgot for this assortment.[5]

I have been occupying myself with Turgot and a few other theorists, in order to track the history of the concept of progress. I am working through the whole plan of the Baudelaire (about whose revision I advised Teddie Wiesengrund in my last letter) from the perspective of epistemology. From this standpoint, the concept of history becomes an important issue, as well as the role that progress plays in it.

---

2   The Declaration of Lima initiated by Roosevelt at the Pan-American Conference at the end of December 1938 announced the inviolability of the American states and their solidarity in the face of any external aggression.
3   The publication of Otto Kirchheimer's *Punishment and Social Structure*, by Columbia University Press, was announced for January 1939. The jurist Otto Kirchheimer (1905–1965), who was a member of the SPD and an intellectual adversary of Carl Schmitt, belonged to the Institute of Social Research from 1934 to 1942.
4   It was listed under the title *A Text and Source Book for the History of Philosophy*, on p. 19f of the brochure.
5   Benjamin incorporated his excerpts from Turgot into File N of the *Arcades Project*.

Shattering the idea of a continuum of culture, as postulated in the essay on Fuchs,[6] must have epistemological consequences, amongst which one of the most important appears to me to be the designation of limits set on the use of the concept of progress in history. To my surprise I found trains of thought in Lotze that offer some support to my considerations.[7]

I will begin the report I mentioned earlier with Nizan's *The Conspiracy*. That Nizan, who writes for *L'Humanité*, has, for now at least, abandoned his attempts to portray proletarian milieus in order to try out a bourgeois one, has been greeted with a sigh of relief.[8] The hapless figure that the workers presented in Nizan's earlier novels is not solely responsible for that. – Nizan was named as one of the candidates of the Prix Goncourt; he was actually awarded the Prix Interallié.[9] Should one wonder what might procure a communist journalist such multilateral sympathies, one would need to look beyond the formal merits of the book. Its composition is skilful, artistic even, and the formulations are often felicitous. But something else was crucial for its success: the book takes the political novel back to the Bildungsroman as executed in the French mode. It is an *éducation sentimentale* of the vintage of 1909. This disenchanting book reveals that, in the opinion of the author (which can be seen as typical of the party hack), the circumstances that inspired the founding of the Popular Front and, above all, the factory occupations, belong in the past.

If things were different, the web that gets torn in the course of the story need not have presented itself as quite so threadbare from the very start. The story tells of a

6   See his essay on 'Eduard Fuchs, The Collector and Storyteller'.
7   See *Arcades Project*, File N.
8   The novel appeared in Paris in 1938. Paul Nizan (1905–1940), a boyhood friend of Jean-Paul Sartre and member of the PCF until September 1939, had previously written the novels *Antoine Bloyé* (1933) and *Le Cheval de Troie* (1935).
9   The critics' prize (30 jurors) was founded in 1930 and was awarded every year in November.

conspiracy between a handful of intellectuals, of whom none is older than twenty-five. The spying activities, which the group undertake in military and industrial organizations, remain chimerical, indeed they are of hardly any interest. The political level of the country prevents the problem of specialists, such as emerged in the Russian Revolution, from developing in any sort of adequate way.

The psychological subject of Nizan's book is the state of the left intelligentsia as represented mainly by their petty-bourgeois offspring. The main character in the story is less the leader of the conspiracy, Bernard Rosenthal, descendant of a Grand Bourgeois, but rather Pluvinage, whose family was hard up. While the former puts an end to his existence, the latter finds his route into life as an informer. The conspiratorial activity is just an interlude for him. If the best part of the book is the part devoted to him, then the reason for this may be sought in the fact that it is only from the perspective of this profligate that we get a good view of the proletarian movement. (Just as one can get a glimpse of the outside world through a broken window, when all the panes are covered with a thick layer of ice.) The book's high point comes in Chapter 21: the informer, who sorrowfully parts from his former comrades, reveals something of their ties. As for him, he returns to the realm that Nizan characterizes as 'a life that unfolds behind the scenes of life'.[10] From now on, he belongs to the family of those whose secret paths, along which they circumnavigate a world built by others, are preordained. ' "The police's secret," Massart resumed, "is that there is no history . . . Little accidents and little men manufacture great events . . . Everybody's unaware of chance working away behind the scenes, and of the secret of little men." ' Everybody, that is, except for the police and some professions connected to it. On one remarkable page the

10   See *The Conspiracy*, Chapter 23.

author describes the complicities that exist between these ostracized professional groupings – informers, prison officials, funeral-bidders – and certain parts of Paris, which are chiefly inhabited by poor people.[11]

Pluvinage's decision to place himself at the disposal of the police is made in the winter of 1931, just as the government began a campaign of intimidation against the Communist Party. Justifying his change of allegiance, Pluvinage observes: 'I had joined an organization destined for victory; it seemed impossible to me to associate myself with a defeat.' Placed at the start of the book, these words are telling. There Nizan characterizes the constitution of the young people he is following. He says of them: 'They liked only victors and reconstructors; they despised the sick, the dying, lost causes. No force could more powerfully seduce young men ... than a philosophy which, like that of Marx, pointed out to them the future victors of history: the workers, destined for what they somewhat hastily judged to be an inevitable victory.' The tendency expressed in this trait is that same one that asserts itself in Pluvinage.

Over ten years ago, when young people still surfed a revolutionary wave, Aragon, incidentally, vindicated the label of traitor as an honourable one for comrades stemming from the bourgeoisie.[12] Nizan interweaves a short history of

---

11   *The Conspiracy*, pp. 200–201.
12   Benjamin is thinking no doubt of Aragon's article 'Surrealism and Revolutionary Becoming', which appeared in *Surrealism in the Service of the Revolution* in December 1931. In this article Aragon, along with Georges Sadoul, attempted to reconcile his Surrealist past with the attitude that he adopted at the Second International Congress of Revolutionary Writers in Kharkov in 1930: 'Not because we are denying our bourgeois origin, but because the dialectical movement of our development has already placed us in opposition to this origin itself. It is this that, strictly speaking, constitutes the position of revolutionary writers, who, if they are of bourgeois origin, present themselves essentially as *traitors to their original class*.' (Louis Aragon, *Chroniques 1, 1918–1932*, edited by Bernard Leuillot, Paris, 1998, p. 441.)

Surrealism into his text. There are passages that could take their place effortlessly in an intellectual biography of Aragon. 'It will be seen later that a historic change occurred, once Hegel and Marx superseded the Schools of Rimbaud and Lautréamont as objects of the younger generation's admiration.' This is how Bernard Rosenthal presents the situation; Aragon had once thought the same way. If it was Nizan's intention to insinuate correspondences between this highly problematic origin of the Surrealists' theoretical position and the far more legitimate origin of their moral position, then he went for an all-too-convenient thesis. Certainly, *communis opinio* from right to left finds it an easy one to adopt.

A well-meaning reviewer wrote recently: 'There is a breakdown of youth for Nizan as there is a breakdown of childhood for Freud.'[13] It would not be possible to be more wrong. If the elite of bourgeois youth seeks its way to the proletariat in vain, it is not the 'constitution' of youth that is to blame. (That would suit the bourgeoisie – and in the end the proletarian leadership too.) The crucial thing is that the campaigns of the working class have forfeited their powers of attraction for the best elements of the bourgeoisie. The isolation of the proletariat is one of the facts that allowed defeat to be predicted and reinforced that defeat. To have taken account of this isolation is the book's achievement, to falsify its analysis is its function. It should be appraised with as much reservation as corresponds to its championing in the bourgeois press.

The current process of decomposition of French literature is even stifling those embryos that appeared designed for a long-lasting development. I am thinking of Apollinaire's aims, which, arguably, could have had an effect

13   Jean-Paul Sartre's review appeared in the *Nouvelle Revue Française* on 1 November 1938.

beyond Surrealism. Apollinaire found a gripping way to connect the *chercheur et curieux* type with an intelligentsia that was innately immune to indoctrination by cultural inheritance. Queneau evokes this dimly. The brashness that combines in him with broad erudition, presented through the medium of fantasy, would not mar the line of succession emanating from Apollinaire, but Queneau is unable to advance beyond the mere rudiments. His *Gueule de pierre*, the first work of his I came across, intimidated me with its incomprehensibility. *Children of Clay*, which I am sending you, afforded me a rather more comfortable entry point. Of course, I doubt that it will win readers for whom it does not open up so readily. I can certainly imagine that it would prompt you into a digressive reading, provided, that is, that you too share some interest in the subject matter. If you check out the seventh book (p. 223), you will find the material that is of the most informational interest. If, following that, you take a look at the first book up to Chapter 10, you will get a good idea of the most diverting part of the volume.[14]

The genre that is being founded here is a most outlandish one. One might label it romantic bibliography. I am impressed by the author's documentation, some of which I can verify. His hero draws up an inventory of books by the mentally ill. He calls it: Encyclopaedia of the Inexact Sciences. – If I was left perplexed by the book I mentioned earlier, I am now able to see why the author had good reason not to show all his cards. He learnt bluffing from Apollinaire,

---

14   At that time, the writer Raymond Queneau (1903–1976) was an employee at Gallimard, where he was responsible for English literature; up until 1929 he was close to the Surrealists. The novel *Gueule de pierre* appeared in 1934. *Les Enfants du limon* (*Children of Clay*) appeared in 1938; Book 7 comprises a presentation of what is supposed to make up the fourth part of the *Encyclopaedia of the Inexact Sciences*. 'History from the coronation of Napoleon I to the abdication of Napoleon III'.

but his trumps are not all out yet. As before, the book fits in with just that sort of material that Paulhan, editor of the *N.R.F.*, whom you know from *Mesures*, is keen on.

You will not be surprised to hear that the *N.R.F.*, which has proven itself to be impermeable to our cause,[15] is putting out a special issue on the College of Sociology[16] with Bataille, Leiris and Caillois.[17] We met Michel Leiris a few years ago socially at Landsberg's. Under the title 'The Sacred in Everyday Life', Leiris clumps together some of his childhood memories. Caillois continues to romp about in ambiguities. His contribution 'Winter Wind' celebrates the 'cold wind' under whose frosty breath all that is weak must perish and in which the fit link together to form a master caste, recognizing each other by their pink cheeks, a shade not induced by shame.[18] Not a single word situates these

---

15 The plan to get a collection of Horkheimer's essays published in France.

16 The July 1938 issue of the *N.R.F.* published the texts by Leiris and Caillois mentioned in the letter, plus an Introduction by Caillois and Bataille's 'The Sorcerer's Apprentice', with the title 'For a College of Sociology'. A few copies appeared – with their own cover – in a special printing.

17 Purely as a matter of curiosity, I'll add: the same goes for Johannes Schmidt's undertaking. Groethuysen also insisted on making this affair his own, that is to say he defanged it [author's note].

18 Benjamin is describing the concluding sentence of 'Winter Wind': 'Those whose circulation is good will be recognized in the exceeding cold by their pink cheeks, their clear skin, their ease, their exhilaration at finally enjoying what they require of life and the great quantity of oxygen their lungs demand. Returned then to their weakness and driven from the scene, the others shrink back, shrivel, and curl up in their holes. The bustlers are paralyzed, the fancy talkers silenced, the comics made invisible. The coast is clear for those who are most able: no obstructions on the roads to impede their progress, none of the countless, melodious warbling to cover up their voices. Let them number and acknowledge each other in this rarefied air, and may winter leave them closely united, shoulder to shoulder, conscious of their strength; then the new spring will be the consecration of their destiny.' In Dennis Hollier (ed.), *The College of Sociology, 1937–39*, trans. Betsy Wing, University of Minnesota Press, Minneapolis, 1988, p. 32.

declarations in any reality. Clearly this silence informs much better than any confession. – With this special issue the *N.R.F.* is declaring what political orientation is the cost of the peremptoriness of its stance against French pacifism in the European crisis in September. At the same time, it legitimates any doubts one might have about the soundness of this decision.

You will have received the latest issue of the Gazette des Amis des Livres, in which Adrienne Monnier takes on anti-Semitism.[19] Clearly, while reading it what springs to mind, first and foremost, is the well-established bourgeoisie of the quartiers and a section of Faubourg St-Germain who make up her clientele. These are people who do not want to know and who would have felt indisposed by any passion in the language or vividness in the reports. After reading it, however, I was left with a peculiar uneasiness. More than anything the weakened moral consciousness of humanity needs nourishment – not medication. Here the words are so precisely measured, the arguments just the right dosage. But the writing lacks any stuff that could be assimilated by a larger circle of readers. It might be the case that the holy writings of the Indo-Germans[20] highly revere earthly goods – with such an allusion, though, one won't eradicate from people's minds the image of the eternal Jew of the stock exchange, roaming the earth with a sack of gold.

Nevertheless one should not lose sight of the fact that Monnier's text serves as a holding place in the fight against anti-Semitism. Its chief service is the attempt to make Jules Romains' position on the matter useable, for it is currently of

---

19   See Adrienne Monnier, 'À propos de l'antisémitisme', in *Gazette des Amis des Livres*, year 1, no. 5, December 1938, pp. 75–88.
20   Adrienne Monnier quotes the Hindu Vedas, particularly the Rig Veda and the ancient Persian Zend-Avesta (the commentary on the Avesta, or 'Holy Text').

considerable importance. It is written in close liaison with him. And Romains is Daladier's *directeur de conscience*. For this reason, the series of lectures, which Romains published at the same time as the journal I mentioned, is valuable as a source of information.[21] The first thing that strikes one about the four speeches, which stem from the period 30 October to 10 December, is the shift in the author's own position. What appears in the first address, to war veterans, to be a bearable arrangement becomes, by the last one, in front of a sophisticated audience, a vast anticlimax (p. 120). This reflects a corresponding change in public opinion. The focus on empire, which is the chief object of the last lecture, signals, in a passage on French immigration policy (p. 128), the dovetailing of Romains' position and Monnier's text. All the same, when it comes to the excesses of the National Socialists against the Jews, the wilful and audible silence of the latter demonstrates a different attitude to that expressed in the grisly euphemisms with which Romains (p. 70) thinks he can dodge these matters.[22] Romains'

21 Edouard Daladier (1874–1970), a member of the Radical Socialist Party, formed a government on 10 April 1938 without the Socialists. His appeasement policies vis-à-vis Hitler, which were reflected in the Munich Accord, were intended to avoid war. Romains' lectures appeared in 1939 in a book titled *Cela dépend de vous*. The first lecture, 'Discourse on Toulouse', states the following: 'For the first time perhaps in history, with such a degree of urgency and with so tragic a shortcut, men existed who struggled until the last possible minute to avoid that which their conscience refused to believe was inevitable. These men are called Chamberlain, Daladier, Georges Bonnet.' (Paris: Flammarion, 1939, p. 7).
22 The passage in Romains' 'How to view the Franco-German Pact'– published in *Paris-Soir* on 6 December 1938, the date of the signing of the non-aggression pact between France and Germany – states: 'Without me having to underline it – you sense that, though having hoped for this friendship and having worked for it, it was with no great enthusiasm that I welcomed the pact that we signed today with a steely Germany that is puffed up with power, bristling with military excitement, aggravated and perhaps intoxicated by fresh annexations; with a Germany that displays its scorn for idealistic values, such as those we hold, a bit too much, and that, in its conduct in respect of the

wife is a Jewess.[23] His presence at the reception held here by the German foreign minister was noted.[24] (The invitations to this reception were composed in German, which was grounds enough for Valéry not to appear.)

Nothing throws a gloomier light on this field than the fact that it is Duhamel who emerges as Romains' antagonist.[25] No genuine political contradiction exists between the two of them. (The narrowness of Duhamel's cultural political horizon, in particular, was something I mentioned in passing in my essay on the artwork in the age of its technical reproducibility.) But at least Duhamel does confront the acute danger for France that goes along with keeping silent about National Socialist misdeeds. Up till now, the *accord de presse*, planned by the two governments, has found an irreconcilable adversary in Duhamel. Romains does not even mention this issue. The passage in which he alludes to the German wish to see a 'strong government' at the helm in France (p. 78) can scarcely be read as a spirited rejection of the invitation that fascism is issuing to the country.

As a writer, Romains has shifted in the same one-way direction as was pioneered by the likes of Clemenceau. That he has moved from the left, and how far he has moved, is best understood by rereading his *Vin blanc de La Villette*.[26] This story arose in connection with a crisis in the pre-war years, when, in response to a threatened general strike,

---

Germans whose forefathers do not correspond to the official doctrine, abuses a bit too much the law that everyone is master in his own house.'

23   Lise Dreyfus was Romains' second wife.

24   The reception was held on 8 December.

25   Georges Duhamel (1884–1966) was a friend of Romains until 1921. In 1935 he was elected to the Académie Française. He wrote regularly in *Le Figaro*. The edition of 9 November 1938 carried his essay opposing the Munich Accord, 'From a Diplomatic Sedan to an Intellectual Sedan'. In 1939, Duhamel published his essays from this period under the title *The White War of 1938*.

26   Appeared in Paris in 1914, originally titled *On the Quays of La Villette*.

troops were amassed in the capital city. It portrays what happens as a result in the head of a common soldier, who belongs to one of the relevant detachments. What the Popular Front might have been can be better gleaned from this book than from any one of those that appeared three years ago as the vanguard for this political formation.

Considering how hopeless the situation of France in Europe is, maybe Romains' foreign political programme – outbuilding within the empire – cannot be opposed. I do not know if it is irreconcilable with the interests of the working class. Given that these interests never get voiced anywhere, not to mention the significance that they have for the salvation of European civilization, the text stays within the orbit of the cabinet from which it emerged. It is an airless atmosphere, not that of the galleries of the Quai d'Orsay,[27] but rather the offices in the prefecture.[28] Thérive noted of the philosophy of the police secretary in Nizan's novel that it is not that far removed from that of the author of *Men of Good Will*.[29] This claim is certainly not repudiated in this little volume. It is no coincidence that it is this mode of thinking that found the most universal expression in France, in the fourteen volumes of that novelistic work. For all its skill, it is highly parochial and, for all its logic, thoroughly deceptive.

A purer wine can be poured from Jacques Madaule, who has published an essay titled 'French Prefascism' in the December edition of *Esprit*.[30] I will convey some of its most

---

27 Metonym for the French Ministry of Foreign Affairs [trans].
28 The body responsible for law enforcement in Paris [trans].
29 A reference to Jules Romains. This discussion by André Thérive (pseudonym of Roger Putheste, 1891–1967), which is meant to have appeared in *Temps*, could not be located.
30 The teacher Jacques Madaule (1898–1993), who was influenced by Claudel's work and by Jacques Maritain, was also a member of the Popular Front and a regular political and cultural chronicler for the magazine *Esprit*; his

trenchant formulations. On Daladier: 'His intentions are perhaps exemplary; Brüning too possessed great qualities. But that cannot distract from the fact that Daladier is the opposite of a leader; his lack of resolution compares only with the energy of his formulations.'[31] On the CGT congress in December, just before it took place: 'Jouhaux will perform the impossible, in order to save the unity of syndicalism. We have to assume that it will be successful. Then we will have one more cracked façade.'[32] On Flandin: 'A fascism that has no other programme than to continuously capitulate, in order to continue enjoying certain possessions, would be a fairly original fascism.'[33] On the domestic political situation: 'France does not exist alone in the world . . . its borders are not impenetrable. Fascism could very well be imposed on the country from the outside. That need not necessarily happen as a result of war.'[34] And: 'The French proletariat is in less of a position than that of other countries to sustain a coalition with the middle classes and the big bourgeoisie in its own right.'[35] The closing sentences of the essay: 'The fatal indecisiveness, which we perceive in France at this moment, shows that the country is still hoping for a solution other than fascism. We, who know what we want, and know even better what we do not want, must summon such energy that

---

contribution 'French Prefascism' is in the volume mentioned, which was devoted as a whole to this theme – his essay is on pp. 327–42.

31   See ibid., p. 337.

32   See ibid., pp. 341f. Léon Henri Jouhaux (1879–1954) was general secretary of the CGT from 1909 to 1947. In 1951 he received the Nobel Peace Prize.

33   See ibid., p. 330; Madaule does not mention the name Pierre-Étienne Flandin (1889–1958) in this passage. Flandin was a deputy of the national and state parliament and a minister. Pétain made him foreign minister on 13 December 1940; he held the post until 9 February 1941.

34   See ibid., p. 338.

35   See ibid., p. 334.

the coming spring does not witness the collapse of the last Free State for humans in continental Europe.'

I shall conclude this survey with a recent book by Claudel, which I managed to see by a happy coincidence.[36] – On 1 July 1925, the Surrealists issued a flyer 'Open Letter to M. Paul Claudel, ambassador to Japan'.[37] This observed that: 'For us, there can be no talk of harmony or great art. The idea of the beautiful is long over. Only the moral idea remains undisputed – for example, the knowledge of why one cannot be a French ambassador and a poet at the same time.' – The jeweller Cartier, 13 rue de la Paix, has just published a 'Mystique of Precious Stones', written for him by Claudel. The word 'published' is, I suppose, not quite accurate; the text is only being distributed to jewellers, not booksellers. It cannot be purchased. It does not seek to teach the reader about the mystical powers of precious stones as they have arisen across history (the most important source on this, the Byzantine Psellos, is not mentioned[38]). Claudel saw himself primarily faced with a diplomatic task: to be the ambassador for a jeweller amongst his customers. The question of whether such a thing is permissible might have its charm for casuists. It is a different question to that posed by the Surrealists, and does not necessarily propose a ready-made answer. Unfortunately, however, the contents of the slim volume release the reader totally from the effort to pursue this further. How Claudel

---

36   Appeared in 1938; see Paul Claudel, *Œuvres en prose*, pp. 339–354; the passages cited by Benjamin can be found on pp. 351, 354 and 352.

37   This was a collective answer to an interview with Claudel, which appeared in *Comœdia* on 24 June and in which he stated that the literature of the Dadaists and Surrealists amounted to homosexuality. The flyer, printed on blood-red paper, was placed under guests' plates at the banquet in honour of Saint-Pol Roux in the Closerie des Lilas on 2 July 1925.

38   The text is *Peri lithon dynameon* by Michael Psellos (c. 1018–c. 1097), which F. de Mély included in the second volume of his three-volume work *Les Lapidaires grecs* (Paris, 1898).

approaches the matter – stolidly, without a trace of irony – means that the least agreeable sides of such an undertaking come to the fore, at the expense of all the others. Claudel is well aware of the devices of exegesis, but the circumstances in which these are appropriate pass him by. Earrings as allegory, for example, appear to him in the following way: 'Right and left of the head, they are . . . the two alerters, sensitive, gently sounding, they are the penetrating counsels of God, which are continuously flanking us humans, the intelligible fire of grace itself' (p. 38).

Cartier appears in the book like the patron in old paintings. Here is the passage verbatim: 'There I was with the greatest jeweller in Paris, with one of the men such as is praised in the Gospels and whose handiwork it is . . . to demand of the sea itself its mystical fabrication – the pearl – the answer . . . to the shudder that arises as God's gaze glides from one horizon to another . . . A poor devil – blind and deaf he is, the weight of the water's mass has burst his eardrum – found it by groping in the depths. And now I am holding them, these virginal, angelic creations, in my cupped hand – this holy nothingness' (pp. 30–1). That is a triptych. If the secret meaning of this advertising brochure is to establish the truly mystical congruence of social and theological hierarchies, it has certainly been achieved in this series of images. There is the dealer, who has his place in the shadow of the Gospels; there is the proletarian whose eardrum has burst in an echo of the curse with which his predecessor, Satan, was once afflicted from God's throne; and lastly there is the customer, the man toward whom this new Beatitude is directed.

It ill behoves one to include the parables of Jesus as an extra for the customer. According to these, the mystical mustard seed of the Gospels appears in the pearl.[39] It is, to be

---

39   See Matthew, 13:31–32.

sure, as Matthew says, the least of all seeds; but once it is full-grown, then it is larger than all the other herbs in the garden and grows into such a tree that the birds of the air come and lodge in its branches. What happens in the garden is child's play compared to the miraculous feats of the pearl within the life of the economy. After a portrayal of money-grubbing capital, which speaks disgustedly of all the blood that sticks to pennies, yet leaves shares aside as an anachronism, Claudel goes on to say: 'The penny has its exchange value. The law prescribes it and Lady Justice guarantees it. But the pearl, the spawn of duration and the fruit of the sea, has no other value than that of its beauty . . . Its appearance on the market devalues all other goods; it changes their price; it brings disquiet to the banks, it threatens the equilibrium of their transactions. For it ushers in an element that escapes every number: I am speaking of its spiritual concupiscence, which emerges from contemplation of it' (pp. 29–30). – Claudel invites the customer into the boutique with sacristan bells. One can no longer deny the idea that the peace we enjoy is named after the Rue de la Paix.

And how long will it last? Should it survive the spring, then I really do trust this year will bring us together. I have been thinking that the World Fair will bring a number of important people to New York. Will you still be able to make some time free for Europe? I very much hope so.

I wish more than anything for you that your nearest and dearest are spared the darkest horrors.[40]

---

40   In his letter of 17 December, Horkheimer wrote: 'Your assumption that I have relatives in Germany is correct. Not only am I called upon to help by countless relatives and acquaintances, but both of my parents are still alive too. My father is 80, my mother 70 years old. As I am an only child, this situation means that I have quite a lot to cope with. Up until the latest events, the old folk had kept themselves quite well and had not requested that I arrange their migration. Of course, that has now changed too.' – Moritz Horkheimer (1858–1946) and Babette Horkheimer (1869–1946) managed to flee to Switzerland at the beginning of July 1939.

Two days ago Germaine Krull came to Paris.[41] She seemed to me to be relatively cheerful; in a more confident mood than last time.

In the next few days, three detailed book reviews[42] will be sent to Löwenthal: Hönigswald's *Philosophy and Language*, Dimier's *From the Spirit to the Word* and Sternberger's *Panorama* – I chose an anagram of my name for the publication of the review in the latest issue: J. E. Mabinn.[43] I hope that, in conjunction with the statement of place, it turns out to be transparent enough for connoisseurs of the journal.

In conclusion, my very best wishes,

Yours
Walter Benjamin

PS. Are you really looking into moving the Institute, as could be inferred from your postscript?[44] I don't suppose you are thinking of Europe.

---

41 The photographer and traveller Germaine Krull (1897–1985) grew up in Paris and was a friend of Horkheimer from 1912. In subsequent years Benjamin stayed in close contact with her; the letters he wrote her are untraceable.

42 These remained unpublished during Benjamin's lifetime. See Walter Benjamin, *Gesammelte Schriften III*, Suhrkamp, Frankfurt am Main, 1989, pp. 564–79.

43 In using this anagram Benjamin, who had wanted to sign as 'Hans Fellner', was complying with a request from Horkheimer: 'We will accommodate your wish that the literary notice appear pseudonymously. My main reason for regretting this is that the publication of this notice in so loose a form is only really justified if its origination with a close associate of the Institute is apparent.' (Horkheimer to Benjamin, 17 December 1938.)

44 'It is very kind of you to wish to assign us *History of the German Book Trade*. For now let me accept the gift with gratitude in the name of the Institute and I am expressly happy to agree that it retains its location with you for the time being. I hope very much that, one way or another, some day you will reside in the same city in which the Institute has its seat. Where that might be is as yet undetermined.' (Ibid.)

.

Notes

Page 5 *Revue de Métaphysique et de Morale* was founded in 1893, and soon established itself as one of the best known French philosophical journals.

Page 7 The AX was a former Parisian bus route.

Janson is the Lycée Janson-de-Sailly.

Odette de Crécy was first the mistress, later the wife, of Charles Swann in Proust's *A la recherche du temps perdu.*

Page 8 Rue Cloche-Perce, etc.: streets in a section of the 4th arrondissement, just behind the Grand Magasin du Bazar de l'Hôtel de Ville, settled by indigent Jewish immigrants from Central Europe (and more recently North Africa). Despite gentrification of the Marais, the nearby Rue des Rosiers still retains something of the ambience described by Nizan.

Page 11 Théodore Fantin-Latour (1836–1904) and Pascal Dagnan-Bouveret (1852–1929) were both best known as society portrait painters.

Page 12 Irish seminarists: the Collège Irlandais still stands in Rue des Irlandais, off Rue Lhomond.

Gare: the Gare d'Austerlitz.

Page 13 Wednesday: a free day in the French educational system.

Page 21 Henri-Joseph-Eugène Gouraud (1867–1946), a distinguished First World War general, served as military governor of Paris from 1923 to 1937.

Page 22 The Belfort Lion, commemorating the successful defence of Belfort in 1870–71, was erected in 1880 on Place Denfert-Rochereau, named after the commanding officer during the siege.

André Tardieu (1876–1945), a minister in Poincaré's government in 1928, was himself to become Prime Minister for the first of three terms in November 1929.

Page 29   Poincaré, at this time (1928) Prime Minister, had been President of the Republic from 1913 to 1920.

Théophile Corret de la Tour d'Auvergne (1743–1800) distinguished himself in the Revolutionary Wars, refused promotion beyond the rank of captain in the grenadiers, and was killed at the Battle of Oberhausen in Bavaria.

Sadi Carnot (1837–1894), grandson of Lazare C. who organized the armies of the French Revolution, was President of the Republic from 1887 until his assassination by an anarchist at Lyon.

Marcelin Berthelot (1827–1907) was an eminent chemist and political figure, father of the philosopher René and the politician Philippe C.

Comte Timoléon de Cossé-Brissac (1775–1848), scion of an old aristocratic family, was created a count of the Empire in 1812.

Comte Jean-Marie-François Lepaige-Dorsenne (1773–1812) was a Napoleonic general who distinguished himself especially in Spain and died of his wounds.

The *Doctrinaires* were a political grouping founded under the Restoration by Pierre-Paul Royer-Collard and François Guizot. Their aim was to give some philosophical foundation to a middle-of-the-road policy of constitutional monarchism, rejecting both popular sovereignty and divine right of kings. Their ideas found expression after 1830 in the July Monarchy.

Page 30   Pierre Casimir-Périer (1777–1832), rich banker and politician, Minister of the Interior under the July Monarchy.

Jean-Paul-Pierre Casimir-Périer (1847–1907), diplomat and politician, President of the Republic 1894–95.

The Chapelle Expiatoire in Boulevard Haussmann was erected under the Restoration, on the site of a small cemetery that had received the bodies of 1,343 victims of the guillotine on

Place de la Concorde during the French Revolution, including those of Louis XVI and Marie Antoinette.

Page 31 Albi is the provincial capital and main railway centre of the Tarn *département*, where Jaurès was first buried at his birthplace, Castres. Les Aubrais is a railway junction near Orléans.

Lucien Herr (1864–1926), librarian, from 1888 until his death, of the Ecole Normale Supérieure. A socialist, he influenced successive generations of *normaliens*, and among others Jaurès and Blum. A prominent supporter of Dreyfus, in 1904 he was among the founders of *L'Humanité*, then an organ of the Socialist Party.

Lucien Lévy-Bruhl (1857–1935), philosopher and social theorist, whose best-known works are concerned with the thought systems of 'primitive' societies.

Palais-Bourbon: seat of the National Assembly.

Page 37 Rodin's *Thinker*, now in the Musée Rodin in Hôtel Biron, in the twenties stood in front of the Panthéon.

Page 38 The Unknown Philosopher: Louis-Claude de Saint-Martin (1743–1803), a mystical (and often obscurantist) 'illuminist' philosopher influenced by freemasonry and theosophy.

Rabbi ben Ezra: Abraham ben Meir Ibn Ezra (1098–1164) Jewish poet, philosopher, grammarian, astronomer and biblical critic, born in Spain, the inspiration for Robert Browning's poem 'Rabbi Ben Ezra'.

Page 41 *Clarté* was a novel published in 1919 by the pacifist socialist Henri Barbusse, who in November of that year founded a journal with the same title, with an associated international committee including such well-known names as Anatole France, Georges Duhamel, Jules Romains, Upton Sinclair, H.G. Wells and Stefan Zweig.

Page 42 See Lenin, *Collected Works*, vol. 33, p. 113.

Page 44 Doktorklub: graduate discussion club at Berlin University in the 1830s and '40s which formed the focal point of the Young Hegelian movement, and in which Marx worked out his early views on philosophy and society. The epigram is taken from a satirical poem by Friedrich Engels and Bruno Bauer's brother Edgar, 'The Triumph of Faith', and reads: 'Our actions are just words, and long they so shall be./ After Abstraction, Practice follows of itself.' (Marx/Engels, *Collected Works*, vol. 2, p. 338).

Page 45   *La mobilisation n'est pas la guerre:* these words are taken from the proclamation accompanying the order of general mobilization on 1 August 1914, signed by President of the Republic Raymond Poincaré, but drafted by Premier René Viviani.

   The *Gazette du Franc* was a financial weekly founded in 1925, which collapsed in 1928.

Page 46   Jean Chiappe (1878–1940) was Prefect of Police in Paris from 1927 to 1934. Known for his far-right sympathies, in 1940 he was appointed High Commissioner in Syria by the Vichy regime, but the plane taking him there was shot down by the RAF.

Page 49   Dolgoruky is the main character in Dostoievsky's *A Raw Youth.*

Page 51   The Vexin was a historic French province, overlapping the border between the modern *départements* of Seine-et-Oise and Eure: Pontoise was the centre of Vexin Français, Gisors of Vexin Normand.

Page 54   Edouard Herriot (1872–1957), leader of the Radical-Socialists, had lost in 1925 a premiership he was not to regain until 1932.

   Philippe Berthelot (1866–1937) was Secretary-General of the Foreign Ministry 1920–33, exerting great influence over successive ministers.

Page 56   'Acquiescence in oneself' is a principal theme of the last two. books of Spinoza's *Ethics.*

Page 61   The Broglie: Place Broglie.

Page 61   Anglo-French glasses: the allusion to a couplet from Alfred de Musset's 'Le Rhin allemand':

Nous l'avons eu, votre Rhin allemand;
Il a tenu dans notre verre.

Gabriel Alapetite (1854–1932) was Commissioner-General of the Republic (or *de facto* Governor) in Alsace-Lorraine, from the time of its transfer from Germany in 1918 until 1924.

Etienne-Alexandre Millerand (1859–1943) was War Minister from 1915 until the Armistice, and became Prime Minister briefly in 1920, before becoming President of the Republic (1920–24).

Page 62   The speech of Touraine is commonly regarded as providing the closest thing to standard French (*mutatis mutandis* roughly equivalent to Hanover German, Tuscan Italian or Oxford English).

Common sense . . . a quotation from Descartes' *Discourse on Method.*

Page 66   The Fosse: Quai de la Fosse.

At the Ecole des Chartes for librarians and archivists, Simon would have studied diplomatics or the science of documentary analysis – in contradistinction to the diplomacy which, for the sake of the pun, Nizan ascribes to the curriculum of the Ecole des Sciences Politiques.

Page 72   'Alain': pen-name of Emile-Auguste Chartier (1868–1951), a product of the Ecole Normale Supérieure and the most influential philosophy teacher in France during the inter-war years, especially thanks to his prolific essays. His main emphasis was on education of the will, creating a personality for oneself that is the product of self-conscious and rational effort.

Page 78   MENE TEKEL PERES: the reference is to the writing on the wall at Belshazzar's feast, see Daniel, 5, vv. 25–8: 'And this is the writing that was written, MENE, MENE, TEKEL, UPHARSIN. This is the interpretation of the thing; MENE – God hath numbered thy kingdom and finished it. TEKEL – Thou art weighed in the balances, and art found wanting.

PERES – Thy kingdom is divided and given to the Medes and Persians.'

Page 89   Italians: by analogy with the post-war chambers in Italy, which had given their support after 1922 to Mussolini and his fascist movement, fuelled by the resentful aspirations of demobilized officers.

Page 92   Georges Duhamel (1884–1966), poet, novelist and playwright; his war novels give an unsparing picture of the horrors of war itself, but a highly sentimentalized one of its victims.

Max Scheler (1874–1928), German phenomenological philosopher and sociologist of knowledge, published the collection of essays *Vom Umsturz der Werte* in Leipzig in 1919.

Page 93   Henri Massis (1886–1970) and Alfred de Tarde (born 1880), under the joint pseudonym Agathon, published a series of influential surveys of public opinion in the years immediately preceding the First World War, notably *L'esprit de la nouvelle Sorbonne* and *Les jeunes gens d'aujourd'hui*. They identified a new generation of French youth, breaking with *fin de siècle* nihilism and narcissism, more open to the appeal of patriotic virtues, indeed specifically more ready to combat Germany – both on the cultural and on the military planes. In the case of Massis, at any rate, the conclusions of the survey were to a large extent tailored to a prewritten script.

Page 101   Auteuil, etc. – fashionable racecourses.

The Company is the Company of Stockbrokers, rough equivalent of a London city guild.

1927 was the year in which Julien Benda's influential *La Trahison des clercs* (Treason of the Intellectuals) was published.

Page 103   Camelots du Roi: youth organization attached to Action Française, a far-right grouping founded in 1899 and led by Charles Maurras and Léon Daudet. Originally republican, after 1908 Action Française became increasingly royalist, Catholic and anti-Semitic, drawing many of its themes from the writings of Edouard Drumont (1844–1917), a prominent anti-Semitic and anti-Dreyfus propagandist, founding editor of *La Libre*

Parole. The Jeunesses Patriotiques formed by Pierre Taittinger represented a proto-fascism which by the twenties had more appeal in France than the royalist nostalgia of Action Française.

Page 103   Rue Saint-Guillaume: site of the then Ecole Nationale des Sciences Politiques.

Page 104   Conciergerie: play on words – the Conciergerie is in fact a famous prison, forming part of the Palais de Justice.

Page 109   Otto I sat on the Greek throne from 1832 to 1862.

Page 112   The Hecatonpylus or 'hundred gates' was Homer's designation for Thebes on the upper Nile.

Page 110   Hédiard's is a luxury food store on Place de la Madeleine in Paris.

Page 111   Palikars: irregulars in the Greek War of Independence, in which Byron, Admiral Andréas Miaoulis, Marcos Botsaris and General Theodoros Kolocotronis played greater or lesser roles. The interior of the Erechtheum dates from the period when it was used as an Ottoman harem.

Page 116   Emile Bréhier (1876–1952) taught philosophy at the Sorbonne 1919–46 and wrote the standard French history of philosophy in seven volumes.

The Power of a Lie, play by the Norwegian author Johan Böjer (1872–1959), published in 1903.

Page 117   André Marty (1886–1956), a prominent Communist leader – who in 1919 had led a mutiny in the French Black Sea fleet; of whom Hemingway was to give an unflattering portrait as a vain and bloodthirsty commissar in *For Whom the Bell Tolls*; but who would be expelled from the Party in his old age for expressing doubts about the role of the Soviet security police – was convicted in 1929 for articles urging soldiers to resist the imperialist warmongers.

Page 121   Bois-Belleau in the *département* of the Aisne was the site of fierce battles in October 1914 and again in July 1918.

Urania was the Muse of Astronomy and Geometry.

The church of Sainte-Clotilde is in the 7th arrondissement in Paris.

Page 122   Grande Mademoiselle: Louise d'Orléans, duchesse de
Montpensier (1627–93), niece of Louis XIII, took an active part
on the side of Condé in the second Fronde, fell in love at the age
of forty-two with a Gascon adventurer named Lauzun. The king
initially consented to their marriage, but changed his mind and
imprisoned Lauzun for ten years. They may then have been
secretly married, but Lauzun, whom she had greatly enriched,
abandoned her. She wrote lively memoirs, and a number of less
interesting novels.

   Pedro I was emperor of Brazil from 1821 to 1831.

Page 124   The Compagnie Général Transatlantique was control-
led by the Péreire family and their Crédit Mobilier.

   The Crédit du Nord challenged the six national banks from
its base in the northern *départements.*

   Eugène Mathon (1860–1935) was a self-made textile manu-
facturer and proponent of corporatism.

Page 125   Joseph Arthur de Gobineau (1816–82), in his novel *Les
Pléiades* (1874), presented his three heroes as 'kings' sons', or
alternatively *calenders* (mendicant dervishes), adrift in a world
populated by fools, brutes and rogues.

   Auguste Scheurer-Kestner (1833–99) was a notable of the
Third Republic, Vice-President of the Senate, uncle to Jules
Ferry's wife, the most eminent of exiled Alsatian politicians after
1870, and one of the foremost defenders of Dreyfus.

Page 126   Pera is a district of Istanbul.

   Diana of the Crossways: eponymous heroine of the novel by
George Meredith.

Page 131   The Hague Conference on the Young Plan was held
from 6 to 31 August 1929. It was designed to provide a final solution to the German post-war reparations problem, and German
acceptance was rewarded by the evacuation of the Rhineland by
June 1930.

   In August 1929 there were major clashes in British-administered
Palestine, following a dispute over Jewish use of the Wailing
Wall in Jerusalem.

Page 132   Chéron, the French Finance Minister, and Snowden, the British Chancellor of the Exchequer, clashed openly over German reparations at the Hague Conference. Henderson was then the British Foreign Secretary, Jaspar the Belgian Premier.

Page 134   Concert Mayol: nightclub similar to the Folies Bergères.

Page 144   Charles Fréminville (1856–1936), engineer, played a large part in introducing Taylorism into France and was President of the first Comité National de l'Organisation Française (1926–32).

Henry le Châtelier (1850–1936) was a chemist and metallurgist, an early French advocate of Taylorism.

The neo-Saint-Simonian movement in France in the twenties was led by such men as Henri Fayol, Ernest Mercier and Eugène Mathon; many of them were graduates of the Ecole Polytechnique, and many of them too had fascist leanings.

Page 155   Perthes-lès-Hurlus: village near Rheims taken by the German army in October 1914, retaken by the French in 1915.

Page 156   Emile Combes (1835–1921), Prime Minister 1902–5, is mainly remembered for his fiercely anti-clerical policies.

At the Tours Congress in December 1920, a majority of the Socialist Party voted to join the Third International, thereafter changing its name to Communist Party.

Page 159   Alfred Jarry monkey: in Jarry's *Gestes et opinions du Docteur Faustroll, pataphysicien* (1911), there is a monkey named Bosse-de-Nage.

Page 162   Stuart Mill: the reference is perhaps to the well-known passage in the second section of John Stuart Mill's *Utilitarianism*, where the author stresses the need to judge the goodness or evil of actions rather than of their perpetrators.

Page 166   Eteocles and Polynices: sons of Oedipus and Jocasta, joint heirs to the kingdom of Thebes, they agreed to serve alternate years, but at the end of the first year Eteocles refused to surrender the throne. Polynices turned for help to Argos, and returned with an army led by seven generals. Eventually the brothers slew each other in individual combat.

Page 178 Mur des Fédérés: site of the mass shooting of 147 survivors of the last resistance put up by the Paris Commune in May 1871.

Page 188 Place du Combat: now renamed Place du Colonel Fabien. Bellevilloise: the Association Bellevilloise, a large cooperative enterprise.

Page 192 Joseph Fouché (1759–1820): politician, member of the Mountain in the Convention, responsible for the Lyon massacres in 1793; he became Minister for Police and Duke of Otranto under the Empire, but betrayed Napoleon after the Hundred Days and kept his post under the Restoration; later ambassador to Dresden and, after his removal from this post, naturalized an Austrian, dying in Trieste.

Raoul Rigault (1846–1871), son of a sub-prefect of the Second Empire, after the latter fell on 4 September 1870 took over the Prefecture of Police and devoted his energies to uncovering the police intelligence techniques of the Empire, making long lists of its police spies. Under the Commune he continued to occupy what was now known as the Ex-Prefecture and became Procureur de la Commune, playing an important role in the final resistance, in which he was killed (in Rue Gay-Lussac).

Police powers in Paris are roughly divided between the *police administrative* or *générale*, and the *police judiciaire* – a plainclothes criminal investigation force. The Prefect of Police in Paris has an exceptional position, with full police powers, autonomous police forces under his control and a large measure of responsibility in the Département de la Seine, in which Paris is situated.

Page 194 Philippe-Auguste, comte de Villiers de l'Isle Adam (1838–1889), novelist and playwright, symbolist, extravagantly romantic – at times almost Gothic.

Page 195 Duke of Otranto – title awarded to Fouché under the Empire.

Page 196 Marie-Jean Hérault de Séchelles (1759–1794), President of the Convention, died on the guillotine with the Dantonists.

Perhaps a reference to *Une visite à Montbard*, in which Hérault quotes Buffon as saying: 'Genius is merely a greater capacity for patience.'

Page 198   Seine Prefecture: adjoining the Hôtel de Ville, it had authority over the Département de la Seine in which Paris was located – smallest but most populous of the French *départements* until it was split up in 1964.

Page 200   Noyau de Poissy is a drink flavoured with cherry kernels. Centre Psychiatrique Sainte-Anne: large mental hospital in Rue Alésia.

Page 210   There was a bloody battle between Berlin workers and the police on 1 May 1929, after a ban on all open-air demonstrations by the Social-Democrat police chief Zörgiebel. Police fire killed 25 and severely wounded 36 workers.

Page 212   The Parc de Bagatelle forms a westward extension of the Bois de Boulogne.

Page 213   Secours Rouge: French section of the Comintern's International Red Aid organization.

Page 218   Georges Dumas (1866–1946), experimental psychologist. Nizan himself was sympathetic to psychoanalysis, and was one of the first to express an interest in the work of the young Jacques Lacan.

Page 219   The Faubourg Montmartre district stretches along the Rue Montmartre, between Les Halles and the *grands boulevards*.
The Croix-Rousse district of Lyon lies on a hill just to the north of the city centre.

Page 220   The Prefecture de Police is situated on Place du Parvis Notre-Dame.

Page 221   Anatole Deibler (1863–1939) was public executioner, like his father and grandfather before him, from 1899 until his death, during which time he supervised over 350 guillotinings.

Page 223   Fauxpasbidet, Peudepièce: derisive names indicating that the foundling in question was the result of an ineffective contraceptive douche, or had been discarded because of over-crowded family accommodation.

Page 225 Cartesian diver: scientific toy consisting of a hollow figure filled partly with water and partly with air, floating in a flexible airtight vessel nearly filled with water. Pressure on the vessel compresses the air within and forces more water through an aperture into the figure, which sinks, to rise again when the pressure is removed.

Page 246 Max Horkheimer Archive at the City and University Library, Frankfurt am Main.